# CUDDLES & CUSTARD

By

## MAGGIE WHITLEY

*Cover illustration by* **Jason Ferdinando**
***www.jasonferdinando.com***

This paperback edition published in
The United Kingdom 2017

by Elm House Publishing
www.elmhousepublishing.com

Copyright © 2017 Maggie Whitley
ISBN-13: 978-1979430104

ALSO BY MAGGIE WHITLEY
The Adventures of the Great Alfonso (and his brother Ronnie)
The Kettles Boil
Bushed!
The Man with the Tattooed Eyebrows

For Albert

# PROLOGUE

So this is what it feels like to be a criminal, thought Alice, looking into the drab, grey, uninviting room. It had no windows and was lit by stark neon lights. Interview Room 2 said the sign on the door.

"Take a seat, Mrs Coalter. I'll be with you shortly."

"It's Coulter."

"I'm sorry?" The man holding the heavy door open looked at her.

"It's *Coulter*. You said *Coalter*. As in *coal*. It's not. It's *Coulter*. As in *cool*."

He nodded vacantly as she stepped inside. "Whatever," he muttered as he closed the door leaving her inside, alone.

"I heard that," she said to no-one.

The only furniture in the room was a table and four chairs. A matt black machine sat on the table, a red light blinking at her. Alice knew it was a recording device – she'd watched enough police programmes. She sat down on one of the chairs and tried to drag it closer to the table but it wouldn't budge. Grey metal bolts held it fast. Alice put her handbag on the floor and straightened her red woollen skirt. Crossing her ankles, she pulled up the collar of her coat, shivering. Looking round she took in the grey walls, grey floor, grey ceiling, grey table, grey chairs. Couldn't they have picked a nice lilac? she thought. Or even a pretty yellow? Shivering again, she pulled her coat tighter. Cold? Or scared? Excited even? This was a first for her. She sighed deeply and stared at the worn surface of the table stained with coffee rings and pock-marked with cigarette burns. I bet there's a story behind each one of those, she thought, running her forefinger round and round a particularly dark circular stain. What if it's blood? Alice wiped her hand vigorously on her skirt.

She was trying to make sense of why she was here, sitting in this cold interview room in Smedley Police Station on a wet April morning. What had she done? She couldn't think of a single thing. She was Mrs Average. Mrs Nobody, truth to tell. Yet here she was, in this bleak, colourless non-descript room that smelled of stale sweat and staler urine, waiting for the return of that annoying young man who couldn't even get her name right but who was hopefully going to tell her why she was here. What crime he thought she was supposed to have committed. Crime? She smiled to herself. She could no more break the law than sprout wings and fly. But this was a room for interviewing suspects, wasn't it? And criminals? Alice wondered how much longer she'd have to wait. For want of something to do, she took a small mirror from her handbag and examined her face closely. Was this the face of a criminal? She smiled again. Hardly. But then what do criminals look like? They couldn't all be tattooed monsters with cropped hair and an IQ to match. She stared hard. Green eyes surrounded by thick pale eyelashes stared back at her. Moving the mirror further away so she could see the whole of her face, Alice tried to be objective. It was a round face with a small button nose and full lips. She preferred to think of it as dimpled rather than creased. She touched her hair. Grey. Like her surroundings. Stray hairs had escaped from an untidy pony tail and Alice tucked them behind her ears. She desperately needed a trim and some highlights but money was tight at the moment. Wasn't it always? Alice sighed. She didn't think herself unattractive. Or even attractive. Truth to tell, she didn't really think about herself much at all. If anyone had asked her, and no-one had, she would have described herself as 'homely', the sort of word her mother would have used. She'd been described as pretty once but that was such a very long time ago. Examining the dark bags under her eyes Alice thought she looked a good ten or even, depressingly, fifteen years older than she was. Well, that's what life did to you. The door opened and she quickly dropped the mirror back in her bag. She half turned in the chair.

"Sorry I was so long." He half smiled. "Things always take longer than you think." He sat down opposite Alice and put a thin blue paper folder down on the table. She took a good long look at him - young, so young. Still uncrumpled. Not creased or dimpled. Yet. What he did have was short brown hair and a matching beard trimmed to within an inch of its life. Piercing blue eyes stared at her. Alice looked away.

"Why am I here? What have I done?" she asked nervously, fingering her wedding ring and staring hard at the folder. She squinted, trying to read what was written across the top of it but it was upside down and too far away.

"All in good time, Mrs Coalter."

"It's *Coulter*, I told you."

"That's right, you did." He sighed loudly.

Then why don't you listen? she said to herself. It's not that difficult. You may have youth and good looks on your side but that's no excuse for not paying attention. Nobody does anymore.

"As I said yesterday on the phone, my name is Inspector Lancaster. James Lancaster. And I asked you here today to answer a few questions."

"Am I under arrest?" asked Alice, clenching and unclenching her hands under the table.

"No, of course not. You came here voluntarily to help us with an ongoing enquiry. When I rang you yesterday and invited you to come down here to the station, I thought I'd explained all that yesterday." Honestly. Some people never listen, he thought.

Alice nodded, remembering the call. It was so unexpected she hadn't really taken it in at the time. The Police? Calling *her*? She did remember someone, it must have been the man in front of her, asking when was a good time to call round. When she'd hesitated, he'd offered to send a car to pick her up and bring her to the station. And here she was.

"Can I just confirm your personal details, Mrs Coulter?"

She nodded and swallowed hard.

"You *are* Mrs Alice Coulter of 46 Greenfields Road, Smedley?"

She nodded again.

"And your date of birth is 24 November 1967?"

"How do you know that?"

"We can check these things," replied the Inspector.

Alice started to chew her bottom lip. So they'd been checking up on her. That couldn't be good, surely?

"Do I need a lawyer?" she asked.

Inspector Lancaster laughed. "Now why would you think that?" He shook his head. "And anyway, it's a solicitor."

"Whatever it's called, do I need one?" Alice asked again.

Inspector Lancaster shook his head. "No, you don't."

"Are you sure? These detective programmes always tell you to get a lawyer."

"You're not under arrest and you don't need a lawyer," he sighed. "Or a solicitor." TV had a lot to answer for. "You've come here of your own volition to answer a few questions as part of our enquiries. You can leave any time you want. Okay? Now, is there anything else?"

Alice looked at the Inspector squarely. "Is this going to take long? It's just I've got quite a lot of things to do."

The policeman nodded. "It may take a wee while. Is that a problem?"

"I suppose not. But I missed breakfast. Any chance of a cup of tea?" she asked.

Inspector Lancaster stood up.

"And a biscuit?" she added tentatively.

He stopped and looked at her. "And a biscuit."

Alice dunked the chocolate digestive in her tea.

"Can we start now?" the Inspector asked her. He opened the blue folder and straightened some loose papers inside.

She smiled and helped herself to another biscuit. She was oddly pleased that he'd bothered to put the biscuits on a plate, even if it was badly chipped and had a crack running all the way through. A bit like my life, she thought ruefully.

"Does the name Ronald Sanders mean anything to you?"

Alice put the biscuit back on the plate. Ah, so that's what this was about.

"I did know him," she said, her chin quivering slightly. "But he's dead."

"I know," said Inspector Lancaster quietly.

"Is that why I'm here? Because he's dead?" asked Alice, more loudly than she intended. "You think I had something to do with it." It wasn't a question. She stood up. The Inspector looked up at her. "I was the one who found him. You know that, don't you?"

"Yes, we do. And please sit down, Mrs Coulter. Or can I call you Alice?"

"Actually, I'd rather you didn't," she said, sitting down. "Mrs Coulter will do."

Inspector Lancaster shrugged his shoulders. Whatever.

"Technically, Ronald Sanders died from a heart attack. The post mortem confirmed that."

Alice looked at him, puzzled. "What do you mean, *technically*? He either did or he didn't."

Inspector Lancaster ignored her question. "Can you tell me how you knew him?"

"He was my next door neighbour. Lived next to me and my husband for years. He was already there when we moved to Greenfields Road."

"Did you know him well?"

"Well enough. We were neighbours, as I said. For over 25 years."

"Just how well did you know him?" asked the Inspector.

"I've just told you," said Alice impatiently. "I knew him for over 25 years."

"What I want to know is how well did you know him?" he repeated, emphasising each word. "It's a simple enough question."

Alice shrugged her shoulders. "Pretty well, I suppose. I used to go in once a day. Sometimes more. To check he was alright."

"A good neighbour?"

"I'd like to think so."

"And what *exactly* did you do for him?" asked the Inspector.

"I took him meals. Well, his dinner. Did some of his washing. A bit of cleaning. Shopping. That sort of thing."

"Anything else?"

"Like what? What are you getting at?"

"There's no easy way of asking this, Mrs Coulter. Did you do anything for him of a…er…a…sexual nature?" The Inspector had the grace to blush.

Her reaction surprised him. He'd expected outrage or indignation at least and got neither. Alice looked down at her hands in her lap, unable to meet his gaze, and asked quietly. "Can I ask you why you're asking that?"

"We've had a complaint," said the Inspector.

"A complaint! What sort of complaint? From who?"

"I can't say," replied the Inspector. "But the complainant alleges that Ronald Sanders' heart attack may have been the result of some unusual…sexual activity."

Alice glared at him. Now she knew. "It's his son, isn't it? Ricky. It has to be. Couldn't be anyone else. In all the time I've lived next to Ronald, I'd never seen his son. Not once. At least, not until the funeral. He never visited his father once, not in all the time I knew him. No Christmas cards. No birthday cards. Nothing!" Alice was aware her voice was getting louder. And angrier. "Ronald had given up on him. Told me that as far as he was concerned, I was the only family he had!" She could feel her face going red and tears starting to well up. "How could you think I had anything to do with his heart attack? How could anyone think that?" She pulled a used tissue out of her coat pocket and blew her nose loudly.

"Mrs Coulter, we don't think you killed him. But we are obliged to investigate any mysterious death."

"But how can it be mysterious if the doctor said he died from a heart attack? He was in his eighties, for goodness sake!"

"Nevertheless, we have a duty to investigate these allegations."

"Allegations made by a no-good, lazy bastard of a son who could never be bothered to visit his father when he was alive! This is unbelievable!" She tore the tissue into shreds.

"Mrs Coulter, an allegation has been made that you were offering sexual services to Ronald and that these put a strain on his heart. It has also been alleged that you were organising these...services for other lonely old men. You were, to use the exact words, running a mobile brothel." He consulted the file. "A sort of Feels on Wheels is how it's been described." The Inspector failed to suppress a smile. They'd had a good laugh about that in the canteen.

"I don't believe this," said Alice, standing up again. "A mobile brothel! I've only got a bike!" She put her hands on her hips and stared down at him. "How dare he! I did nothing for Ronald but care for him. And if that sometimes meant a bit of...well, I don't call it sexual services. There was no sex involved. Well, not really. I mean...for goodness sake!"

"What would you call it, Mrs Coulter? If you don't call it sexual services, what would you call it? And please sit down."

Alice sat. "I'd call it...friendship. Companionship. Caring. Being neighbourly. That's what I'd call it."

"And when did this 'being neighbourly' start?" asked the Inspector snidely.

"I can't remember." Alice shrugged her shoulders. "Years ago. Does it matter?"

"Mrs Coulter, I'm investigating an allegation that you offered these services to influence Ronald's will."

If this wasn't so serious, it would be funny. Alice looked at him.

"Will? What will? I don't know anything about a will. That's Ricky again, isn't it? He doesn't know what he's talking about. Ronald had bugger all." She laughed wryly. "Money!"

"What?"

"Money. It always comes down to money. That's what this is all about. Not the fact that poor Ronald was a lonely old man whose son couldn't be bothered with him when he was alive. But when he's dead,

God rest his soul, and his lazy, no-good…shit of a son thinks he might be worth something, *then* he's interested. Like a maggot crawling out of a dead dog's arse." Alice's cheeks were on fire. She didn't often swear but now it seemed right. And actually, it felt rather good.

"Please calm down, Mrs Coulter."

Alice was finding it difficult to keep calm. The mere thought of Ricky was sending her blood pressure through the roof. She took several deep breaths.

"Can you tell me what you know about Ronald's financial affairs," asked the Inspector.

"His financial affairs? Why, nothing. Why would I?" Alice was mystified. Ronald had told her from time to time that he had a bit of money stashed away but she'd always thought he was joking. "I really have no idea. He gave me a little bit of money every now and then, money he kept in a tin, for food and…things." Alice thought she wouldn't say anything more at the moment unless she was pressed. "Money in a tin. But that was it."

"It's claimed that your next door neighbour was a very wealthy man."

Alice stared at him, her mouth open. "Somebody's pulling your chain!" she laughed dryly. "I don't know where you're getting your information from but I can tell you for sure, Ronald did not have any money. You know where he lived. Greenfields Road, for goodness sake! Hardly Millionaire's Row!" She sighed deeply. "And anyway, I still don't understand what this has got to do with me?" She paused, remembering a letter that had arrived yesterday from Snatchet, Crumbs and Stollen, Solicitors, asking her to make an appointment to see them. Could that have something to do with all this? Maybe if the Inspector wouldn't explain what was going on, the solicitors might be able to shed some light on the matter.

The young policeman rubbed the back of his neck. Something told him this was going to be a very long day. "I'm not sure what it's got to do with you either," he admitted. "So why don't you tell me about Ronald? How all this being neighbourly began? Could you do that? Starting at the very beginning?"

Alice Coulter leaned forward, her elbows on the table, her head in her hands. "Right from the very beginning?"

"If you don't mind."

Alice closed her eyes and nodded. Right. From the very beginning.

# CHAPTER 1

## BANGERS AND MASH

"Show us yer tits!"

"Ronald!"

"Go on! Flash 'em!"

"I can't believe you just said that," said Alice, laughing. "You really are a dirty old man. An old rogue. Disgusting, that's what you are!"

Ronald laughed. "Go on! You're a handsome woman. Show me what you've got! You've got a nice body. I want to see more of it! I want to see your hooters! Your gazongas! Your bristols!"

"If you don't stop this nonsense now, Ronald Sanders, I'm going out that front door and I won't be coming back!" She put a plate of food down in front of him.

Ronald sighed, glared at her then smiled.

"Bangers and mash. Onion gravy. My favourite. Good wholesome food. Like the woman who cooks it. No fuss. No frills. Just the way I like it."

Alice smiled. A back-handed compliment if ever there was one. She watched him as he ate. Ronald looked old. Small, his body folding in on itself, he sat hunched in his chair, a tartan blanket across his knees. His skin was almost transparent, dry and heavily lined, his white wispy hair escaping from under a woollen hat. His eyes were deep. Sunken. Alice couldn't be sure of their colour, brown possibly. But there was still a sparkle in them. She had no idea exactly how old he was. Somewhere in his eighties, possibly older. While Ronald happily tucked into his dinner, Alice looked round the room. An old man's room. Small, all four walls covered in the same floral wallpaper which had long since lost its colour; brown curtains which didn't shut completely and a stained, thin, red carpet. There was one small armchair pulled up close to the three bar electric fire, a small television in the corner, a table in the window on which Ronald sometimes ate his meals, two mismatching plastic chairs and a wooden sideboard on which stood several framed photos and an assortment of yellowing newspapers. There was a pervading smell of cabbage – nothing to do with the food that Ronald was eating so heartily – and damp. Ronald cleaned up the last of the gravy and peas with a spoon and sat back. He licked his lips and leaned back contentedly.

"Lovely stuff. Thank you, Alice. Any pudding?"

"Sorry. Not today, Ronald. I didn't have time. Maybe tomorrow."

"You're a grand woman, you know that. You remind me of my Shirley." He nodded his head towards the largest of the photographs on the sideboard, black and white in an ornate silver frame. Alice picked it up. It showed a young couple on a sandy beach, holding hands, their backs to a stormy sea. The pretty, dark-haired girl was trying to hold down her coat with her free hand and the handsome young man held onto his hat. Despite the grim weather, they were both smiling broadly "That was our honeymoon. Scarborough. In June. Though you wouldn't know it from the weather." Ronald took the photo from Alice and held it in both hands. His eyes misted over as he looked at it. "That was my Shirley," he said quietly. "Lovely lass. Best in the world. Shame you never met her. You'd have liked her." He sighed and handed the photo back to Alice who returned it carefully to its exact place on the sideboard. "I do miss her you know."

"I know," said Alice softly, wondering what it felt like to be missed like that.

"It'll be fifty two years tomorrow exactly."

"What will?"

"My Shirley. Fifty two years since the day she died."

"Oh, I'm so sorry, Ronald, I had no idea."

Ronald wiped a tear from her eye. "Died in labour she did. Would have been a daughter, But it was too much for them both." He examined the liver spots on the back of his hands.

Alice couldn't think of anything to say. What do you say to say to someone who was still grieving, fifty two years later?

They sat in silence for a while.

"I'd better be off," she said. "You be alright?"

Ronald looked up. "See you tomorrow?" he asked her quietly.

Alice picked up the dirty plate and cutlery and washed them up in the small kitchen as she waited for the kettle to boil.

"Here's your tea," she said, handing Ronald a mug with Happy Birthday written on it.

"Tomorrow?" he asked again.

"Tomorrow."

"A tenner."

"What?" She stopped in her tracks.

"I'll give you a tenner. If you show us yer tits! Your melons!" The doleful mood was gone.

"I thought you'd stopped that nonsense!"

"Twenty quid then. A tenner for each!"

"Ronald, no! I'll see you tomorrow."

"Think about my offer. Twenty quid is twenty quid. You could treat yourself. Get something nice."

Or put it towards a new coat, thought Alice. Goodness knows, I need one. She dismissed the idea immediately. "Now, is there anything else you need before I go?"

Ronald shook his head. He smiled at her and winked. "See you tomorrow?" he asked again.

"Tomorrow." She closed the door behind her.

"Do you know what Ronald just asked me to do?" said Alice addressing a man who was slumped in an armchair only feet in front of a blaring television set. The room was identical in shape and size to Ronald's but it seemed much smaller because it was dominated by a huge flat screen tv which had cost them – her – a small fortune. The price of their holiday, in fact. Alice couldn't look at it without feeling sick. This monstrosity represented a week away, together. Their first holiday in years. A coach trip through the Borders. Northumberland and southern Scotland. She'd been so excited, looking at the brochure over and over again. Memorising each and every detail of the tour. Small family hotels. Nothing posh. All their meals included. Castles to visit. Gardens and stately homes. Mountains to see. Even a boat trip on a lake. And all included in the price. Nothing else to pay for except maybe the odd glass of wine or even a nice gin and tonic. She would be on holiday, after all. Nothing to worry about except having a good time and forgetting about work. She'd been so excited. A proper holiday! Then three weeks ago, the day before she was going to go into Broad'n Your Horizonz in the town centre to book the holiday and pay the small deposit, there had been a knock on the door. A pimply youth dressed in jeans and a brown cotton jacket with 'Darby & Sons' embroidered on the pocket with a matching baseball cap on back-to-front stood there clutching a clipboard.

"Delivery for Coulter."

"There must be some mistake," said Alice. "We've not ordered anything."

14

"You are Coulter?"

"Yes."

"And this is 46 Greenfields Road?"

Alice nodded. She'd never been able to work out why it was called Greenfields Road. Maybe there had been fields around here once but if there had, it was a very long time ago. She looked up and down the seemingly endless street at the two-up two-down, brick-built, terraced houses facing each other, identical apart from differently coloured front doors. At least nearly all the houses here in Greenfields Road are lived in, she thought to herself. Not like some of the other streets in town where most of the old Victorian houses were boarded up and abandoned. Must be awful trying to live somewhere like that. Waiting for the developers to come in. Except they never do. Run out of money, the council says. So they stand empty and forgotten. Most of the houses on Greenfields Road were well looked-after; one or two even had wooden flower boxes under the windows although at this time of year they were empty. There might not be much money round here but most people made a bit of an effort. The houses were small, no doubt about that. But then they'd been built for factory workers in the days when there was a factory at the end of almost every street and space was considered a luxury. Like most people, Alice and Frank had moved the bathroom from the ground floor upstairs cutting one of the bedrooms almost in half in the process. It gave them a bigger kitchen but Alice, if she'd had a say in the matter, would have preferred a proper hall. She had never liked the fact that the front door opened straight into the living room. Cold, she'd said to Frank. Brings the weather straight into the house. But that would have cost a lot more money and her husband had decided that having an upstairs bathroom was more important.

"I said, this is Smedley, isn't it?" said the youth loudly and very slowly. He obviously thought her deaf as well as dim.

"Yes, sorry. Yes it is," replied Alice. "But we haven't ordered anything," she repeated.

"Sign here please." He handed her the clipboard with a pen attached to it by a piece of string. As she looked at the invoice he lugged a huge cardboard box out of the white van which he'd parked half on the pavement outside the house. "My, this is a big bugger," he said, wrestling it through the open door and into the lounge, past Alice standing open-mouthed and incredulous. He put it down in the middle of the floor.

"But it says here," said Alice almost in tears, tapping the invoice with her finger, "it says it's a 60 inch television. We didn't order this. We've already got one." She pointed to a small television set sitting in the corner of the room, framed by the open doors of a faux wood cabinet. "And this is a huge amount of money." She stared at the invoice. "It has to be a mistake." At that moment, an overweight, untidily dressed man had shuffled into the lounge from the kitchen, hands in pockets. Her husband. Then it dawned on her.

"Do you know anything about this, Frank? Did you order a television?"

Frank's face lit up, his eyes bright. "It's here! Great!" He took the invoice from Alice, signed it and stuffed the copy he was given down the back of the armchair. Fumbling in his trouser pocket for some change, he gave a few coins to the youth who looked at them in disgust then left, muttering. Tearing at the cardboard he started to unpack the tv whilst Alice looked on, speechless. "Fantastic!" he enthused. "Look, princess, isn't it brilliant?"

Alice retrieved the invoice and stared at it again. "Frank, tell me you didn't order this."

"Of course I did. Why d'you think he delivered it? You can be such a lemon at times, you know. People only deliver stuff that gets ordered."

"But the cost! This can't be right. We don't have this sort of money." She read the bottom line of the invoice again. "Where's this money come from?"

Frank stopped what he was doing and shuffled his slippered feet, looking at her sheepishly. Something else dawned on her.

"This was our holiday money, wasn't it?" Alice was having difficulty speaking.

"I've got to have some pleasure in life, haven't I? You can't deny me a bit of fun, can you?" He reached his hand towards her but Alice backed away from him.

"Tell me this isn't our holiday money. Tell me you bought it out of your own money." But she already knew the answer. Frank had no money of his own. Never had, never would have.

"I'll replace it, princess. Honest I will."

"Don't *princess* me!" Alice slumped into the armchair.

"But you are my princess. You always have been. Always will."

16

Alice felt sick. "That money was for our holiday. I saved years for that. Years." She felt physically sick.

"I know, pet. But you can't deny me a bit of happiness, can you?"

"Happiness? Happiness? What about me, Frank? What about me?"

"But it was in the sale. It was a real bargain. Half price it was. And the delivery was free. Give me some credit, love."

"Frank, I don't ask much. I work all hours god sends at the factory making those bloody biscuits. I don't do it because I love it. I do it so we can have a roof over our heads, can pay our bills, and occasionally, just very occasionally, we can have a treat. Nothing fancy. I don't ask for much, God only knows. Just something. Something different. Once in a while. Can't you understand that? "

"Of course I can," said Frank, trying again to reach for his wife's hand. "But when you think about it, this is more of an investment. After all, what would we have to show for a holiday in Scotland, eh? A few days away, soon forgotten. Bad backs from uncomfortable beds. Strange food. Having to talk to people we don't know. This way we've got something to show for our money. This tv will still be here long after any holiday. Every day we can look at it and consider it money well spent."

"*My* money spent, not yours."

"Stop going on about whose money it was. It's not important. And look on the bright side, we'll be able to get rid of that tv cabinet you've always hated."

Alice looked at her husband in disbelief. What did I ever do to deserve you? she asked herself. Frank smiled weakly at her then turned his attention back to unpacking the television. The matter was over as far as he was concerned. He heaved it out of box, tore off the bubble wrap and plugged it in. His face positively glowed with delight as the picture came on and two men materialised chasing a ball.

"Look, football," he whispered, mesmerised, as if he'd just witnessed the Second Coming. He had.

"I'll be in the kitchen ironing," said Alice, closing the lounge door. He didn't even notice she'd gone.

"Do you know what Ronald just asked me to do?" Alice repeated. Still no response. She looked at her husband. It was almost impossible to tell where the chair began and her husband ended. Like one of those horror films, she thought. Frank had morphed into a piece of furniture.

He had become the armchair, inseparable and inextricably linked, condemned to a future of shared entropy. Both had seen better days, much better days, and both looked as if the stuffing was coming out of them. At least the armchair retained some of its original colour, faded reds and browns, which was more than could be said of Frank. He was washed out. Colourless. Not surprising, since he never saw daylight. She couldn't remember the last time he'd stepped outside the front door. He had the grey pallor of an addict, afraid of the sun. Afraid of reality. His world revolved round the tv and there was nothing else. Even the armchair has more personality, thought Alice. Perhaps I should give it a name and talk to it instead. She coughed loudly. Frank tore his gaze away from the screen and looked at her.

"Oh, hello, love. Didn't see you there. Alright?" He turned back to whatever he was watching.

Alice looked at him. He was slouched deep as he could, the top of his head level with the back of the armchair. His arms rested across his beer-swollen belly, comforting it, the remote control in his right hand like a sixth finger. What little hair he had was thin and lank. His fat face was round, child-like and his snub nose and tiny eyes gave him a porcine appearance. He wore his usual stained vest, once white, and black tracksuit bottoms encased his fat legs which were stretched out in front of him. A tin of beer was on the floor, within arm's reach.

"Do you know what Ronald has just asked me to do, Frank?" said Alice, for the third time.

"Mmm? Ronald? Ronald who?"

"Ronald. Our next door neighbour for over twenty five years? That Ronald."

"Oh, him."

"He has offered me ten pounds to…"

"Sshh a minute. It's the final of the 100 meters. Sorry, love. Can't miss this."

Alice stared at her husband as he watched ten sleek, toned, athletic bodies hurtling down a track, arms and legs pumping. It seemed to be over before it had even started. Like life, she thought.

"As I predicted," said Frank smugly. "I knew he'd do it. After his performance in the Europeans, he could hardly fail." He nodded satisfactorily. "Now, what were you saying?"

"Nothing," replied Alice. "It's not important. You watch your telly."

"Ok, princess. Did I hear you say you were putting the kettle on?"

# CHAPTER 2

## CHICKEN PIE WITH LEEKS

Alice reached out a hand from under the duvet and groping in the dark, turned the alarm clock off. Frank grunted but didn't move. She lay there, yawning and rubbing the sleep from her eyes, reluctant to get out of bed. Another day. She heard the rain lash against the window, feeling the draught as the wind rattled the panes. Shivering, Alice yawned again then got up. Without turning the bedside light on she put on her slippers and shuffled across the room, taking her dressing gown off the hook on the bedroom door. She didn't need a light. Alice had done this thousands of times, so many times she could do it in her sleep. Most mornings it felt as if she did. She crossed the landing to the bathroom and turned on the light. Blinking hard, Alice undressed and climbed into the bath, shivering. She turned the hot water tap on full and stared at the cheap rubber shower spray in her hand, waiting. The water ran cold for several minutes before it was warm enough to use. It could hardly be described as hot. Maybe that £20 that Ronald offered would mean we could have the water on for a bit longer, she thought and I could have a hot shower in the morning instead of a tepid one. Maybe we could even have the central heating on for a bit longer too, especially now that the nights were really cold. December had been relatively dry and mild, thank goodness, and she'd been able to persuade Frank not to have the heating on too much to save on bills. But now, mid January, the weather was doing what it usually did in January. Being cold and wet and thoroughly miserable. But what difference would twenty quid make? A drop in the ocean. When Alice thought about what she'd have to do to get it, she couldn't help but smile. Stepping out of the bath, she dried herself on one of the thin towels draped over the cold radiator and stood in front of the mirror above the sink. She could only see herself from the waist up but that was more than enough. Alice shook her head in dismay as she looked at her breasts. There's only one word for them. Droopy. Like one of the Seven Dwarves. She could remember when her finest attributes pointed to heaven. Well, Rochdale at least. She smiled again. Are these really worth twenty quid? Ronald seemed to think so. Alice examined her face closely in the mirror, shook her head sadly, then squeezed the last of the moisturiser out of the tube and dabbed some under her eyes.

It made no difference. Nothing would make those bags disappear. They'd headed south too. Same direction as her breasts. She ran a brush through her hair and sighed heavily. Onward and downward, she thought.

Alice decided to skip breakfast. She was running late as usual, and would grab something at work in the staff canteen. Whilst the kettle boiled she looked round the small kitchen with its dated cupboards and worn counter tops. The cracked lino floor and the old electric cooker, the rings lined with silver foil. The stainless steel sink which belied its name. The sash window which wouldn't open. If I won the lottery, she thought, I'd have one of those modern kitchens. One with an island in the middle. Fancy! An island. A kitchen where I could cook. Really cook. Try out some of those exotic recipes I've been saving all these years. Ones from the glossy magazines that Valerie gives me. Or torn surreptitiously from magazines in the doctors' surgery, coughing loudly to disguise the sound of ripping paper and stuffing them into my handbag when no-one's looking. She smiled to herself. Wonderful recipes for food that was more than just a belly-filler. Exciting food. Fancy food. But who'd eat it? Ronald? Certainly not Frank. No, he'd be more than happy with the chicken pie and leeks she was going to cook tonight using the left-overs from yesterday's roast. Nothing fancy for him. Alice sighed deeply. Bland is as bland does.

The kettle switched itself off and she made a mug of tea which she took upstairs to Frank. He lay on his back, snoring.

"Here you are, sloth. Your early morning cuppa. Be sure to take it easy today. Wouldn't want you exerting yourself." She prodded the sleeping mound with her finger. "Tea," she said loudly.

Frank muttered and rolled over on to his side. He opened one eye.

"Whassup?"

"Tea."

"Mmm." The eye closed.

"You're welcome. Please don't mention it."

Alice turned on the overhead bedroom light. Frank didn't stir. Not a muscle. She slammed the bedroom door hard. Back in the kitchen she put on a plain green head scarf and her only coat. A brown wool affair that had seen better days. I'm going to get soaked, she thought as she peered out of the window. The rain had not eased off. If anything, it was worse. It was only a ten minute ride to work but in this downpour, it might well have been ten times that. She opened the back door and dashed to the small outhouse where she kept her bike. The back yard was under half an inch of water and she could feel it seeping through the soles of her shoes. "Damn and blast!" Wheeling the bike out into the yard, Alice glanced up at the bedroom window. The light was off. So Frank had got out of bed, turned the light off, got back into bed and was presumably now asleep once more. If she'd had the energy and it hadn't been pouring with rain, Alice would have been tempted to throw something up at the window, even if it had only been words. But the longer she stood there, the wetter she got. Angrily she turned the headlamp on so she could see to unbolt the wooden door that opened onto the alley. Wheeling the bike towards a streetlight where the alley met the road, Alice carefully avoided black bin bags full of rubbish and the occasional abandoned item of furniture, her feet sliding on the wet, moss-slick cobblestones. Under the light, she mounted her bike and headed off to work.

After fifteen minutes of furiously pedalling into a headwind which threatened to knock her off her bike, Alice rode through the imposing factory gates. An illuminated sign on an arched, black wrought-iron frame above the gates read 'Bercow's Biscuits – Baked with 'utter for a Better Bite.' The 'B' from 'Butter' had long since gone. The joke amongst the workers was that the butter had never been there in the first place. Of all the ingredients that went into making Bercow's Biscuits, butter was not one of them. Alice dismounted and walked her bike round to the back of the building to the covered bike sheds. Always reminds me of schooldays, she thought. She rammed her bike into the metal rack, not bothering locking it – the bike was so old and knackered, it wasn't worth pinching. Just like me, she thought wryly. Her feet squelched as she made her way round to the staff entrance.

Not long ago she would have been welcomed by a smiling, uniformed Raymond whose job it was to watch the comings and goings of staff. His proper title was Security Officer but all he ever did was to sit in a small office drinking tea and read the racing section of the Smedley Sun. He could have no more protected the factory or its workers than knit marshmallows, everyone knew that. He was a throwback to the days when Bertram Bercow, the founder of Bercow's Biscuits way back in 1930, liked his workers to be greeted when they arrived for their shift. He thought it would make them feel worthwhile, valued. A pay increase would be even more effective in making us feel appreciated, one worker had been audacious enough to tell the great man. That rash comment had resulted in his employment being terminated with immediate effect. But cutbacks meant Raymond had to go. As did the shifts. Times were so difficult now that twenty-four hour biscuit-making at Bercow's was a thing of the past. It wasn't that people were eating fewer biscuits. They were eating even more if you believed what you read in the papers. Everyone was eating more of everything. It was just that, like everything else, biscuits were made overseas. Labour was cheaper and workers not as fussy. Eastern Europe? Western Europe? Alice wouldn't be surprised if some biscuits weren't made in China. So no more shifts now. They were all on days. Great to be able to get a good night's sleep, but come payday, it hurt. Everyone was chasing occasional overtime, rare as rocking horse poo, just to make ends meet. Bercow's was not the place it was. At its peak, over 400 people had worked in the factory and Bercow's Biscuits was a household name, known far and wide. Some of the biscuits were even shipped as far away as Australia and New Zealand. A little taste of home for those far away, they used to say. Not any more. There was only the domestic market now and even that was being undercut by cheap imports. And fewer than 60 people worked at the factory today. Bercow's Biscuits was struggling to survive.

Once inside and out of the rain, Alice took a card bearing her name from a rack on the wall and put it in the slot of the clocking-in machine. It made a satisfying clunk - not as satisfying a clunk as the one at the end of the day. That was the best sound of all. She made her way along dark brick-lined corridors to the staff room, her wet shoes making unpleasant squelching, farting noises. The staff room, which doubled as a changing room for the female staff - the men had to use the toilets as their changing room - was lined on three sides with grey metal lockers and a couple of cupboards and on the fourth by a stainless steel sink and draining board. A large rectangular table occupied most of the room and half a dozen plastic chairs were scattered about. It was functional, not designed for comfort or spending time in. Despite the hour the place was quiet. Alice shook as much rain out of her coat as she could then hung it inside her locker. Taking off her wet shoes, she grabbed some paper towels from a dispenser above the sink and dried her feet as best she could. The dye from her shoes had stained her toes and heels blue. She sighed. Another pair of tights ruined. Then she turned her attention to the shoes themselves. A few more paper towels were stuffed into the toes in an attempt to soak up some of the rainwater. New shoes time, no question. New shoes. New coat. If only. Wriggling her toes, Alice looked down at her stockinged feet. Why 'stockinged feet'? she mused. I've got tights on, so why not call them 'tighted feet' or simply 'tight feet'? As she pondered one of life's unanswerable questions, shoes in one hand, paper towels in the other, the door opened. In walked a tall Asian woman dressed in a long green waterproof coat, matching hat and pink wellington boots.

"Morning Alice," she said, smiling. "Awful weather!"

"Hello, Shanti," Alice replied, gesturing with a shoe. "Wet feet."

The woman nodded in sympathy as she shrugged off her coat to reveal jeans and a light blue fleece. She sat down to pull off her boots and Alice watched her enviously as she went to her locker and took out a dry pair of trainers. Alice was kicking herself. Last week she'd had to throw away the spare pair of shoes she kept in her locker – holier than a string vest in church - and she couldn't believe she'd forgotten to replace them. How could she have been so stupid? If only she'd remembered, she wouldn't have to work all day in wet shoes with wet feet. Shanti took two clean white overalls from one cupboard and two hairnets from another and gave one of each to Alice. Effortlessly coiling up her long, lustrous black hair, she tucked it into the hairnet. Not a single strand was missed.

"Do you know, Shanti, you'd look good in a flour sack with a cupcake on your head! It's so unfair," said Alice as she wrestled her damp grey hair first into a pony tail then into its protective headgear. "You're the only person I know who can look stunning in an overall. I think I hate you!" And she was right. Shanti did look stunning. The bleached white overall set off her flawless golden skin. High cheek bones with deep-set almond-shaped black eyes surrounded by the longest lashes you could ever imagine. Shanti exuded class. Elegance. Sophistication. Everything that Alice didn't. "Yes, it's official. I hate you!"

Shanti laughed. "You look good too, Alice. How's things?"

Alice shrugged. "Same old. Same old."

"I take it you mean Frank?"

"I mean Frank. He's the same and he's old. Makes me feel old too."

Shanti put her arm round Alice's shoulders. "You're not old. You're in your prime. I like you just the way you are. Don't ever change." A lump unexpectedly appeared in Alice's throat. Shanti squeezed tighter. "Why don't you leave the old goat? Divorce him."

"What?" Alice looked at her.

"Don't tell me you've never thought about doing it."

"Well, I, er, I mean, not really. Well, yes, I have. Maybe," she admitted.

"Why don't you then?"

"What would he do? He couldn't cope without me. He's disabled you know."

"No he's not."

"Shanti, you can't say that! He's on Disability Benefit. Has been for years."

"The only thing that's disabled about your Frank is his Get Up and Go! It got up and went years ago and it's not coming back. Ever. He's as fit as the next man. And as able. He just chooses not to be." Shanti folded her arms. "You spoil him. Wait on him hand and foot. Why not leave him? He's never going to change. Make a new life for yourself. While you've still got time. Find a new man. Or not. Your choice. But get out there, girl! Live!"

Alice looked at her friend open-mouthed. Where had this suddenly come from? She'd known Shanti for years and she'd never said anything like this before. She'd put into words thoughts Alice had had so many times but put out of her mind as soon as they'd risen to the surface. And here was Shanti saying what she'd didn't dare think about. "I couldn't possibly divorce him." She folded her arms. "And anyway," she added as an afterthought, "who'd have me?"

"You're kidding me, right? Alice, you are the most kind-hearted, wonderful woman I know. Anybody would have you. I'd have you. Come and live with me."

Alice looked down at the shoe in her hand, embarrassed.

"Ok, then. You won't divorce him. What about bumping him off?"

"Bumping him off? You mean…kill him? I can't believe you just said that." Alice stared at her friend, open-mouthed.

In the distance, a klaxon sounded. Alice looked at the clock on the wall.

"Shit! We're going to be late!" She pulled her wet shoes back on quickly, shivering in disgust. And too late now to grab something from the canteen. She'd have to wait until lunchtime. Another missed breakfast. "Where are you this week?"

Shanti consulted a roster pinned to the back of the door. "I'm Cumberland Creams. You?"

Alice found her name. "Wafers." She was heading out of the door and down the corridor. "See you at lunchtime?" she shouted over her shoulder.

"Alice?" Turning round, she saw Shanti was smiling at her. "Just think about it, that's all I'm saying."

# CHAPTER 3

## MACARONI CHEESE

Think about it? That's all Alice did for the next nine and a half hours. That was one thing about working for Bercow's Biscuits – it gave you plenty of time to think. The work wasn't demanding, not even physically, even though there was a lot of standing involved. Most of the production was automated so it was simply a question of keeping an eye on things, pressing a few buttons or pulling the odd lever just to add to the excitement. What it didn't require was intelligence. You didn't even really need to pay attention, not unless something went wrong. The weekly roster dictated which biscuit or part-biscuit manufacture she would oversee and this week it was Pink Wafers. Her role this week was to stand next to a large noisy machine, one of many on the factory floor connected to each other by a series of conveyor belts, tubes and ducting, whose sole function was to mix the pink paste that sandwiched the same unnaturally-coloured wafers together. Someone else further up the food chain was responsible for making the wafers which appeared in front of her on a slow-moving conveyor belt. All she had to do was to mix the filling and oversee the machine that sandwiched them into place.

She started the process by watching the yellow gloop, a mixture of flour, sugar and fat (definitely not butter) go round and round, round and round, in the giant stainless steel blending bowl. After ten minutes, when the consistency was deemed to be just right, Alice pressed a button which dispensed a specified amount of fluorescent pink colouring into the mix via a thin metal tube which was connected to a large plastic container mounted high above the mixing machine. After three minutes she pressed another button which caused a cocktail of preservatives and additives to be added to the bowl from another similarly located container. After a final further stir of three minutes, Alice pulled a lever and the rotating paddle in the bowl rose slowly then stopped. She scraped off any mixture that was still attached to it then scooped the pink confection into what looked like a large syringe with a fluted nozzle which she positioned over the conveyor belt. Pressing yet another button caused a dollop of pink filling to be deposited on each wafer and she quickly pressed another wafer on top, forming a sandwich. And that was it. Someone else downstream was responsible for the packaging and distribution. When she'd finished the current batch, Alice would press a red button and watch the machine grind to a halt and fall silent. It made no difference to the overall cacophony on the factory floor, with all its various machines for the different types of biscuits that Bercow's made and all the noisy complex processes involved and Alice didn't notice any lessening of the incessant background noise; her ear plugs blocked out most of the racket. The only time the building was completely silent was at the end of each day when all the biscuits had been mixed, shaped, baked, cooled, decorated (where appropriate), wrapped and boxed ready for distribution. Otherwise there was a constant thrum of ageing, failing machinery urged on by a team of three engineers who spent their time coaxing, cajoling and sweet-talking the giant machines to keep them going for just one more hour, one more day.

The men who tended the machines were known whimsically as the S&M engineers, or Serious Maintenance engineers. Most of the time they were successful in getting a recalcitrant machine back up and running, but it was usually more by luck than skill. But sometimes they failed and the machine refused to listen to the engineers' wheedling entreaties (or more usually, swearing) and ignored the blows of a hammer or a surreptitious kick. And when a machine broke down and ground to a halt, the lucky biscuit maker snatched a few minutes of relative peace. Nothing to do but wait until the problem was solved. A few moments of unheralded idleness at the company's expense. Unless the breakdown proved truly problematic and the machine couldn't be repaired quickly in which case that particular biscuit section would have to be closed down and the worker deployed elsewhere until the fault was remedied. All the biscuit workers, or Bercow's Biscuit Biddies as they were referred to glibly by Management, (for some reason all the staff on the factory floor who actually made the biscuits were women), could be sent to help out somewhere else in the processing plant. All the Biddies could do every part of every biscuit-making – there were so few of them now that they had to be able to turn their hand to anything - Marshmallow Moments, Chocolate Dropsies, Caribbean Crunch, Hazelnut Hearts, Lemon Licks, Caramel Curls. Alice, like her fellow workers, could do each and every part of the manufacture of each and every biscuit that Bercow's made in her sleep – and sometimes did. It required no thought process, no intellectual involvement. It did require a robust constitution and strong legs as the

Biddies were on their feet for most of the day. But the only skill any of them needed was an ability to push the right buttons at the right time. Which meant Alice could switch off and think about what Shanti had said.

When did it all become so...*samey*? When did she wake up and realise that Frank was no longer the handsome, young and to be honest, incredibly sexy, man that she married so long ago? When did he go to seed? At which precise moment did he decide to give up and become a slob? Alice stretched her back and rolled her shoulders. She was getting too old for this game. She pressed the button and added the pink colouring. When did they stop being in love and become just *there*? Because no doubt about it, she had loved him. Had? Yes, had. Loved him passionately. Furiously. But that was a very long time ago. She couldn't remember the last time she felt anything for her husband except apathy. Or irritation. When did she grow so cold? Oh, it was long before the incident with the television and Frank stealing all her holiday money. Long, long before that. Truth to tell, Alice had hoped that the holiday in the Borders might have re-kindled some of what they had once felt for each other. A bit of romance. Maybe even a bit of passion? Alice smiled wryly. *Passion?* When did passion last come into it? Too late now. They'd missed the boat. His new 60 inch television had seen to that. And what now for the future? An endless round of Bercow's Biscuits. A long, lonely retirement like poor Ronald next door? Maybe she should divorce Frank, like Shanti said. Alice laughed out loud. Bella, another of Bercow's Biddies, working on a machine opposite her, (Shortbread Sweeties?) looked up at the inappropriate and unusual sound. Embarrassed, Alice waved to her and Bella returned to what she was doing. But maybe Shanti was right. I should divorce him and have a bit of life while there's still time. What would I do? What *could* I do? I've got no skills, no talents. All I can do is make these wretched biscuits. But what Shanti said about bumping Frank off. She was joking, wasn't she? Ordinary people didn't go around killing their husbands. Though sometimes you read about it in the paper or saw it on the telly. And when their neighbours were interviewed, they always said that the murderer or murderess was a lovely person, the kindest person you would ever wish to meet, there had to be some mistake, surely. So maybe I could, thought Alice, as she pressed the button adding the preservatives to the now pink mixture. I could put something deadly in his pudding one day. Or lace his beer with poison. But knowing my luck, I'd get caught. End up going to prison. Mind you, that would be no bad thing. Three square meals a day and I wouldn't have to get up at the crack of dawn to go and make bloody biscuits. But why square meals, she mused. Could I ask for *round* meals or a triangular one? And I'd have a nice warm room. Wouldn't have to worry about heating bills and I bet there'd be bags of hot water. Might not be that bad after all. She shook her head. Fantasy, that's all it was. She wasn't going to murder Frank or leave him. Couldn't do it. And, anyway, what about poor Ronald? Who'd look after him if I murdered Frank and went to prison? Alice turned off the machine and scraped the mixing blade. No, it's not going to happen. Nothing's ever going to change.

"Do you know what Ronald said to me the other day?" said Alice, leaning forward.
"Who's Ronald?"
Alice sat back, folded her arms and looked at the woman sitting opposite her. Theirs could not have been a more unlikely friendship. They had nothing in common. Valerie was everything Alice was not, including inattentive. Elegant, sophisticated, thin. Always immaculately dressed with never a hair out of place. But then Valerie worked in Accounts and didn't have to hide her hair under one of those sexless protective hairnets designed to stop 'Foreign Matter' falling into the mixes. Foreign Matter in the mixes was a hanging offence at Bercow's and there were regular checks for any hygiene breaches. Valerie would never be found guilty of hygiene breaches of any sort She was perfect. And working upstairs, she could wear make-up and nail polish, unlike Alice, whose work on the factory floor prohibited any outward display of femininity. Valerie was the same age as Alice but looked ten years younger. That's what money does for you, thought Alice. It buys you time. Either with a stylish cut with highlights, or a Pilates sessions, or homemade salads. She wasn't sure that Valerie hadn't had a bit of that Botox thing, but she'd never ask. Yes, they could not have been less alike. But the main difference between them was that Valerie didn't have to work. She lived in Meadowbank, the posh part of Smedley, and drove to work each day. She had money. That was thanks to seeing off two husbands, Valerie had explained. You didn't murder them? Alice had asked her incredulously. Valerie had doubled up with laughter.

Murdered them? No, not murdered them! Just divorced them and taken them for every penny she could. So now she worked because she chose to, for something to do, for companionship. Unlike Alice who worked because she and Frank needed to eat and she needed to pay the bills. Alice envied Valerie her strong chiselled cheekbones, her flawless skin, her finely etched eyebrows, her toned body and her fitted, designer-label clothes. She adored her but that didn't mean that Valerie didn't annoy the hell out of her when she didn't pay attention.

It was the lunch break and the two of them were sitting at one of a dozen or so plastic-topped tables in the staff canteen, half of which were occupied. Even here it wasn't quiet. A buzz of chatter filled the room which was too small for its current use. It used to be the printing room for the labels which were stuck onto the packets of biscuits by hand, but two years ago, this had been taken over by Pious Printers in nearby Wedgefield who did the whole lot, packaging and labels combined, for half the cost and with twice the imagination. Sales had actually increased initially when they had taken over this part of the manufacturing process – they had re-designed most of the packets and although the contents had not improved, the exteriors had. Bright, jolly, fun packaging made the customers think they were getting something new. They soon found out otherwise and sales had quickly fallen back to what they had been. And so the old printing room had been converted into a newer – and too small - staff canteen. It was lit by harsh neon strip lights with two stainless steel and glass cabinets against one wall. One contained ready-made sandwiches, the other plated pastries and slices of cake, sheathed in Clingfilm to prevent them going even staler. A drinks machine dispensed coffee and tea – there was a prize for anyone who could tell the difference. On a small table near the door were two plates of assorted Bercow's Biscuits and an honesty box. Management thought this was a nice touch. The workers could help themselves to the fruit of their labours and pay for the privilege. The workers thought otherwise. The plates were full and the box remained empty - staff were so fed up with sight of Bercow's Biscuits that the last thing they wanted to do was to eat them. And even if they ever did fancy one, they could surreptitiously pinch one off the line and who would know? Rarely was anyone tempted - they knew what went into them. The same applied to the bags of broken biscuits that anyone who worked at Bercow's could buy at a knock-down price.

30

No-one did. In a futile attempt to brighten and personalise the canteen, half a dozen photos of some of the workers hung on the walls – ones who had 'made a difference' as Bertram Bercow Junior (aged 63), BBJ as he liked to be known, was fond of saying. Alice was up there, one of the few of the great and the good. She had won the 2005 Bercow Biscuit Bonanza. This was BBJ's idea – something to give the staff pride in what they were doing. Loyalty to the firm, that sort of thing. But it was an act of desperation, a thinly-disguised means of stealing any good ideas about how to inject a new flavour, a new life, into a dying business. If someone could come up with a recipe for a new biscuit, a taste that would set the world on fire, it would guarantee them a place on the Wall of Fame, a handshake from BBJ himself and a £100 prize. It didn't happen often. Alice had been the last winner and that was over five years ago. Her recipe for Almond and Apple Alouettes had so impressed BBJ that he had decreed that her name would appear on every packet. And it did. The factory turned out over 10,000 packs every week and although it hadn't quite set the world on fire, it was still one of Bercow's best-sellers. The recipe had been one of her mum's and sometimes, when she wasn't too tired, Alice made them at home – properly, with real butter. Frank - and Ronald - loved them.

Alice was proud of winning – and even more delighted with the prize money – but she hated the photo. But then she hated any photo of herself. This one, however, was particularly bad. There she'd stood, dressed in her white overall and hair net, glowering at Jason from HR, a pimply youth who looked about 14, as he'd snapped half a dozen shots of her. Smile, he'd kept saying. She'd tried but the final result made her look as if she was suffering from gastric reflux. Grimacing, she clutched a silver cookie the size of a dinner plate engraved with her name. She hadn't even been allowed to take the award home. It was kept in the display cabinet in Reception alongside dusty packets of biscuits from when the factory first opened. No-one was interested – visitors to the factory were rare and the only thing the few reps who still occasionally visited were interested in was chatting up Kitty, the Receptionist, or dropping off their expenses claims before heading to the pub round the corner.

Alice had a plastic cup of something white and frothy in front of her – it might have been a coffee or possibly a particularly exuberant tea.

She also had a plastic-wrapped sandwich, grey bread curling over a yellow filling dotted with green bits. Coronation Chicken? Egg and Cress? Brie and Botulism? There were no obvious clues as to what it was but she was hungry, having missed breakfast. A piece of carrot cake sat between her and Valerie. She only knew it was carrot cake because the label said so. Valerie sipped from a bottle of mineral water and picked at a home-made couscous strewn with finely sliced roasted vegetables.

"Who's Ronald?" repeated Valerie.

"The old man who lives next door. You remember."

"Oh him. Your neighbour. The one you feed. Your friend."

Alice nodded. "Him. Well, you know I pop round every day. Make sure he's alright and that."

Valerie nodded. "You're an angel, that's what you are. I don't know anyone else who would do what you do."

Alice looked embarrassed. "I don't do anything special," she said. "I'm sure there's loads of people out there who do the same thing."

Valerie wasn't convinced. "What's on the menu tonight, then?"

"Macaroni Cheese."

"You spoil him, you really do," said Valerie.

Alice wasn't sure if she was being sarcastic or not. "Not really. I'm cooking for the two of us, for Frank and me, so it makes no difference to cook for one more. Besides, he's all on his own. It's a bit of company for him. And if I didn't take him his tea of an evening, I'm not sure he'd eat. I don't think he'd be able to cook for himself."

"What about the Council? Meals on Wheels? That sort of thing. They should be doing that, not you."

Alice shrugged her shoulders. "I'm just being neighbourly. I don't mind. Really. And as I say, I'm sure lots of other people do it."

"I don't think so, Alice. You're a one-off." She reached over and squeezed Alice's hand.

"Well, anyway," said Alice, shrugging her shoulders, "I was telling you what he said to me. You'll never guess." Valerie looked at her expectantly. "He said he would give me ten pounds if I showed him my...my you know. Bosoms! Actually, *tits* was what he said!" She leaned close to her friend and whispered the words. "*I'll give you £10 if you show me your tits!*"

"Ten pounds!" shrieked Valerie, covering her hand with her mouth. The canteen fell silent. "*Ten pounds!*" she repeated, whispering this time.

32

Alice nodded. "Then he upped it to £10 for each…you know, two bosoms. Both of them!"

"Twenty pounds! The dirty old dog! No way, girl!"

"That's what I thought," said Alice. "Awful! I was gob-smacked!"

"Too right! They're worth a lot more than that!"

"Valerie, you're as bad as he is! I meant that I couldn't possibly do it. I didn't mean that the money wasn't enough!" Alice sat back in her chair and looked at Valerie. She hadn't expected this reaction from her friend.

"So what are you going to do? Are you going to take the money?"

Alice looked at her friend in amazement. "Of course not! How could I? I mean, you wouldn't, would you?"

"Not for twenty quid, I wouldn't! And you're right. You shouldn't either. As I said, they're worth a lot more!"

"Valerie!"

"Look out! Here comes Funeral Dog. Back to work before he eats you!"

Valerie nodded towards the door of the canteen where a man in white overalls and a blue hairnet was scanning the room, clearly looking for someone. It was Iris, another Bercow Biddy, who'd given him the nickname and Alice could see why. He wouldn't look out of place moping along behind a hearse. Or lying on the tomb of his dead master, pining. Never had Alice seen anyone with a more hangdog expression. But she thought the nickname cruel and only ever thought of him by his real name; Graham. He was a tall man but always walked with hunched shoulders as if to make himself smaller and less noticeable. Sad looking, with a permanent frown and downcast eyes, he rarely smiled and clearly found it uncomfortable being around people. He was one of two supervisors on the factory floor. Spotting Valerie, he weaved his way through the tables.

"Valerie. Alice." He stood in front of them, hands in pockets, looking truly miserable.

"Graham," Alice acknowledged him. Why so sad? she thought. What has life done to you? Maybe you've got a Frank at home too. Or someone like him.

"Mr Bercow would like to see you as soon as possible, Valerie," said Graham. "If you don't mind," he added apologetically.

Valerie stood up. "Gotta go. I didn't want a full lunch break anyway."

Graham looked embarrassed, as if he was personally responsible for curtailing her lunch. His shoulders slumped even further. "Wonder what his nibs wants this time. See you later, Alice."

Alice nodded. Graham followed Valerie as she made her way out of the canteen and Alice, looking at her uneaten sandwich and carrot cake, decided she wasn't hungry after all. She left the sandwich but wrapped the cake in a paper serviette and put it in the pocket of her overalls. She'd give it to Ronald tonight.

# CHAPTER 4

## SPAGHETTI BOLOGNAISE

"Have you thought any more about my offer?" asked Ronald.

"What offer's that?" asked Alice, innocently.

"You know. Twenty quid to see your bazoomas!"

"I was hoping you'd forgotten all about that. That was ages ago."

"I'd never forget a thing like that. I meant every word I said."

"How was that?" she asked, nodding at his empty plate.

"Great." Ronald wiped his mouth with the back of his hand. "I like it that you cut the spaghetti up for me. Difficult for me with my arthritis and never could work out how to eat the bloody stuff anyway. Slipping off your fork and all. Now, how about you for pudding?"

"Sorry, Ronald. You'll just have to make do with apple crumble and custard."

"Shame. Not that I don't like your crumble – best in the world – but I'd rather see your tits. Forty quid and that's my final offer!"

Alice laughed as she put his pudding in front of him.

"Fifty quid then! Not a penny more!"

"No, Ronald! Eat, will you, so I can go home."

"Sixty quid!" He picked up the spoon and took a mouthful.

Was he kidding? Sixty pounds was serious money. "You haven't got sixty pounds," she said.

"Oh, haven't I? Just you have a look in that tin over there." Ronald pointed to the sideboard. "There. In the bottom. On the right."

Alice did as she was told. With difficulty she opened the stiff door of the old wooden sideboard and found a metal tea caddy with 1953 Coronation written on it, tucked away right at the back. A faded picture of the Queen smiled enigmatically at her. "This one, you mean?"

Ronald nodded. "Go on, open it."

Alice pulled out a roll of bank notes from the tin, mostly twenties but some tens and one fifty pound note. She stared at the money in disbelief.

"Where did you get this from?" she asked. "There must be hundreds here."

"Over four hundred quid," said Ronald proudly.

"But where…I mean…where has it come from?"

"I got it from the cash point in the corner shop. Up the road."

"That's not what I meant, Ronald, and you know it. Where's it from?"

"It's mine. I've got money you know." He ate another spoonful of pudding, licking his lips appreciatively. "Good custard this." Clearly he wasn't going to tell her.

"Well, you shouldn't be keeping money like this in a tin, just lying around. Anyone could pinch it."

"Alice, the only person who comes to see me is you. It's not as if I have thousands of visitors. So nobody's going to pinch it. It's safe enough." Alice put the roll of money back in the tin. "Anyway, sixty quid is yours if you want it." Alice looked at him. He was serious. Sixty pounds. What she could do with sixty pounds. That would be a new coat with some spare, if she was careful. Wasn't she always? "I'll make it a round hundred if you throw in a cuddle." Alice looked at him, put the tin back where she'd found it and angrily slammed the sideboard door shut, making the photos on top rattle. She had to admit, she was tempted. And that was what was making her cross. Sixty pounds was sixty pounds. It was a lot of money. But a *hundred* pounds? That was even more! She could do a lot with a hundred pounds. But there was no way that she could take his money. And she wouldn't do, couldn't do, what he was asking. Still angry, she stood up.

"I'll see you tomorrow, Ronald," she said, her face tight.

"Don't be cross, Alice, please. I'm sorry if I offended you. I'm just lonely. And I miss my Sheila. I miss her cuddles. I miss touching someone." Ronald looked as if he would cry. Her heart went out to him. She picked up his thin, bony hand and squeezed it gently.

"I'm not cross, not really," she said quietly. "It's just it's a bit of an unusual request, you have to admit."

"Then you'll do it?" he asked excitedly. "You'll do it? Show me yer tits for sixty and give me a cuddle for another forty?" His eyes were bright.

Alice threw his hand down in disgust.

"You're hopeless, Ronald Sanders! Hopeless!" Alice grabbed her handbag and stormed out. "See you tomorrow," he called after her.

"I do not believe that man!" said Alice, hanging her coat up.

"Mmm," mumbled Frank, staring at the television screen. "What's he done now?"

36

Alice stood between her husband and the television set, hands on hips. Frank tried to peer round her but she didn't move.

"Alice, please. It's the highlights from York races. It's the Fit as a Butcher's Dog Stakes next. You know how much I like to see the horses. Don't spoil it for me." Alice didn't move. She stared hard at her husband. "Ok," he said, realising she was not going to budge, "tell me what he's done."

"He's only gone and offered me £100! That's what he's done!"

"What's the matter with that? Sounds brilliant. That's a real chunk of money. Have you taken it?"

Alice's nostrils flared. "For your information, Frank, he has offered to give me £60 if I show him my, er, my bosoms and an extra £40 if I give him a cuddle."

Frank burst out laughing, the horse-racing completely forgotten. "But that's great. I hope you've agreed? I could well use that sort of money. £100. Wow! It's a small fortune."

Alice could hardly speak. She didn't know whether she was angrier with him because he didn't care about another man seeing her 'bits' or because he automatically assumed the money would be his.

"Don't you care?" she yelled, beside herself with anger. "Don't you care that another man, our next-door neighbour, wants to see bits of me with no clothes on? Doesn't it bother you?" She could not remember ever having felt so angry.

"£100 is £100, Alice. Think of the money. And anyway," he added, "your tits are nothing to write home about. They've seen better days now, haven't they, love? Admit it."

Alice started at him in disbelief. And pure, white rage. This was her husband talking. Agreeing that she should display herself to Ronald because, after all, what she was going to show him were past their sell-by date. She felt as if she'd been thumped in the stomach. Frank looked up from his armchair at her.

"What?" he asked.

Too upset to speak, Alice shook her head and left him to his horses.

Alice stomped noisily upstairs, slamming the bedroom door shut so hard that the window panes rattled. She sat down on the bed, the mattress sagging, and cried quietly. So this was what it all boiled down to. She'd known for a long time that theirs was a passionless marriage and that her husband had stopped loving her a long time ago. Maybe the same time she stopped loving him. But it hadn't always been like that. Alice smiled through her tears as she remembered the day she first met Frank. She was working in the shoe shop on the High Street. Soles it was called. Everyone in the town called it RSoles and Alice was embarrassed to work there. But it was a job and it paid, after a fashion, and with only three O levels to her name, Domestic Science, Art and Chemistry, of all things, she was glad to have it. It was one rainy Friday afternoon and the shop had been quiet all day. The manageress was talking about closing early, business being so slow and Alice was really excited at the thought of getting away early. That didn't happen every day. She was sweeping the floor in preparation for closing when in walked this tall, skinny, handsome man with dark eyes and a smile as bright as the Blackpool illuminations. Hello Cinders, he'd said to her. A little princess sweeping the floor. Want to be my princess? Corny or what? Pass me a bucket, she'd thought to herself, but she was mesmerised by his sparkling eyes even if his wit wasn't of the same calibre. Want a new pair of smart shoes, he said. For dancing and the like. Worn the others out, he'd boasted. She'd sold him a pair of black leather lace-ups and a tin of matching Cherry Blossom polish. How about helping me put them through their paces? he'd asked her. To see if they work. Let me take my little princess to the ball. She'd agreed, against her better judgment, even though the ball turned out to be a disco in the Ritzy Roller above the Co-op. And that was it. Their first date was one of many and soon everyone considered them an item. They got married in the Register Office six months after they met. Looking back now, it all seemed so inevitable. Frank worked as a plasterer, earning good money and at first things were good. With them both working they were able to save and put a deposit on one of the small terraced houses that could be found all over Smedley. They liked their own company and kept themselves pretty much to themselves. Disco nights still happened occasionally on a weekend when they both liked to dress in their best and dance until the early hours. Apart from the odd dance and once in a while, a meal in the pub down the road, The Escaped Goat, long since torn down, they didn't go out much. But they were happy, to start with. Then Frank hurt his back at work one day. Fell off a roof, though what he was doing up there in the first place was anyone's guess. He certainly wasn't plastering. Fooling around was the verdict from the subsequent Health & Safety enquiry. Showing off, thought Alice. So no compensation. And that put an end to the meagre social life he and Alice had enjoyed. No more discos, no more meals out. And although the accident put paid to his plastering days, Frank could easily have done something less physical. But he chose not to. He milked the accident for all it was worth and to add insult to the unfortunate injury, he decided he had a dodgy heart. In his mind, he could never work again. So he didn't. Alice left Soles and went to work in Bercow's making biscuits. It was shift work then, the pay was better and there was as much overtime as anyone wanted. And she wanted it and needed it. With only one wage now coming in - Frank insisted his Disability Benefit was for him alone; after all, it was *his* disability - it was a struggle and a one-sided struggle at that. Alice worked all the hours she could and eventually, over the years she paid off the small mortgage and just about managed to keep the wolf from the door. And Frank? He stopped caring and gave up. His body shrank downwards as he grew outwards. He got fat. And his once luxuriant dark locks thinned, greyed, then almost disappeared altogether. He was no longer the smart handsome young man Alice had fallen in love with. He was old and grizzled and there. And he stopped caring about her too. He still called her his little princess but that was as far as any terms of endearment went. And as for romance – Alice couldn't remember the last time Frank had kissed her or even held her hand. Love had got up and walked out the front door and it wasn't coming back. She had to admit that she'd stopped trying too. She'd let herself go. Why not? What was the point in making an effort? Her once-slim figure now relied increasingly on elasticated waistbands and large knickers to accommodate it. Her slim shapely legs, once elongated by high heels were now lumpen with a hint of varicose veins and any shoes with more than half an inch heel made her calves ache. Her long, shiny, black hair which was the envy of her few girlfriends, was now grey, lank, tied back in an unflattering pony tail. She felt old. Lumpy. Worn out. Frank was right. She *was* past her sell-by date. But he didn't have to say it. Telling her that her bosoms had seen better days. Bastard! It hurt, him suggesting she was past it. Washed-up. A has-been. He clearly didn't care about her. The only thing he cared about was his damned television. She was nothing in his eyes. She'd known this for a very long time but the difference now was that he'd come right out and practically said it. And it wounded her even more that he didn't care if she showed her body to another man for money. He wanted her to! Well, sod him! she thought. The miserable, fat, useless, lazy pig! She'd show him. She didn't know how, but she bloody well would. She wiped her eyes with the back of her hand and sniffed loudly. I hate you, Frank Coulter. I hate you so much. I've put up with your idleness and indifference for too long now. She stood up, automatically straightened the duvet then started to pace up and down beside the bed, her arms folded. I mean nothing to you, Frank. I wonder if I ever did. I'm just your meal ticket. Your skivvy. Up and down she strode, the floorboards complaining under the threadbare carpet, the tears continuing to roll down her face. A knock at the bedroom door stopped her mid-stride. That had never happened before. Frank never knocked. Tentatively the door opened and Frank's disembodied head peered round. He's come to apologise, she thought. He's come to say sorry for the awful things he just said.

"Are you alright, princess?" he asked. Alice nodded, overwhelmed that he'd come upstairs to see how she was. So he did care, really. "It's just that you walking up and down is making a hell of a racket downstairs. I can hardly hear the commentary. Can you keep it down a bit?" She looked at him, incredulous. Before she could stop herself, she nodded. "Atta girl," said Frank, closing the door behind him. Alice stared where his head had been, almost forgetting to breathe. Bastard! Bastard! Bastard! she muttered under her breath, each one louder than the last so there was a real danger that she might actually say the word out loud. I so hate you, Frank Coulter! She sat back down on the bed and thought about what Shanti had said. Maybe she should leave him. What had she got to lose? She could manage on her own, there was no doubt about that. She was totally independent, doing everything now. Earning the money to almost pay the bills; keeping a roof over their heads; feeding them. She'd even managed to put away enough money for the little trip to the Borders until Frank had stolen it to buy that humungous television set. Selfish, selfish bastard! She tried to remember the last time he'd contributed anything. Money? Time? Effort? Alice couldn't think of a single occasion. She ran the show. Lock, stock and stinking barrel. He'd miss her if she went. But only because he'd have to finally get up off his so very fat arse and do things for himself. Like get a job! Ha! That was so never going to happen. Maybe, Alice mused, it would be easier to bump him off. Save him the bother of having to earn a living. That would be kinder than simply leaving him. Rat poison? Would that do? She'd read somewhere that it was untraceable. Once you'd drunk it, it couldn't be detected in the body. Foolproof. Or was that something else she was thinking of? She'd have to get it right. Alice sighed. None of this was ever going to happen. She'd never leave him and she was never going to kill him with rat poison. But she could always dream.

# CHAPTER 5

## TUNA BAKE

"So what are we going to do for your birthday?" asked a very large woman sitting opposite Alice. It was the lunch break and they were in the staff canteen. This was Iris, the Bercow Biddy who'd given Graham, the floor supervisor, his unkind but apposite nickname. Despite her best efforts, the woman's badly-dyed blonde hair poked out from under her hair net. Her body was similarly doing its utmost to escape from her overalls which stretched tight over her enormous bosom and gargantuan hips and the rolls of fat that were layered tidily one on top of the other round her middle. Buttons strained and it was only a matter of time before they gave up the ghost altogether and went pinging off into the distance. She re-arranged her buttocks on the uncomfortably small plastic seat.

"I'd forgotten all about it, to be honest, Iris," said Alice.

"How can you forget your own birthday, Alice?" asked a much younger girl sitting next to her. She was totally different from Iris in every respect – petite, dark, quiet, and she lived up to her name. Grace. "You never forget any of ours."

Alice shrugged. "Just a lot on my mind at the moment."

Another woman joined them. She was dark, Mediterranean, with deep brown almond-shaped eyes. Bella.

"Hi Bella!" said Iris. "We were just talking about what we're going to do for Alice's birthday."

"Birth'? Doan mention birth' to me. Pah! Las' birth' my no-good lazy boyfrien' gave me a new iron." She pronounced it eye-ron. "I was so disappoint'. Mortify even." Bella was Spanish and had the endearing habit of missing the ends off words. Alice could never work out if this was laziness or whether she simply got bored with a word half-way through and gave up on it. "An iron? I mean, I ask. I would be amuse' if it was not so sad." Bella looked at Alice. "What you wan' do for your birth'? It have to be cheap. I got no money."

"I don't think any of us have," said Iris. She sighed. "What about you, Grace? Any ideas?"

"Cheap is good for me too. I'm flat broke," she replied. She looked downcast.

"Perhaps we shouldn't bother this time," suggested Alice. "I mean, we're all feeling the pinch at the moment. Maybe we should leave it until things are better?"

"No way," said Iris, shaking her head. "If we wait until things get better, we'll wait forever."

"Is true," added Bella. "If we wait for better, it never come. I still wait for better boyfrien'. He never 'appen."

"Alright then. What about a curry?" suggested Iris.

"Suits me," said Alice. "What about the rest of you?" There were nods of assent from Grace and Bella. "I'm sure Valerie will be up for it. And I'll check with Shanti too. Is that ok then? Shall I book for the six of us for next Thursday?"

"What's Frank getting you for your birthday?" Grace asked her.

Alice couldn't help but laugh. "You are joking aren't you? I can't remember the last time he got me a birthday present."

"At least he no get you an iron," said Bella.

"I'd be thrilled if he did," said Alice. "At least it would show that he'd remembered, if nothing else."

"Maybe he'll surprise you this year," suggested Grace.

"Well, there's always a first time!"

A klaxon announced the end of the meal break. Reluctantly the women stood up, dutifully obeyed the notice on the wall which told them to clear their own trays and headed out of the canteen, back to the factory floor. Alice walked back with Grace who was unusually quiet.

"Are you alright, Grace?" she asked. "You seem a bit out of sorts."

Grace shook her head. "Nothing that several hundred pounds wouldn't cure."

"Are things that bad?"

"Ivan lost his job at the carpet shop. They laid off half the staff. Don't need as many fitters because nobody's buying carpets. So now it's only my wages that are coming in. Not sure how we're going to pay the rent this month, to be honest. And Shawn desperately needs a new pair of shoes for school."

"Oh Grace, I'm so sorry. Is there anything I can do to help?"

Grace put her hand on Alice's arm. She knew that Alice was in the same boat as her. The same boat as all of them. Money was tight but it was typical that Alice would offer to help. She would if she could, Grace knew that.

"We'll manage, Alice. But thanks anyway."

Alice stood in the corridor staring at Grace's back as her friend returned to Chocolate Dropsies. She had met Grace's partner, Ivan and their son, Shawn, in town one day. Nice family. Worked hard. She shook her head despondently. Shit always happened to the nicest people.

Alice slammed a plateful of tuna bake down in front of her husband. She hadn't forgiven him for his crass comments from the other day. She didn't know that she ever would.

"Only tuna?" Frank asked tentatively.

"You give me some money," she said, sharply, "and I'll give you fillet steak with truffles."

"Now there's no need to be sarcastic, princess. I'm just saying, that's all."

"Perhaps if you contributed to the household finances, we could have something a bit more than *only* tuna."

"What's gotten into you? You know I can't work. I'm disabled." He clutched his back and groaned quietly to emphasise the point. "I *do* give you some of my Disability Benefit when I can."

"Really? When was the last time that happened?"

"You really are in a mood, aren't you? Time of the month, is it?" Alice felt like grabbing her tweezers and plucking the hairs from his nostrils one by painful one. Time of the month? She'd show him! "And anyway, if we're struggling, then we can't afford to feed old buggerlugs next door, can we? He should fend for himself, mean old sod. I bet he's loaded. What about that £100 he offered you? Why not take it? Then we could have a bit of steak or something?"

The only stake that Alice could envisage was one that she would like to drive through his heart, slowly, inch by inch, starting at his fat arse-end and working upwards. She smiled at the thought.

"I feed him because he's a lonely old man."

"And I'm not? How do you think I feel when you're out at work all day? I'm on my own too, you know."

Alice looked at him in disbelief. "You've got that thundering great television to keep you company," she shouted. "Or you could get off that fat backside of yours and go out for a change. You know. Out into the big wide world? Maybe even get a job! Or maybe I should give up work and stay home to keep *you* company? Then see how we manage to eat!"

Frank's mouth fell open. Dramatically he clutched his chest making strange bleating noises. He gasped for air. Alice was unmoved. She'd seen it all before. Sighing, she turned away.

"You used to be my princess," he whispered.

"I used to be a lot of things," she said quietly, going into the kitchen to plate up Ronald's tuna bake. At least *he* wouldn't complain.

"You're quiet tonight," said Ronald, as Alice put his dinner down in front of him. "Not your usual ebullient self. Why are you not ebulling?" Alice didn't reply. "Is everything alright?"

"Fine. It's just one of the girls at work. Money problems. Wish I could help, that's all."

"You'd help everybody out if you could. Too kind-hearted, that's your problem."

Alice sighed and watched Ronald tuck in. Here was a man who loved her food, whatever she gave him. He appreciated her, even if her slob of a husband didn't. He never complained, whatever she served up. And he always thanked her.

"That offer's still on the table, you know. The £100. If you won't take it for yourself, Alice, you could give it to someone who needs it." Ronald scratched his chin. "You know, I've been thinking. I bet quite a few of the old folk I see at the Day Centre I go to - you know, my monthly trip into town to meet up with the other crumblies - I bet lots of them are lonely just like me. Men who just want a bit of a cuddle. Women too, probably. A bit of company. And happy to pay for it. No funny business, just a bit of comfort now and again." Alice hadn't really thought about it but now that he'd mentioned it, she could imagine lots of people just like Ronald. All on their own and lonely. And for some of them, all they had was Evergreens, the council-run day centre for the elderly in the middle of town next to the library. Evergreens. Where did they get the name from? The last thing those who attended the day centre were, was evergreen. On the first Tuesday of every month, a white minibus pulled up outside Ronald's house, the name of the centre emblazoned on the side in bright green and a silhouette of a fir tree on the sliding door and whisked him off for a day of giddy delights. He'd told her that nearly every weekday, this minibus, with Simon at the wheel, trundled round a different part of

Smedley and the outlying villages, collecting the old and lonely and taking them to Evergreens for an action-packed day of bingo, dominoes, sedentary calisthenics and tea and biscuits. Bercow's, of course. A light lunch was provided, though sometimes this turned out to be no more than a sandwich. For some of these once-a-month visitors, the trip into town might be the only human contact they had. Alice thought that was the saddest thing imaginable. At least Ron had her to pop in every day to talk to him and check he was alright. But what if you had absolutely no-one? No-one at all? Alice couldn't imagine it. Okay, the only family she had was Frank and he didn't count. But she did have some wonderful friends and she couldn't imagine what it would it be like if she didn't have them.

Ronald brought her back to earth with a bump. "Maybe I could mention it to one or two of them at Evergreens?" suggested Ronald. "See if any of them fancy a bit of a cuddle? Perhaps one of your friends at work might be interested? You know, the one with no money? Maybe if she had someone like me it could help pay her bills. What d'you think?"

Alice tried to imagine Grace showing her bosoms to some sad old man. She couldn't. Even though hers were almost certainly worth looking at and hadn't yet headed south, like Alice's. She wondered what Grace's reaction would be if she suggested it. Horror? Disgust? She'd probably never speak to Alice again. No, Alice didn't think she'd mention it. Not if she wanted to keep her as a friend. She took Ronald's empty plate into his small kitchen.

"Just think about it, that's all I'm saying," he said. "If you can't use the money, I'm sure someone else can."

"I'll think about it," agreed Alice, surprising herself.

Ronald's face lit up like a Christmas tree. "You will? You know it makes sense," he said. "It'll make all the difference in the world. Just you wait and see!"

Frank looked up as Alice came in the front door and into the lounge. There was a boxing match on the television.

"How is the old goat?" he asked her. Alice ignored him. "Offer you any more money, did he? Offer to pay you to take your clothes off?" He smirked at her. "You know, you could be on to a winner there. Think about it."

"Oh, I am," she replied. "I am."

Frank looked at her, surprised. "Seriously?" he asked.

"Whyever not? As you said, my bits have seen better days so the fact that Ronald is offering me good money to show them to him...well, it's a bonus. As long as he doesn't mind a bit of sagging and a few wrinkles here and there, there's good money to be made."

Frank said nothing but look sheepish. He reached for her hand but Alice moved away from him. "I'm sorry what I said the other day. About your bits having seen better days. I didn't mean it. Really."

"Then why did you say it?" asked Alice.

"I just said it without thinking. You know, the old foot in mouth disease."

Yet another of your many disabilities, Alice thought.

Frank smiled at her. "I don't really want you showing your parts to anyone else."

"Apart from you, you mean?" she asked. When did you last show any interest in seeing any of my bits?

"Well, yes. You're my wife and I don't like the idea of you parading round naked in front of others. Nobody else should see you like that but me."

"Even for £100?" Alice asked.

Frank nodded. "Even for £100," he agreed. Reluctantly, Alice thought.

He looked back at the screen where the two boxers were thumping the hell out of each other, spittle and sweat flying everywhere. One of them had a cut above his eyebrow and it was bleeding copiously. Alice looked at the fighters in disgust.

"And when was the last time you saw them?" Alice asked him, tearing her eyes away from the sweat and gore.

"Sorry, love. Saw what?" It didn't take much to distract him.

"When was the last time you saw my breasts? I'm trying hard to remember the last time you saw me with no clothes on. And I can't."

Frank blushed, clearly uncomfortable. "Well, you know how it is."

"No I don't Frank. How is it, exactly?" Alice was not going to let this lie. Her husband was getting more and more embarrassed and she was going to milk it for all it was worth. Payback time for his hurtful comments. "Tell me how it is. I don't mind people seeing me with my clothes off. Especially if there's money in it. And to be honest, Frank, I don't think I'll limit it to just Ronald. I'm sure he's got lots of friends who'd pay good money to see me."

"Now stop being so daft, Alice. This isn't funny any more. You're just being silly. It's not going to happen and that's the end of it. I was a bit silly with some of the things I said the other day, but I was having a laugh. We both were. I mean, some of my bits have sagged too." He laughed. Alice didn't. She could not have agreed more. "So let's just forget what I said and go back to the way we were. We shouldn't bicker so much. It's not good for us. Friends?" He held out his hand to her just as the audience on the television erupted with delight as one of the boxers felled the other with a mighty blow to the head. Down he went and didn't get up. The crowd bayed with delight. "I've just missed the best bit," said Frank, crossly, not even aware that Alice had not taken his proffered hand. She sighed and turning her back on him, went to seek solace in the ironing.

# CHAPTER 6

## BEANS ON TOAST

"Looking forward to Thursday?" Valerie asked. Alice nodded. It had been a long morning on Marshmallow Moments, the cutting machine that was supposed to divide the gooey mixture into equal amounts had failed to do its job and the lumps of brilliantly white marshmallow on the conveyor belt in front of her were misshapen and uneven. She'd called Graham over and he'd looked at the mismatched blobs with dismay, abstractedly scratching his head, before summoning one of the S&M guys to sort it out. When the engineer finally arrived, he looked at the machine as if it was something he'd never seen before and sucked his breath noisily through his teeth, shaking his head slowly. He rather thought it wouldn't be a quick fix.

"Why don't you go and grab a cuppa?" Graham suggested.

Alice looked at him. "You sure?" Normally if a machine was going to be out of action for any length of time, you were sent off to do something else.

"Go on, why not. You work hard enough."

"Well, thank you, Graham," Alice said. "That's really kind of you."

He half smiled and fiddled with the top button of his overall. "I'll come and find you when it's fixed."

Alice was surprised to find Valerie sitting in the canteen, nursing a bottle of mineral water. There was no-one else there.

"Looking forward to your birthday curry?" Valerie asked as Alice sat down.

"Enormously. It's going to be good to have an evening out for a change. Nice to get away from Frank and that interminable television. Do you know, it's on from the moment he gets up in the morning until he goes to bed at night? And all he watches is bloody sport. It's not even as if he watches anything sensible like the news or documentaries. It's just sport, sport, sport."

Valerie smiled. "Best make the most of it then."

"What? What do you mean? Best make the most of what? My night out?" Valerie nodded. "Why?" asked Alice. "What are you on about?"

Valerie looked round the empty canteen to make sure she wouldn't be overheard. She leaned forward, getting as close as she could to Alice without actually sitting in her lap. "Might be your last chance for a while."

"What are you talking about?" Alice was growing concerned.

"Mr Bercow's going to make an announcement, probably next week. Not sure when. But he's going to close the factory." She sat back, looking grim.

Alice felt as if she'd been struck by lightning. "You can't mean that. It's not possible. He can't. I mean, what will we all do?" Like everyone else, she'd known for years that the factory was struggling but she didn't think it would ever come to this.

Valerie looked round the empty room again. "Bercow's is in trouble. Serious trouble. I shouldn't be telling you this. I'm not supposed to say anything but you'd best start looking for another job."

"*Another job?*" Alice screeched. Valerie put her hand on her arm in a futile attempt to quieten her. "Where am I going to find another job at my age? And round here? In Smedley?"

"I'm sorry," said Valerie, "I know it'll be difficult."

"Difficult? Too right it's going to be difficult. It's going to be bloody impossible." The enormity of what was going to happen was sinking in fast. "It's alright for you. You don't need to work. You've got plenty of money."

Valerie looked hurt and took her hand away. Alice's face fell. "Oh, I'm so sorry," she said, reaching for her friend's hand which she held tightly between hers. "I didn't mean that."

"I know you didn't," said Valerie. "I'd best be getting back. Mr Bercow is going through all the accounts for the past five years to get things ready for the administrators."

"But what about the others? Iris and Bella? Shanti? Shouldn't we tell them?"

Valerie shook her head emphatically. "No, best not. I'm not supposed to have said anything, remember. And they may as well enjoy things while they can."

"But what about our curry night? If we're all going to be made redundant soon, we're going to need every penny we have. Grace can't even afford a new pair of shoes for her son."

"I don't really think one night out at the Indian is going to make any difference in the overall scheme of things. Let's go and have a good night out. It'll probably be the last one we all have for a long time." Valerie stood up and, squeezing her friend on the shoulder, left Alice to think about her future. Or at least that's what she would have done if Graham hadn't come into the canteen to tell her that the cutting machine was working now and she could get back to work. Alice examined his face closely. Did he know about the factory closure? He gave no sign of it but then he never gave much sign of anything.

"Enjoy your wee break?" he asked, but Alice was too upset to do more than nod. Her long morning had just become even longer.

As she cycled home, Alice thought about whether to tell Frank her momentous news straightaway or to save it until later? Do I tell him now? Or wait until it's official? You never know, maybe somebody would buy the factory and all their jobs would be safe. Alice had heard about that happening before, on the news. Factories going into receivership then at the 11th hour, somebody stepped in and everybody's jobs were saved and they were happy. She was usually an optimist but somehow she didn't believe that it would happen this time. What would she and Frank do? How would they manage? Fine, the house was theirs; through her hard work and as much overtime as she could get when it was on offer, Alice had paid off the mortgage, but there were still bills to pay and they had to eat. Maybe she would have to stop feeding Ronald after all. Maybe she could get another job, like Valerie suggested. But Smedley was what the local politicians called an 'unemployment hotspot' and the prospects of finding something locally were virtually nil. Once home, Alice sat down at the kitchen table and put her head in her hands. Any thoughts she'd ever had of a fabulous kitchen with an island were coming back to bite her. New kitchen? Pah! Pigs would fly first. I wonder how much notice we'll get? she thought. And whether there'll be any redundancy pay. And what about her pension? It wouldn't have been much anyway, but would it be anything at all now? Frank was going to have to give up more of his Disability Benefit, no question. He wouldn't be happy. Tough. If things had been bad before, they were going to get an awful lot worse. And not just for me, she sighed. What about the rest of the girls? Grace, who couldn't afford the rent this month and or new shoes for her son. And Iris? She'd moved back in with her mother after her divorce because she had no money. That couldn't have been a barrel of laughs. And Bella? She wasn't sure what her boyfriend did. Shanti would probably be ok. Alice knew she was married but she never talked about her husband. She got the impression there was money there. Another

Valerie? Worked because she chose to? Whatever, things were going to change for them all and Alice was not looking forward to it.

She decided against telling Frank just yet. There'd be time enough. Alice was going to enjoy her birthday, come what may. It might be the last chance she would have to spend it with her girlfriends. Once they'd lost their jobs that would be it. There'd be no spare money for luxuries like curries or girls' nights out. Or any nights out, for that matter. But she decided she'd tell Ronald. Why would I tell him and not my husband? she pondered. Easy. Because Ronald would accept the news for what it was. Bad news but not the end of the world. Something would turn up, Ron, the optimist, would tell her. Frank, on the other hand was a moron who would panic. He'd have a set of kittens. What would happen with no money coming in? How would they eat? How would he manage without his milch cow? What would happen to them? How would he be able to afford his beer and whatever else he spent his money on? She could hear it now. No, Alice would enjoy her birthday and then she'd tell him.

The fact that it was only beans on toast for dinner tonight seemed appropriate. A sign of things to come. As Alice buttered the toast she thought that if Frank said one word, just one word, she would tip his dinner in his lap. Fortunately, after his recent comments about the tuna bake, he had the sense to hold his peace. And whilst Alice was not prepared to apologise to Frank for the meagre dinner, she felt Ronald warranted an explanation.

"Just beans on toast tonight, I'm afraid, Ron."

Ronald was sitting in his armchair, blanket over his knees, waiting to be fed. "I don't mind, lass," he said. "Anything will do." He tucked in. "I'm not a fussy eater. I like anything simple."

"That's just as well," she said, "as we might be having a lot more simple meals. Things may start to get a bit difficult."

"What do you mean?"

"I'm not supposed to tell you so you mustn't say anything, especially to Frank."

"Good lord, woman, when do I ever speak to your husband?" he asked her. "Or him to me?"

"Well, you mustn't say anything to him or to anyone. Promise?"

Ronald nodded his head and crossed his heart. "Your secret's safe with me."

"Bercow's is closing. We're all being made redundant, Ron. We're all losing our jobs." Alice's chin quivered. "I haven't told Frank yet. Thought I'd enjoy my birthday first."

Ronald looked sadder than she had seen him for a long time. "When's this going to happen?"

"Not sure. I expect they'll try and find somebody to buy the company and when that fails, we'll all be out on the street. Could be next week. Could be a bit longer than that." She shrugged her shoulders.

"Oh, Alice, I'm so sorry. What will you do?"

"I don't know, Ron. A woman my age? What is there for me? I'm probably too old to get another job and anyway, jobs round here are as rare as free beer tomorrow, as my Dad used to say."

"Something'll turn up, I'm sure." Ron squeezed her hand. "What will Frank do?"

"Frank? I expect he'll panic. Then he'll panic some more. Then he'll go back to watching his television."

"Will he try and get a job?" Ronald suggested.

"Oh, you are a hoot, Ronald Sanders. Frank? Get a job? There's about as much chance of that happening as me winning Miss World!"

"And what's this about a birthday?"

"Oh, nothing really. It's my birthday on Thursday and me and the girls are going out for a curry. But they don't know about Bercow's yet. My friend in accounts told me and I'm not supposed to say anything. So this will probably be the last night out I have with my friends because sure as eggs is eggs, once we're all redundant, that'll be it for birthdays. And Christmases. And everything."

"You don't know that, Alice," said Ronald. "Sometimes things happen."

"Yes, Ron. And more often than not, they don't."

"Alice, sit down." She sat, turning round one of the wooden chairs until she faced him, their knees almost touching. He leaned forward. "I've been dealt some rough hands over the years, Alice. I lost my wife when she was only twenty-five. And my unborn baby. It would have been a little girl. Our second child. Our family would have been complete. But these things happen. And they happen for a reason. I'm not sure what the reason is but that's what I believe. But I've never lost hope. I've come pretty close once or twice but I've never given up. Think positive. That's what I did and that's what you must do. If you don't, then there's no point going on. Something'll turn up, just you wait and see." He leaned back in his armchair, clearly tired. "You make sure you have a nice birthday, d'you hear?"

Alice stood up and put the chair back. Then on impulse she leaned over and kissed him on the forehead. She smiled broadly at him. "You're a tonic for the soul, Ronald Sanders. You make me smile."

"How about making me smile then?" he asked, mischievously.

"Not that again! You don't give up, do you?"

"£100. That's a lot of money for someone who's not going to have a job soon."

Alice stood over him, looking down. He was right. More so than ever. £100 was a great deal of money. And she was going to need every penny she could get. But not just me, she thought. Everyone else would too. Some of her friends were worse off than she was. She kept coming back to Grace and her son's shoes. Alice made her mind up.

"Does that offer of £40 for a cuddle still stand?" she asked him, the words coming out before she could stop them.

Ronald smiled. "Of course it does. And the £60 to show us your tits!"

"No, Ron. Just a cuddle. Fully clothed. Nothing else. No groping. No naughty touching. What about it?"

"I thought you'd never ask. Hop aboard!" He pulled the blanket off his knees exposing thin legs encased in worn green corduroys.

"But I'm far too heavy for you," cried Alice, hesitating. "I'll squash you!"

"I'm stronger than I look," beamed Ronald. "Especially where this sort of thing is concerned."

Gingerly, Alice lowered herself down onto Ronald's lap. She couldn't work out if the noise he made was simply a sigh or it was her squashing all the air out of him. For a few moments no-one said anything.

"Are you alright?" she asked.

"Never better," Ronald whispered. "Can I put my arms round you?"

"I said no touching," Alice reminded him.

"But all you're doing is sitting on my lap. This isn't a cuddle in my book."

What harm would it do? Alice nodded her agreement. Quick as a flash Ronald's bony arms encircled most of her waist. He leaned his head on her shoulder and closed his eyes. "Lovely," he sighed. "You should be able to get this sort of thing on the NHS!" Alice was trying to decide how long to sit there. How long should she give him for his £40? "Don't want to change your mind, do you?"

"About what?"

"Another £60?"

"No, Ronald, I don't. And I think that's enough for today."

"What? You mean there'll be more tomorrow?"

"No, Ron. It was just a figure of speech."

"The only figure I'm interested in is the one sat on my lap. Waited a long time for this, I can tell you. Fine, mighty fine."

Alice looked at him. His face was wreathed in smiles. She couldn't help but smile back. Was this all it took to make this old man happy? Gently she took his hands from her waist and put them down on the arm rests. Slowly she stood up.

"Thank you, Alice. You've no idea how much that meant to me. It was grand. Simply grand. Now go and take your £40 from the tin in the cupboard."

Alice shook her head. "No Ron, have it on me. I can't take your money."

"Now then! We had an agreement. You've stuck to your side of the bargain and I'm going to stick to mine."

"It was only a cuddle. I can't take your money just for a cuddle."

"You can and you will. I insist. If you won't take it, I'll never let you come here again. I mean it, Alice Coulter. A deal is a deal." He crossed his arms for emphasis.

Reluctantly Alice went to the sideboard and retrieved the Coronation tin. She handed it to Ron who opened it and took out £40. Silently he gave it to her.

Alice looked at the notes as if she couldn't quite believe they were real. "Thank you," she whispered.

"Thank *you*." said Ronald. "You've made me so happy. You've no idea how much better that's made me feel. See you tomorrow?"

Alice bent down to kiss him on the cheek. "See you tomorrow."

# CHAPTER 7

## CORNED BEEF HASH

"I did it!" whispered Alice.

"Did what?" asked Valerie, selecting a black olive from her multi-coloured salad and popping it onto her mouth. Alice's canteen sandwich looked unappetising in comparison. What was it? Ham? Anaemic cheese? Carpet tile? There was no label to give the game away.

"You know, Val. Ronald." Valerie looked blank. "You know. The old man next door. The one who keeps offering me money to show him my…assets!"

Valerie looked at her friend, her face undergoing a complete transformation as she realised what Alice was telling her. "You never!"

Alice smiled broadly. "Well, not quite. But the next best thing."

"What's the next best thing?"

"Well, I…oh, bother, here come the others. Later." Alice smiled as Iris, Bella and Shanti walked into the canteen followed by Grace. She grabbed a couple of extra chairs for them from a nearby table. "Everyone good for tonight?" she asked, as they all sat down. "Table's booked for 7.30."

"I should say so," beamed Iris, producing a large pork pie and a packet of crisps from a carrier bag. "Haven't had a curry for weeks. Happy birthday, by the way." The others chorused their birthday wishes. Alice nodded her thanks.

"Have you had a nice day so far?" asked Grace.

"Well, if you can call a morning spent battling with Caribbean Crunch and losing, 'nice', then I suppose the answer is yes!"

"What did Frank get you for your birth'?" asked Bella.

"Nothing. I didn't really expect anything. He never remembers birthdays. But you never know, he may just surprise me when I get home." Alice was trying to be charitable.

"Oohooh! You should be so lucky!" bellowed Iris, nudging Alice in the ribs.

Alice blushed. "Somehow, Iris, I think not."

"You mean you an' Frank don' do the lovin' any more?" asked Bella, innocently.

"You shouldn't ask things like that, Bella," hissed Grace. "It's rude."

"It doesn't matter, Grace. I don't mind. No," she said, turning to Bella, "we don' do the lovin' any more. In fact, I can't remember the last time we did do the lovin'."

"That's what I was telling you," said Shanti. "Get out and live. Find some lovin', girl. It's out there just waiting for you!"

"Not in Smedley it isn't," Iris shook her head. "I know. I keep looking. There's about as much lovin' in this town as there is in the bottom of my mother's airing cupboard."

"I'll second that," added Valerie. "Not that I've ever been in the bottom of your mother's airing cupboard. But I know what you mean. Smedley is not the best place for hot sex."

Alice laughed.

"Where is?" asked Bella. "You tell me anywhere in Englan' where sex is hot. This country too damn cold for sex. An' wet. An' English men?" She shook her head in disgust. Clearly Bella didn't think much of English men but then if her boyfriend bought her an iron for her birthday, one could hardly blame her.

"Why do you stay then?" asked Grace.

Bella shrugged her shoulders. "No work in Spain."

Valerie and Alice exchanged glances but said nothing. Soon, there wouldn't be too much work in Smedley either.

"Not eating, Grace?" Alice asked, changing the subject.

"No. Trying to lose a bit of weight."

"That, my girl, is one thing you don't need to do," said Iris, stuffing another piece of pork pie into her mouth. "You're as thin as a rake as it is. Not like me."

"Din' you say you were goin' to have that barbaric surgery?" Bella asked her. The table erupted with laughter. "What? What did I say?"

"It's called *bariatric* surgery," explained Alice.

Bella shrugged her shoulders. "Same thing. Why you no have it, Iris?"

"Because, me dear Bella, Mr Richards, my despicable ex-husband, may he rot in hell and his willy fall off, decided that even if I'd had the surgery and lost a shed load of weight, it wouldn't turn back the years as far as he was concerned and the pneumatic bottle-blonde who works in the fish and chip shop on Riley Street and always smells of vinegar, was a better proposition. So now I have no husband, no money and I have to live with my mother. I could no more find the money for *barbaric* surgery than I could for a drink from the fountain of youth." She sighed deeply.

"Bast'! All men are bast'!" said Bella philosophically.

"There, my dear, you are absolutely right!" agreed Shanti. She stood up. "See you tonight, girls."

One by one the women slowly got up and followed her back to work. At the canteen door, Alice grabbed Grace by the arm.

"Here, Grace. I want you to take this." Alice thrust the £40 from last night's activity with Ronald into Grace's hand.

"What? What's this?" asked Grace, perplexed.

"It's for you. For Shawn's shoes."

"I can't take this." Grace tried to shove the money back into Alice's pocket. "I can't."

"You can." Alice took a step back out of reach. "It's money I didn't expect to have and anyway, I'd just spend it." She tried to laugh it off. "Honest."

Grace looked at the money. "Alice, it's £40. I can't possibly take it." There were tears in her eyes. She was torn. Shawn desperately needed new shoes but she couldn't take money from Alice like this. It wasn't right.

"Please. You'd make me really happy if you took it. Honestly you would."

Grace burst into tears. "I don't know what to say." Alice put her arm round her friend's shoulder.

"Don't say anything."

"I'll pay it back, honest I will," she sniffed. "It's your birthday. I should be buying you something and here you are giving *me* money. It's just not right."

"You'd do the same for me if I were in your shoes. Now then, you are still coming tonight, aren't you?" Grace nodded. "Great stuff. See you later." As Alice turned away, she happened to glance back into the canteen. Graham was sitting on his own at one of the tables. She hadn't noticed him there earlier. He'd clearly seen everything that had gone on between her and Grace. Alice blushed and gave him a half smile. Embarrassed, he acknowledged her with a slight nod of his head then resumed eating.

"What are those?" asked Frank, pointing to a large bunch of flowers which lay on the floor just inside the front door. Alice picked then up and smelled them. There were white chrysanthemums, pale pink lilies and deep red roses.

"I could be wrong," replied Alice, "but I think they're called flowers."

"I know what they're called, Alice. No need to be sarcastic. I was wondering who they were from."

Alice inhaled the fragrances again. They made her feel quite light-headed. Flowers. When was the last time anyone bought her flowers? She found a small white envelope tucked among the blooms and opened it. 'Happy Birthday' it said simply. 'From Ronald.'

"They're from Ronald, next door. Isn't that nice?"

"They were delivered just before you got home. Now why would the old geezer next door go to the expense of buying you flowers? Eh? What have you been doing for him? What have you been up to?"

"I think, Frank, he's bought me flowers, because it's my birthday. I think there might be some sort of cause and effect there."

Frank looked at her. Then the penny dropped. "Your birthday? Of course. Why didn't you say?"

"Because I shouldn't have to."

"Oh, princess." He dug deep into the pocket of his track suit bottoms and pulled out a crumpled £5 note which he tried to straighten out. "Here, love, treat yourself to something nice." Alice looked at the money in her hand. "Happy birthday," said Frank.

Tempted as she was to screw the note up and throw it back at him, Alice murmured something under her breath. It might have been thanks, it might not. She put it in her handbag.

"So something special for dinner tonight, is it?" Frank asked.

"Yes," she replied. "Well, it is for me. You've got corned beef hash. I'm going out."

"Out? Out where? Without me? On your birthday?"

"You could have asked me, Frank. You could have taken me out to dinner. But you didn't ask. You didn't even remember my birthday so I made my own plans."

"I thought we were struggling. But you can afford to go out to dinner?"

You don't know the half of it, thought Alice. Just you wait until you hear the real news. I wonder how you're going to like it when I lose my job. What will you do then?

"I'm only going out for a curry with the girls, Frank. It's hardly the Ritz. I'll make you your dinner before I go but don't wait up for me."

Frank looked truly crestfallen. "But I like curry," he whimpered. "I want to go out." He sounded like a small child who'd had his sweets taken away from him. Any minute now Alice expected him to burst into tears. Man up, she thought, and went upstairs to get ready.

"Well, don't you look a million dollars!"

Alice beamed. She looked nothing like a million dollars and she knew it, but it made her day to hear someone say so.

"If I had my own teeth, I'd give you a wolf whistle!" Ronald stuck two fingers in his mouth and made a spitting sound. "Go on. Turn around. Let's have a look at you."

Alice turned slowly, soaking in the fact that someone appreciated the effort she'd made. She'd spent longer than usual in the shower, letting the hot water run completely cold. Bugger Frank. He'd have to wash in cold water tonight. As she washed her hair, she momentarily rued the fact that she'd given Grace the £40. She could have had a really good cut and blow dry for that, with some highlights too. Got rid of this awful pony tail and jazzed it up a bit. But Grace's - or Shawn's - needs were greater. She'd taken special care blow drying her hair before deciding that nothing she did was going to make any difference. It would still be grey and it would still be boring. So Alice had scrunched it back into its usual pony tail, allowing a few stray wisps to float free round her face, softening her features. Picking the right dress had taken even longer. It wasn't as if she had a lot to choose from; it was more a question of finding one that still fitted. Somehow every time Alice came to try something on, everything always seemed to be a little tighter. She eventually settled on a favourite, something she hadn't worn in years; a deep blue cotton frock with a tiny white daisy motif. It had short sleeves which would show off her bingo wings to a T but the v-neck would make her face look thinner. She'd struggled to do the zip up. Drat, she thought, I really must make an effort to lose some weight. I can remember when this used to fit like a glove. But she'd be ok as long as she didn't breathe too much! The colour of the dress set off her grey hair, and matching dangly glass earrings added yet more brightness to her face. A bit of eye-liner and some mascara made her face come alive. Eking out the last of her lipstick, Alice examined the result critically in the bathroom mirror. Could do better, she thought.

A lot better. But it would have to do. I should wear make-up more often. I do feel better for it and goodness knows, I need it. Finally she'd upended her perfume bottle, Eau de Souci, and dabbed the last remaining drops behind her ears and on her wrists. She'd looked the name up once. French it was. It meant marigold but Alice liked it because it sounded like 'saucy'. Saucy water! If only. She sniffed the perfume on her wrists. It didn't smell as good as it used to. Did perfume go off? This bottle was ancient - she couldn't even remember when she'd bought it. She sniffed again. Something wasn't quite right. It was less like marigold flowers and more like the insides of a rubber glove. Yes, it was definitely a bit whiffy. Ah, well, like everything else, it would have to do. And speaking of making do, it was such a shame she'd have to wear the same old brown woollen coat but as it was the only one she had, there was no choice in the matter. Never mind. She'd smiled at herself. Alice felt good and she hadn't done that for a long time. She was about to lose her job and her and Frank's money worries would pile up. Her friends would be even worse off than she was. Why, then, was she happy? Alice had no idea but tonight, at least, she was going to enjoy herself.

Frank didn't say much as she came downstairs. He looked her up and down then returned to the television, sulking. "Too bloody good for a curry house," she heard him mutter. Why couldn't he tell her she looked nice, just once? Alice decided to ignore him. There was no way he was going to spoil her night out. Not tonight. He sniffed the air loudly. "Perfume?" he asked, wrinkling his nose as if there was something unmentionable in the air. "For a curry?" In his view, this was clearly going overboard. I don't care, Frank Coulter, she thought. I really don't care.

Dinner took ten minutes to get ready – open a few tins, mix the contents together and warm them through in a pan. It was hardly haute cuisine but it was cheap and filling and she had to be somewhere. Ronald's reaction to the meal was more enthusiastic than Frank's. Looking at a beautiful woman increased his appetite, he told her.

"What did he get you for your birthday?" asked Ronald.

"Who?"

"Your husband, of course." Alice produced the £5 note, still crumpled, from her handbag and showed it to him. Ronald clicked his tongue in disgust. "That's it? You should leave him," he said emphatically.

"What?" Why was everyone telling her the same thing?

"He doesn't deserve you. Come and live with me. I'll take care of you. I'd look after you."

Alice shook her head. "It would more likely be the other way round, Ronald. I'd be taking care of you."

"What are you going to do with that £5?" He nodded at the money still in her hand.

Alice shrugged her shoulders. "Not much, that's for sure."

"What did you do with the £40? The cuddle money?" She didn't answer. "You gave it away, didn't you?"

"Someone needed it more than me. She said she'll pay me back."

"Let me add something to that measly fiver from your husband. Treat yourself to something nice."

"Oh, I couldn't, Ronald. You got me those lovely flowers. I haven't thanked you for them yet. They are so beautiful. You've no idea how thrilled I was when I saw them. I cannot remember the last time somebody bought me flowers. Thank you."

"Well, just you have a nice time tonight. Enjoy yourself. You deserve to."

"Thank you, Ronald. I plan to."

And nothing was going to spoil it for her.

# CHAPTER 8

## CHICKEN KORMA AND RICE

"So that's two chicken kormas, one lamb rogan josh, one chicken biryani, one beef dopiaza, one vegetable curry, and three plain rice," repeated the waiter. He was young, Asian, with a broad Smedley accent. "Any naan with that?" He counted the nods and wrote something down on his pad. "Ten minutes," he said and left them to it.

It was Thursday night and they were in the Hackney Cabbage celebrating Alice's birthday. The Hackney Cabbage was the best Indian restaurant in town and had got its name because late at night some drunken wag had climbed onto the shoulders of his equally drunken friend and, armed with a pot of paint, had changed the 'Rs' of the restaurant's name into 'Bs'. Seeing as spelling was not the strong point of either of the acrobatic inebriated vandals, it had become the Hackney Cabbiage, but everyone in town knew it as the Hackney Cabbage. And no-one could ever explain why a restaurant in Smedley was named after a taxi cab, including the people who worked there. One of life's enigmas. But as enigmas went, it served a pretty mean curry. The six women were all dressed in their finest and done up to the nines; Alice squashed into her blue and white flowered dress; Valerie, dressed to kill in a tailored body-hugging plain black dress with her hair piled high; Shanti in a multi-coloured floral silk suit which brightened the restaurant considerably; Grace was in black trousers with an almost sheer black top adorned with sequined butterflies in silver; Bella was in a bright red trouser suit with a matching bow in her jet-black hair; and Iris was dressed in what looked like a gold lamé marquee. The air was thick with half a dozen different perfumes and Alice was convinced that hers was eye-wateringly pungent compared with the delicate flowery overtones of the others'. The six women sat round a circular table with an empty bottle of sauvignon blanc in front of them.

"Another bottle?" suggested Iris, draining what was left in her glass. "That one didn't last long."

"It never does when you're around," laughed Valerie. "I'm game."

Iris waved her hand in the air, trying to catch the eye of their waiter. She managed to attract his attention and that of everyone else in the restaurant by picking up the empty wine bottle and waving it in the air.

She'd made her intentions clear. The waiter brought a fresh bottle over and as he re-filled each of their glasses, Valerie reached into her handbag and produced a small present wrapped in pink birthday paper. She handed it to Alice.

"Happy birthday, Alice. This is for you," she added unnecessarily.

Alice was embarrassed. The girls had a rule amongst themselves never to buy each other birthday presents. Presents costs money and they would rather treat themselves to a girls' night out to celebrate their birthdays.

Slowly Alice opened the present, savouring the moment. Presents were such a rarity. Inside, wrapped in green tissue paper, was a tiny piece of delicate black and red lace. Alice held it up between her thumb and forefinger. She had never seen anything so beautiful or so inappropriate. There were murmurs of appreciation from round the table. Even the waiter stopped what he was doing to add his nod of approval.

"It's a thong," smiled Valerie.

"I know what it is, Valerie. The question is, why?"

"It's in recognition of your new status."

"What do you mean?" asked Alice.

"Yes," said Shanti. "What new status? Have you got a lover?"

"Your new status, Alice, as a femme fatale. You know. Ronald."

"Ronald?" cried Iris and Grace in unison. "Who's Ronald?"

Bella interrupted them. "Look, girls! Look who's just come in."

All eyes turned to the door. Funeral Dog had walked into the restaurant and was shaking the rain off his coat. Looking round, he saw the women and nodded at them, embarrassed. Without thinking, Alice gave him a gentle wave, thong still in hand. Realising what she'd done she thrust her hand into her lap and looked away.

"He looks different without his hairnet," said Grace. "Better."

"I suppose you can say that about most men," laughed Iris. "I've never yet met a man who looks good in one."

Alice looked across at Graham surreptitiously. Grace was right. She'd never seen him before with his hair uncovered and she was surprised to find how much better he looked. Less deflated. His hair suits him, she mused. Grey peppered with a bit of black. He looked younger too. Are you like me? she thought. Old before your time or is it just the Bercow effect? She watched him as he ordered from the takeaway menu then sit down at a table near the door to await his order. "D'you think we should ask him to join us?" suggested Alice.

"What!" cried Bella. "You are havin' a joke."

"Just for a drink, I meant. He's obviously all on his own."

"This looking after stray lambs is going to your head," said Valerie. "But it's your birthday, so if you want to ask him, then it's up to you." A couple of the other girls nodded in agreement. Alice got up, tucked the thong under her serviette and walked over to her supervisor.

"Hello Graham," she said. "It's my birthday and I, er we, that is me and the girls, couldn't help notice. I mean, would you like to join us. Just for a drink. Nothing else." Alice realised how awful that sounded as soon as she'd said it.

Graham stood up. "Thank you. I can't. I have to get home. But thank you." Alice turned to go back to her friends. "Oh, and Alice. Happy birthday."

She nodded her thanks and went back to the table.

"That was a 'no' then, was it?" asked Valerie. Alice drained half her glass of wine in one. "Everything ok?" her friend asked. She nodded.

"What's all this about being a femme fatale, then?" queried Iris, as the waiter appeared laden with dishes. "What are you not telling us?"

"It's nothing really," said Alice, clearly not wanting to talk about it. She spooned some rice onto her plate.

"If it's nothing, then why has Valerie broken the no-present rule and bought you a thong?" asked Shanti. She wanted to hear all about it.

"If you don't tell them, then I will," said Valerie.

Alice gave her the blackest look imaginable which Valerie ignored.

"Honestly. Talk about mountains out of molehills. It's nothing, honestly."

"Is it a man?" asked Bella. "You have a new man in your life? For the lovin'?" She started to help herself to some chicken curry then stopped, spoon mid-air. "I know. Is him!" She pointed to where Funeral Dog still sat. "Is him!" Six pairs of eyes turned to stare. Graham happened to look across at their table just at that precise moment. He was like a rabbit caught in the headlights. Never had flock wallpaper been so desperately interesting. Alice felt for him, she really did.

"No, Bella. Don't be daft. It's not him. It's not anybody." This was getting beyond a joke. Alice swallowed the rest of her wine. "Can I have half a lager, please?" she called out to a passing waiter. Why was it so hot in here? "Valerie has bought me this thong, and thank you very much, Valerie. I can honestly say I've never been bought or owned one of these before." She held it up for the rest of the table to see. There were more appreciative noises from the assembled company. And from a couple at the next table too. "But that's all there is to it. Honest!" Alice desperately wished they'd all drop the subject.

"What Alice is trying to say, but won't," explained Valerie, "is that the old man next door who she cooks for, well, she offers him a bit more than just meat and two veg these days!"

"Valerie!"

"Well, it's true. That's what you told me earlier."

"That's a pretty crude way of putting it," said Alice, indignantly. She glared at her friend. No-one was eating except Iris.

"Do you mean to say that you're having sex with your next-door-neighbour?" asked Iris incredulously.

"Oh, for Pete's sake! No, I am not! How many times must I say it?"

"Then what's going on?" asked Grace, smiling at Alice. "We only want to know because we care."

"And 'cos we like a smutty story," added Iris.

"There's nothing smutty about it," said Alice, defensively. "If you must know, I keep an eye on the old man who lives next door. I take him his supper and just make sure he's ok. He's all alone and to be honest, I feel sorry for him. He's got a son, apparently, but he never sees him. Never comes to visit. So I just take care of him. That's all."

"There's got to be more to it than that," said Shanti. "Valerie wouldn't call you a femme fatale and buy you a thong if all you were doing was rustling up the odd cheese sandwich or two. Come on girl. Spill the beans!"

Alice ate a spoonful of korma and washed it down with a mouthful of lager. She signalled to the waiter to bring her another half. "A few months ago, Ronald, that's his name, started offering me money for…extras."

"Extras? Like what?" asked Iris, her eyes enormous.

"Well, he offered me money for a cuddle, for starters."

"A cuddle? Just a cuddle?" asked Grace. Alice nodded. "Nothing else?"

"Well, yes. But he settled for a cuddle."

"Let me get this right," said Iris, putting down her knife and fork. Not much made her stop eating but this had. "He offered you money if you let him have a cuddle. That's it?" Alice nodded again. Iris thought about it some more. "Brilliant, girl! Easy money!"

"But hang on," said Shanti, "you said *for starters*. You said he offered you money for a cuddle *for starters*?" Trust Shanti to pay attention. "What else did he want?"

Alice squirmed in her seat. "He wanted to see my 'you know whats'!" She pointed in the general direction of her chest.

"He wan' to see your busts?" asked Bella, seeking clarification.

"Exactly."

"And he offered you money? To show him your *busts*? I mean *bust*. Wow!" This was from Grace. She shook her head but Alice couldn't tell whether it was in disbelief or because she disapproved.

"What does Frank think?" asked Shanti.

Alice sighed. "He knows about Ronald's offers but I haven't told him about the cuddle yet?" She cringed when she remembered her husband's wounding comments.

"You don't have to tell him anything and it doesn't matter what he thinks. It's your money. You should spend it how you want." She looked at Alice. "I mean, I take it you have done the business?"

"When you say *done the business*, Shanti, I take it you don't mean *doing the business*?" asked Valerie.

"Girls! For your information, I have not *done the business* with Ronald. And I don't intend to. I have given him a cuddle for which I received payment. Nothing more nothing less."

"Is that no' like selling your body? For money? Like prostration?" asked Bella.

"I think you mean *prostitution*," said Valerie. "And no, it's not. Very definitely not. It's being kind to a very lonely old man. And if it just happens to generate a bit of extra cash, then it's not to be sniffed at."

"He likes to sniff too?" Bella couldn't believe what she was hearing. These English people!

"No, Bella," explained Alice. "He likes a bit of company, that's all it is."

"I say go for it!" said Shanti. "Absolutely!"

"Me too," agreed Iris. "He hasn't got any friends, has he? I could do with an extra few bob or two." She finished what was on her plate. "To be honest, I could do with a cuddle as well. I've been a bit lonely since Mr Richards upped sticks and left. He didn't have many good points but he was good at cuddles."

Alice smiled. "I'll give you one on the house," she offered. "Shall we have another drink before we get the bill?"

"Well, you've really let the cat out of the bag, Valerie," said Alice, as she leaned heavily on her friend's arm. She wasn't used to drinking this much and she felt decidedly wobbly. The two of them were walking down the High Street, Alice heading for the last bus home and Valerie towards the taxi rank. They'd said their goodbyes to the other girls outside the restaurant, everyone agreeing that Alice could take the doggy bag containing the uneaten curry back for Ronald.

"Got to take care of your bosom pal," Irish had chortled. "Geddit? *Bosom* pal?"

Alice had got it but didn't find it even remotely funny.

The rain had finally stopped and there was a nip of a frost in the air.

"I just thought they should know, that's all. You're not upset with me, are you?"

"No, how could I poshibly be upshet with my besht friend?"

"Tell me you're not drunk?"

Alice giggled. "A bit." She exhaled loudly, watching her breath whiten in front of her face. She did it again.

"When are you going to tell Frank? Or *are* you going to tell him?"

"I expect I'll tell him when I tell him about Bercow's. Soften the blow a bit."

"Soften the blow? Don't you think it'll make things worse?" Valerie asked.

"Not if he knows there's money coming in. Frank won't be bothered about where it comes from as long as it comes."

They walked on in silence.

"I'm going to miss it, you know," said Valerie.

"Miss what?"

"Bercow's. Us. The girls." She sighed. "It's not much of a job but it's been good fun."

"What will you do?"

"I don't know. Maybe what you're doing. Offer my services to lonely old men!"

"Valerie!"

"Well, why not? It's like a public service, isn't it? And I think there's a market for it."

"That's what Ronald says."

Valerie stopped and looked at her friend. "Really?"

"That's what he says." Alice swayed slightly. "He says that lots of the old folks, women as well as men, at Evergreens. You know, the day care centre he goes to. He says lots of them are lonely. They live on their own and haven't got anyone. Crying out for a cuddle, they are."

"Well, there you are. I've proved my point. Now, here you are. I'll see you tomorrow." Valerie gave Alice a peck on the cheek and leaving her at the bus stop, teetered off on her high heels to get a taxi.

"Thank you, Valerie," Alice shouted after her.

Her friend turned. "For what?"

Alice had forgotten what she was going to say. "Everything," she said. "Thank you for everything."

Valerie smiled, waved and headed off down the street.

Getting the key in the lock proved much more difficult than usual for some reason but Alice finally managed it. It was dark inside the house. He hasn't even left a light on for me, she thought. Miserable git. She slipped off her shoes and padded through to the kitchen where she poured herself a glass of water. She downed it in one and poured herself another. Upstairs Frank was snoring softly so Alice went into the bathroom to undress in case she woke him. As she wiped her make-up off and cleaned her teeth, she realised just how much had enjoyed herself tonight and was quietly glad that Valerie had made her tell her friends about Ronald. It was all out in the open now, apart from Frank. Alice tiptoed as quietly as she could back across the hallway and without putting the bedroom light on, groped under her pillow for her nightie. Slipping it over her head she slid in beside her husband. At least the sleeping behemoth had warmed the bed for her. She giggled quietly to herself. Alice could not remember the last time she'd had so much to drink. She'd pay for it in the morning, for sure. She lay back, thinking about the girls' reaction to Ronald and his propositions. None of them had been horrified or disgusted. Bella obviously, had her reservations but she seemed to be the only one. Shanti seemed to think it was the most natural thing in the world. She would! Even Valerie had said she might do something similar when she lost her job. She was kidding, though. Valerie would never do anything like that. But maybe what Ronald was proposing wasn't so unnatural after all. Maybe Alice was still an attractive woman. Ronald clearly thought so. And now she had a thong. How wicked was that! Alice turned over and spooned Frank. He grunted. Her arm crept tentatively and with some considerable difficulty, over and around his enormous stomach. Frank stopped breathing and held his breath. He was awake now. Wide awake. She found the cord of his pyjama bottoms and started tugging.

"What are you doing, woman?" he hissed.

"Come on, Frank. When was the last time we…you know?" Alice knew it was the alcohol talking but she couldn't stop herself. She certainly couldn't have done it if she'd been sober. "I'm a passionate woman."

"Alice, you know I can't. I'm incapacitated." This was a big word for Frank.

"No you're not. There's nothing the matter with you at all. Don't you want to?" Alice's hand inched down inside his pyjamas. "Not even a little bit?" He tried to wriggle away from her. "But Frank, I have needs!"

Frank sat bolt upright in bed. "I have needs too and I need to get some sleep! Now stop being silly, woman. Leave me be." He lay back down, as far away from her as he could get without sleeping on the floor. Within seconds he was snoring again.

Alice lay there, tears coursing down her cheeks. An attractive woman, am I? And the tears fell faster.

# CHAPTER 9

## FISH FINGERS AND CHIPS

Alice sat with her head in her hands. She had a monumental hangover and could barely keep her eyes open. Fortunately her auto-pilot had kicked otherwise she would never have made it to work. The morning had started badly when she'd found it almost impossible to get out of bed. Why had they gone out on a Thursday night when they could have left it a day with the weekend to recover? With great difficulty she got up and pulled on her clothes but she couldn't face breakfast. The thought of eating was a bridge too far. She decided against making Frank his usual cup of tea – Alice wasn't sure she was sufficiently co-ordinated to handle both boiling water and a tea-bag. Anyway, bugger him! After his behaviour last night, he could make his own tea. She slammed the back door shut as loudly as she could then immediately regretted it as the noise vibrated through her whole body. The bike-ride to work had been precarious but at least it wasn't raining and the fresh air seemed to help clear her head a bit. She managed to get her overalls on without too much difficulty although matching the buttons to the button holes proved problematic. But getting all her hair under its protective cover almost defeated her. Finally she succeeded and stood up just as Grace walked into the staff room. Her friend smiled broadly at her. Without saying a word, Grace walked over and re-buttoned Alice's overalls so that the buttons and button-holes were correctly aligned.

"Are you alright?" she asked Alice.

"I think so."

"You don't look so good."

"No. I have felt better. I'm never going to drink again, that's a promise."

"I must admit," said Grace, "that's the most I've ever seen you drink." She laughed. "But it was a good night and it was good to have a few hours without having to worry about things. I enjoyed myself."

"Me too. I think," said Alice.

"Alice, you know what Valerie said about you being a femme fatale and stuff. Is that true?"

"I'm afraid so. Apart from the femme fatale bit, I mean. I really don't think I qualify on that score."

"Is that where the £40 came from that you gave me? For Shawn's shoes? From your cuddle money?" Alice nodded. "Then I can't take it," she said, reaching for her purse. "That's yours. You earned it."

"Yes, I did. But I enjoyed earning it. So that doesn't count."

"How do you work that out?" asked Grace.

"I have no idea," said Alice, putting her hand on top of Grace's to stop her. "But you can take it. It's yours. I've given it to you."

Grace threw her arms round Alice and was still hugging her when Shanti walked in.

"Interrupting anything, am I?" she asked, smiling. "Can anyone join in?" Alice and Grace opened their arms to include her. "Well, aren't you the dark horse, Alice Coulter? You and your new man friend. Go girl!"

Alice released herself and sat back down. Being upright was just a bit too challenging at the moment. God knows how she was going to get through the day. Thank goodness she was still on Caribbean Crunch. That particular biscuit demanded even less attention than all the others. And she had the weekend to recover.

"How long have you been doing it?" asked Grace.

"Doing what?" asked Alice.

"You know. The man next door thing."

"Well, the cuddles thing only started last week. That was the first time. But as for looking after him and cooking him his dinner. I honestly can't remember." Alice tried hard to think. Today it was particularly difficult. When *did* she start cooking an extra meal and taking it next door? It seemed that Ronald had always been there. He was certainly there the day they moved in. First off, she and Frank didn't have much to do with him. They kept themselves to themselves, a young married couple. They passed the time of day with Ronald, said good morning and that sort of thing, but that was it. He was on his own and he seemed to cope fine. It was one day, a couple of years ago, maybe longer, when she came home from an early shift at the factory to see Ronald standing in his open door looking up and down the street as if he was waiting for someone. "Everything alright?" she'd asked him, noticing how sad and lost he looked. All of a sudden he realised she was talking to him.

"Oh, yes. Sorry, Alice. I thought my son might come today."

72

"I didn't even know you had a son, Ronald. What's his name?" He'd never mentioned a son before but then conversation had not been much more than pleasantries and smalltalk. She'd never really asked him anything about himself. In fact, when she thought about it, she hardly knew anything about her next-door-neighbour at all.

"Ricky. He's called Ricky." Ronald's face looked even sadder.

"Why did you think he was coming today? Did he say he would?"

Ronald looked confused. "No. No, he didn't. I just had a feeling, that's all."

Alice felt desperately sorry for him. She knew he lived alone and that he never had any visitors. For some reason today he'd thought he might see his son and clearly it wasn't going to happen.

"Here," she said, holding out a bag of broken biscuits. "I got these at the factory where I work. Bercow's. Would you like them?" It almost broke her heart to see the way his face lit up.

"For me?" She nodded. "Why, thank you."

"They're only the broken ones. But they are assorted," she added, as if this would make up for the fact that they weren't perfect.

"What a treat," he said, surreptitiously wiping a tear from the corner of his eye. That was the moment that Alice's heart completely broke. She'd given this old man a bag of assorted broken biscuits and you'd have thought she'd given him a cup of ambrosia from the tree of life. Or something. He turned the bag over and over in his hands. There was an awkward silence as Ronald stared at his unexpected gift.

"My favourites are the Caramel Curls," she lied, desperate for something to say.

"Oh, I remember those from when I was a kid," said Ronald, his face lighting up. "And Lemon Licks. Do they still make those?"

"We do. There should be some in there."

"I don't suppose…? No."

"What?"

"No, it doesn't matter."

"What? Come on. You were going to say something."

Ronald looked at her sheepishly. "You wouldn't like to come in and have a cup of tea with me, would you? A cup of tea and a biscuit?" He held the packet high, tempting her.

Alice smiled at him broadly. "I can't think of anything else I would rather do," she said. And she meant it. And that was how it started. Ever since that day, she'd cooked an extra meal at dinner time and, much to the increasing annoyance of her husband, had taken it next door to Ronald. But even after all this time, she didn't know that much about her neighbour except he'd had a wife, Sheila, who'd died in childbirth, and he had a son, Ricky, who never came to visit. And that was pretty much it. But she did know what he liked to eat, she knew that he enjoyed her company, and she knew that he was her friend.

"Planet Earth to Alice! Planet Earth calling Alice!" It was Shanti shaking her shoulder gently.

"Sorry, I was miles away," said Alice.

"Thinking about Ronald?" asked Grace.

"Well, yes, actually. I was."

Grace and Shanti grabbed an arm each and pulled Alice to her feet.

"Come on, girl. Time for work. Those Caribbean Crunches won't bake themselves."

If only they would, thought Alice.

The end of the day could not come soon enough for Alice but only because she knew that as the day progressed she would start to feel more like normal as her hangover slowly disappeared and, when tomorrow finally came, it would be gone altogether and she'd feel a hundred times better. But as much as she wanted the day to be over, she really did not want to go home. Not just yet. She'd have to face Frank and she didn't feel quite up to it yet. The morning had been long; the afternoon even longer. Even her usual lunch break with the girls did little to lift her spirits. They all assumed she was quiet because she was hung over but there was more to it than that. Much more. It was everything. The thought of Bercow's closing and her imminent unemployment. Ronald's obvious loneliness. Frank's rejection of her last night. Yes, Frank certainly had a lot to do with it. Last night, for once, Alice had felt attractive and ready to enjoy herself, and that was before she'd had a skinful. Today she felt unloved and unlovely. Thank you, Frank, she thought. She'd made a fool of herself in front of him. Humiliated herself, laid her needs bare. And for what? What on earth would she say to him when she got home? How do you go about acting normally after last night? Alice took her time changing out of her work clothes in the staff room and she waited at the factory gates for Valerie to appear. When she finally saw her, Valerie's face was dark.

"You ok?" Alice asked her.

"There's going to be an announcement next week. Monday."

"About the closure, you mean?"

"They can't find a buyer so we're going into receivership. That's the end of Bercow's."

Alice gulped. Finally, it was here. No more Bercow's. No more work. No more a lot of things. Oh boy!

"Do you want to go for a coffee or something?" she asked. "I don't feel much like going home straight away."

"Everything alright?" asked Valerie.

"Yes, fine. It's just I'm not in a hurry to go home. I'll probably be spending a lot more time there soon, anyway."

"Yeh. You're right. Why not?"

Arm in arm they made their way to The Bottomless Cup, a small café round the corner from Bercow's. It wasn't very busy because despite the name, it didn't serve endless cups of coffee or tea; the local joke was that the measures were so small, it was as if the bottom had never been in the cup in the first place. Some attempt had been made to make the place welcoming – it was painted bright yellow with outlines of teapots drawn on the walls. A display cabinet on the counter offered cakes and scones that looked a bit dry and sad. Alice wasn't even remotely tempted, even if she hadn't been hung over. There was a slight smell of disinfectant but at least the café was empty. They took their coffees to a table in the window.

"What's up?" asked Valerie, her hands wrapped round a skinny latte.

"Oh, I don't know. Nothing. Something. Everything."

"Whoa! Sounds confusing. Care to share?"

Alice stirred her cappuccino. "I don't know what's the matter with me. I just feel like I'm ready for a change."

"I think you're about to get your wish, girl," said Valerie. "A change is what we're all going to get. Whether we like it or not."

"No, I don't just mean work-wise."

"Frank?" Trust Valerie to get to the nub of things quickly.

"Yes and no." Valerie put her hand comfortingly on Alice's arm and squeezed it. "Don't you ever feel that you're stuck? It's like you're on a treadmill and you can't get off. Like one of those hamster wheels. That just go round and round. Everything's the same and is going to stay that way forever."

"Sometimes, yes. But things are about to change big-style," Valerie reminded her.

"Yes, I know. We're going to lose our jobs. That's a huge change. For all of us. But other things stay the same. Just the same old rut, day after day. Week in week out. Forever."

"Frank?" Valerie asked again.

Before she could stop herself, Alice burst into tears and told Valerie what had happened when she'd got home last night. "I feel such a fool," she sobbed, searching for a tissue. Valerie stood up and went to put her arms round her friend. "I'm so ashamed," sobbed Alice.

"Why? You've got nothing to be ashamed of, girl. You're only human," said Valerie.

"Shanti says I should leave him. She said I should go and live with her."

"Of course she'd say that. She'd have you like a shot. Fancies you something rotten."

Alice was so shocked she stopped crying. "What? What are you talking about?"

"Shanti has always had a soft spot for you. Didn't you know?"

"You don't mean she's...gay, do you?" Alice was incredulous. How long had she known Shanti? Ten, twelve years? It wasn't that her friend was gay but that all this time, Alice hadn't known. "Gay? Are you sure?"

Valerie nodded matter of factly. "You must be the only person who doesn't know."

"Nobody's ever said anything. Iris or Bella."

"Why would they?"

"But I thought she was happily married."

"She is. She lives with her partner."

Alice thought about it some more. "A man, I mean. I just assumed she lived with a man. A husband."

"Shanti lives with Carol from Marketing. Honestly, Alice, You should see your face."

"Carol? Marketing?" All this was too much for Alice. "But if she's got a partner, how can you say she fancies me?"

"Don't be so naïve, Alice. You can't stop people looking, can you? Or straying. And she happens to think you're quite a catch."

Alice stirred her coffee vigorously. "Wow!" was the most she could manage. She didn't know what was surprising her more; the fact that Shanti was gay, the fact she didn't know she was gay, or because someone found her attractive.

76

"So why don't you leave Frank? Like Shanti says. Why do you stay with him? Do you love him?"

"I don't know anymore." She looked out of the window at the few pedestrians, heads down, heading home at the end of the day. Maybe they have something good to go home to, she thought. Someone good. "I just don't know."

"Well, I wouldn't make any snap decisions until we know what sort of redundancy package is on the table. That might make your mind up for you."

Alice drank the rest of her coffee. "Thanks for listening, Val. I'd better be getting home. See you Monday."

Valerie gave her a hug. "Try not to worry. Things have a way of working out."

"That's what Ronald says."

"Well, there you go then. Have a good weekend."

It'll be anything *but* when Frank hears the news about Bercow's, thought Alice. Whatever the weekend was going to be, it was not going to be good.


What struck Alice as soon as she walked through the back door was the smell. Something was cooking. She sniffed the air. Grease? Frank stood with his back to the stove so she couldn't see what was on it. He said nothing but pointed her towards the lounge. Alice was amazed at how tidy the lounge looked. Whilst it couldn't be described as spotless, it was certainly cleaner than usual. There were no newspapers or magazines on the floor, no beer cans or dirty mugs anywhere to be seen. The house seemed different and apart from the smell of frying, there was a underlying scent of lavender. Air freshener? Frank had used air freshener? And the television was switched off. Frank appeared from the kitchen, an apron stretched over his burgeoning stomach.

"You're home later than usual," he said, by way of a greeting.

"I went for a coffee with Valerie after work," said Alice, still unable to take in the transformation. "What's going on?" She pointed vaguely round the lounge.

"I just thought I'd have a bit of a tidy up, that's all."

Alice blinked several times. A tidy up? She didn't think Frank knew what those words meant.

"Anyway, your dinner's nearly ready." Dinner? What dinner? Frank had cooked her *dinner*? At least that explained the smell. History was being made here. Frank had cooked a meal for her. "Go and take your coat off. It'll be five minutes."

"Have I got time to take Ronald his meal in first?" she asked him.

"If you're quick. I don't want this to spoil."

Alice was intrigued. Frank preceded her into the kitchen and resumed his stance in front of the stove, hiding whatever delicacy he was cooking. She took the foil container from last night's curry in the Indian restaurant out of the fridge, emptied the chicken korma and rice into an old plastic ice-cream tub and shoved it into the microwave. After a couple of minutes, she extracted it and holding it in carefully in both hands, carried it next door to Ronald.

"Can't stay tonight, Ron. Sorry. Frank's cooking dinner." She tipped the contents of the container onto a plate and handed it to him.

"Why?" he asked. "He's never done that before."

Alice didn't know what to say. "It's complicated," she said eventually.

"What? The food he's cooking or the reason he's doing it?"

She laughed. "Oh, it can only be the latter. Hope you like curry, by the way. I'm afraid it's only leftovers from my dinner with the girls last night, but the food was very good and I hate waste."

"It'll be wonderful, I'm sure. Off you go then. Enjoy your meal. Bon appetit, as they say. See you tomorrow."

Alice sat in the lounge staring at the blank television screen as Frank busied himself in the kitchen. She could hear him swearing under his breath. Whatever it was clearly involved a lot of pots and pans. She was intrigued but uncomfortable. Would he mention last night? God, she hoped not.

"Come and get it!" yelled Frank. "Dinner's on the table."

Alice stood in the kitchen doorway looking at what Frank had served up. She couldn't bring herself to speak.

"I found the fish fingers and peas in the freezer but had to go round the corner shop to get some frozen chips," he said proudly. "I got crinkly ones." He pointed at the plates as if what he'd served up was worthy of at least one Michelin star. "And look!" He brandished a bottle, wiping the dust off it with a tea towel. "I thought we'd have a treat. I bought some wine too." Alice sat down as Frank poured her a glass. She took a sip. It was warm and sweet. Trying hard not to grimace, she tried to smile. She failed on both counts. "Tuck in. before it gets cold." Frank ate heartily and had cleared his plate by the time she was only half way through hers. "Not bad. Not bad at all, though I say it myself."

"It was lovely, thank you Frank. But I'm full," she said, laying down her knife and fork.

"Don't you want the rest of that?" he asked, pointing at her plate. When she shook her head, he swapped plates and ate what she'd left. He burped loudly, smiled, then raised his glass. "To us," he said simply.

Alice raised her glass and nodded. To us? she thought.

"I've been thinking," he said, "and I've decided that things need to be different between us. Better." Oh God, he's going to mention last night. She couldn't handle the humiliation again. But no, he didn't. "I'm going to change," he told her. "I can and I will. I'm going to try harder."

No, thought Alice, I don't think you can change. It's too late for that. And anyway, I'm not sure I could get used to a new Frank. It's been hard enough getting used to this one.

"I'm going to make more effort round the house and I'll even have a go at cooking now and then. I know you work hard, so I'm going to do more. And I'll economise. I'm going to buy roll-ups instead of proper cigarettes."

"But you don't smoke," Alice pointed out.

"Well, if I did, I could make a saving there."

What are you talking about? she thought. Gibberish.

"And I can cut down on the beer. Then we'll have a little bit of extra money for some luxuries and things." Alice decided this was perhaps not the best time to tell him she was about to be made redundant. Luxuries were going to be the last thing on the list. "Things are going to get better," he promised. "Just you wait and see." Alice felt sick, not sure if it was Frank's cooking or the feeling of impending doom which was making her stomach churn. "Are you alright, princess? You look a bit pale."

"Tired, that's all. It's been a long week. Would you mind if I had an early night?"

"No, of course, love. Off you go. I'll tidy this lot up."

The television was on before she was half way up the stairs. She knew he'd forget to wash the dishes and clean up the kitchen. It would all be waiting for her tomorrow morning. Same old same old. Alice sighed deeply and her stomach churned even more.

# CHAPTER 10

## LANCASHIRE HOT POT

Alice was in the mood to cook. She had no plans for the weekend and she felt like doing what she did best. There was something about cooking, making a really delicious meal from scratch that made her feel what? Fulfilled? Happy? The butcher round the corner was doing a half-price offer on neck of lamb so she decided to make a hot pot. While she browned the meat in a frying pan, she thought about Frank's promises last night and wondered if he'd truly meant what he'd said. Was it possible he could change? Sadly, she knew the answer. He would never change. He'd made promises before he couldn't keep. Even little ones, like cleaning up the kitchen. Alice had to do it before she'd gone out shopping. It was a given. She shuddered at the thought of the congealed fat in the grill - how can anyone get fat from grilled fish fingers? Then there was the pan from the oven chips. They were supposed to be more or less fat-free. But Frank had somehow managed to coat them in grease. Please, let him not do any more cooking. That was one promise she'd rather he didn't keep. She'd pretended to be asleep when he'd come up to bed last night – she doubted if Frank's promise to change would extend to anything on the romantic front but after her abject humiliation the other night, she wasn't sure that she wanted it to. As she'd cleaned up the kitchen, Alice found the empty bottle of awful wine. Frank had finished it off but at least it meant she didn't have to drink any more of the dreadful stuff.

Alice chopped the onions and thinly sliced the potatoes ready for the topping. She really should have told Frank last night about Bercow's but the timing wasn't right. When would it ever be? It was going to change everything and he had a right to know. But after all the effort he'd made, what with the dinner, even if it was just fish fingers and chips, and the wine, she hadn't had the heart. Maybe she should wait until it was official. Just in case there was an 11$^{th}$ hour reprieve, as everyone was praying for. Alice decided she'd wait and see what Monday brought before she said anything. Why worry him if she didn't need to. She put the meat and onions in a casserole dish with some mushrooms and stock, layered the potatoes on top and put the dish into the oven, checking the temperature was not too high. Nice and slow, she thought. Three hours or so and the meat'll be falling off the bone. Delicious. Alice put the kettle on and made herself a cup of instant coffee but no sooner had she sat down to drink it than the postman started stuffing the mail through the too-small letterbox. Alice picked up the half dozen or so letters off the mat and flicked through them. A couple of circulars; a reminder from her dentist to book a check-up - that would have to wait; a letter from her bank offering to extend her overdraft facility – she might need that sooner rather than later; a new summer brochure from Broad'n Your Horizonz which went straight into the bin. She wasn't even going to look to see what she was missing. But the last letter really got her attention. It was an electricity bill. A red one. With considerable trepidation she opened the envelope. The bill was for £189. £189! How did that happen? She couldn't remember having seen any reminder let alone a first bill. Where did they get to? They do still send you a reminder, don't they? Before they send you the red one threatening to cut you off and sell your children? And that was an awful lot of electricity for a quarter. Frank and his bloody television, on all day long. But Alice was really worried that this was a red bill. Surely she couldn't have missed the first one and the reminder. She might have missed one but not both. That wasn't possible. Unless she'd suddenly got dementia. Maybe that was it. This was the first sign of her losing her marbles. But Alice was assiduous in paying bills. She had to be. There was not much to spare at the end of the month or at any time of the month, for that matter. But she always made sure the bills were paid on time. Where was she going to find £189? She looked at the bill again. In seven days it said. Or else. She didn't have that sort of money. And it was still two weeks till payday. Assuming she was still going to have a job in two weeks time and that there would be a payday. Alice collapsed into Frank's armchair. Maybe she could borrow from Valerie? No, not an option. She was cursing herself for being so hasty in giving Grace that £40. What a fool she was! But she'd have to find the money somehow. She sat there, racking her brains trying to remember having seen an electricity bill and a reminder. But she couldn't. She *knew* she hadn't seen them. Which meant one of two things. Either the postman hadn't delivered them – highly unlikely that both of them hadn't arrived – or someone had hidden them from her. Frank! She stood up. That had to be it. It was the only answer. The original bill and the reminder had arrived and Frank had kept them from her. Bastard! Calm down, she told herself, he may have a logical explanation. Boy, it had better be a good one.

Alice stomped up the stairs. Despite the fact it was late afternoon (and there was goodness knows what riveting sport on the television), Frank was still in bed. Must have been the rest of the bottle of wine that did it, she thought. She'd taken him his usual cup of tea before she'd gone out shopping this morning but it was untouched on his bedside table. How could anybody sleep so much?

"Frank!" she yelled. "Frank. What do you know about this?"

Frank rolled over and looked at her. "About what?"

"This!" And she waved the red bill in his face.

"What is it? I can't see." He rubbed his eyes.

"It's a final demand for the electricity! For £189! £189!" Alice was aware she was shouting. "What happened to the first bill? And the reminder?"

"Oh, that."

"Yes, that!"

With some effort, Frank sat up in bed. "I meant to tell you, princess." He tried to smile.

"Tell me what?"

"You know. That the bills had come in. But I must have forgotten."

"Forgotten! Forgotten! How can you forget to tell me, you…fool!" It was the best she could do for the moment.

"Now then, love."

"Don't you *love* me, you…you…cretin!" She was getting better. "Why didn't you just put the bills on the mantelpiece, where they always go? That way I can see them and remember that they need paying." Frank looked sheepish. "Now I've got to find £189 in seven days or they'll cut us off."

"Oh, I'm sure they won't," said Frank. "They don't do that sort of thing."

"They do and they will!" screamed Alice. How could her husband be so unbelievably stupid? How could *she* have been so unutterably stupid as to marry such an idiot? "Unless *you've* got the money to pay the bill?"

"Now, don't be so daft. You know I haven't. That's a silly thing to say."

Alice looked at him. She was so angry she couldn't speak.

"And anyway, I did it for you."

"*Me?*"

82

"Yes, you. I didn't want you worrying about it."

She could not believe what she was hearing. What was there inside this man's head? Cat litter? Grated cheese? It wasn't brains, that was for certain. Alice shook her head in astonishment. Her husband never ceased to amaze her and for all the wrong reasons. "What about all your promises last night, Frank? Your promises to change? And then you go and do this?" She waved the bill in front of his face then sank to the floor. Frank reached out his hand. Alice shrank away from him. "Don't you touch me!" she spat.

"Don't be like that, princess. It'll be alright." He looked at her helplessly from the bed.

"No, it won't be," she sobbed. "It won't be alright."

"It won't happen again," he promised.

"Too bloody right it won't!"

"What d'you mean by that?" he asked.

Alice struggled to her feet. "This," she said dramatically, shoving the bill under his nose, "is the final straw! You…you…arse!" Her best yet.

Exhausted, Alice stumbled down the stairs and grabbing her coat, she stormed out of the house, tears of frustration running down her face, the electricity bill still in her hand.

Alice had no idea where she was going but she knew she had to get out of the house and as far away from Frank as quickly as she could. She headed down Greenfields Road, crossed over at the lights, wandered down Spenser Road and along Chaucer Avenue. Before she knew it, she was at the park, the only green space in this part of Smedley. On a Saturday afternoon it was busy, despite the strong wind and the dark rain clouds which threatened a deluge at any minute. Children played on the few swings and the seesaw that had not been totally vandalised; teenagers hung about sulkily in a group near the dilapidated bandstand, furtively passing a cigarette between them. Shame, she thought, distractedly. They can only afford one cigarette between them, but at least it was a big fat one. Alice found a bench that was mostly free from bird droppings and sat down. It was only then that she realised that in her hurry to get out of the house, away from Frank, she'd come out without her handbag or door keys. Stupid, stupid, stupid! This prompted a fresh onset of tears. She'd have to go back, cap in hand, and knock at her own front door to be let in. Alice bent her head and cried. When did it all go so wrong? She felt tired;

tired of Frank; tired of everything. The wind was getting even stronger and spots of rain dotted the path. One of the young girls in the bandstand ran to get a child down from the swing. Her child? Surely not. She only looked a child herself. Twelve if she was a day. She must be minding it for someone else. "Aw mam!" screamed the child as she was bundled into a bright pink coat. Hers, then. The girl grabbed the little girl by the hand and ran to the park entrance. Other teenagers from the bandstand followed suit, grabbing children and fleeing as the rain became heavier. Suddenly the park was empty. Still she sat, oblivious to the drenching rain and the gusting wind, the electricity bill still clutched firmly in her hand.

A man dressed in jeans and a fleece with a black and white mongrel dog on a lead rushed past her, heading for the exit on the other side of the park. He stopped and turned. "You ok, love?" he asked.

"What?" Alice looked up, dazed.

"I said are you okay? You look a bit upset."

"I'm fine, thank you." She was touched by the stranger's concern and started crying again.

"Are you sure? Best get out of the rain. You'll catch your death."

Alice looked up at the sky, noticing the storm for the first time. She shivered. "Yes, you're right. Thank you. I will." She stood up and looked around her, not knowing which way to turn.

The man turned his collar up. "Lost are you?" he asked her.

You don't know how, she thought. "No, I'm fine. I'm fine."

The dog tugged impatiently at his lead, whining, eager to be off and out of the rain. Alice started to walk away. The man watched her for a few seconds then made a run for it. Once he got to the park gate, he looked back but Alice was gone. There's some queer folk about, he thought. Daft old bat. Sitting out in the rain like that. You'd think she didn't have a home to go to.

Alice left the park quickly and huddled in the first bus shelter she came to. Her feet were wet and her woollen coat did little to keep the wind and rain out. Her wet hair lay plastered to her head and raindrops ran coldly down her neck. She shivered and rubbed her hands together to try and get them warm. It didn't work. Where could she go? Her purse was in her handbag, at home. Alice optimistically checked her coat pockets to see if there were any odd coins but came up with nothing. With not a penny on her, she couldn't even get on a bus and go over to Meadowbank to see Valerie. Who would probably not be at home anyway, not on a Saturday afternoon. Her friend had something called a 'life', something Alice wished *she* had. No doubt Valerie would be out shopping or seeing friends. Or maybe having her hair done. That's what normal women did. Alice didn't resent what her friend had, but that didn't mean she couldn't envy her. She sighed. Not even the wherewithal for a cup of tea in a café. Somewhere where she could sit in the warmth and dry out a bit. She was destitute. And this is what it'll feel like when I lose my job, she thought. I'll have no money and nowhere to go. My life will be empty. The rain started to ease slightly. I'm not going to be able to find another job. Not at my age. What will I do? Alice felt nothing but overwhelming despair. Everything was falling apart and all at the same time. Her marriage, her life, her future. Nothing good was coming her way. Alice was a born optimist, or at least she used to be. Now all she could see on the horizon were black clouds and blacker days. She shivered uncontrollably. Alice was cold. Very cold. And sitting here in this bus shelter was not improving things. She couldn't get any wetter if she tried. Make a run for it? Go home and dry out? Or stay here and catch my death? Home was the sensible option. Survive the weekend and see what Monday brought. Alice couldn't think any further ahead than that. Monday. Everything on hold until then. Pulling her collar up, she ran out into what was now a fine drizzle and dashed back across the park. The kind man and his dog had long since gone and the place was still deserted. It was getting dark, the storm making it seem later than it was. She hurried home.

Alice ran down Greenfields Road but instead of going straight home, she stopped suddenly outside Ronald's house. The curtains were drawn but she could see through the gap that he was sitting in front of his electric fire reading. That looks a lot more welcoming than what I've got waiting for me, she thought. Knocking on the door she went in. Ronald's face lit up as soon as he saw her but fell when he saw how wet she was.

"What have you been doing?" he asked, putting his book down. "You're soaked. Come and sit by the fire." With difficulty he stood up then bent down to turn up the fire up to three bars. "Come and sit here."

Alice did as she was told. She took off her coat, handed it to Ronald and gratefully sank into his armchair. Slipping off her sodden shoes, she pointed her toes at the heat. Bliss! It was impossible to keep her eyes open as the warmth seeped slowly into her bones. She must have dozed for a few minutes because the next thing she knew was Ronald putting a mug of tea down on the table next to her.

"Makes a change for me to look after you," he laughed. "Want a biscuit?" With difficulty he sat down on one of the hard chairs.

"Here, Ronald," said Alice, rising, "come and sit here."

"Absolutely not. You stay where you are. I'm fine here." Alice sat back down and stared at the fire. "Want to tell me about it?" he said.

So she did. She told Ronald everything. She told him about how Frank had used their holiday money to buy the over-sized television they didn't need and couldn't afford. She told him about how he still insisted that he was disabled and couldn't work although there was nothing really wrong with him. She told him how she was certain she no longer loved him, how they barely tolerated each other. She told him how she feared for her future once she was made redundant. How she feared growing old. Old and unloved. And finally she told him about the electricity bill and how Frank had hidden the first bill and the reminder from her. She told him everything. Everything that is, except the bit about her husband spurning her drunken amorous advances. That was just too humiliating. Then she burst into tears. It had been a day for crying. Ronald had sat throughout her story of woe, saying nothing, his chin resting on his steepled hands, watching her closely. But when he saw Alice's tears it was more than he could bear. He stood up as quickly as his old bones would allow and put his arm round her shoulders. She sobbed even louder.

"Hush," he said quietly. "We'll work something out."

Alice raised her face. "What?" she asked. "I can't see a way out of any of this. I've got a husband I can't trust, a marriage that's over, a job I'm going to lose, a huge bill I can't pay. I have no future. Nothing. What am I going to do?"

Ronald smiled at her. "Don't worry, Alice. We'll think of something."

Alice cried even harder.

# CHAPTER 11

## WESLH RAREBIT

Alice couldn't face being under the same roof as Frank. Not for the entire day. Yesterday had been bad enough. He'd been very quiet when she'd knocked on the front door after her wet visit to the park. Forgot my keys, she'd murmured, as he let her in. If he'd noticed her red eyes and tear-stained cheeks, he'd said nothing. Silently she'd taken the hotpot out of the oven, ladled some into two large bowls, one of which she'd left on the kitchen table for Frank. The other she'd taken next door to Ronald, but Alice wasn't in the mood for company of any sort, even Ronald's, so once she'd made sure he was alright, she went back home. He was disappointed that she wasn't going to spend time with him, even if it was just to sit with him while he ate, but he could see she was upset. Alice had no appetite, not even for her own cooking. She wanted to be on her own and knowing she'd be unable to have any sort of reasonable conversation with her husband, especially if he was engrossed in the tv as usual, she'd gone straight to bed.

Early Sunday morning, Alice contemplated ringing Valerie to see if she was free then decided against it. She'd be busy. Valerie would be doing things. Living her life. Best find something else to fill her day. But what? Alice peered out the window. The weather was a lot nicer than yesterday, the wind had dropped and there were patches of blue sky. It was a day for being outdoors. Where could she go that wouldn't cost much? Or even better, that was free? There was nowhere in Smedley and to be honest, Alice wanted to be away from the town, out in the real fresh air. And the best place for fresh air as far as Alice was concerned was the seaside. So she decided on a trip to the coast. Apart from the bus fare and maybe something to eat when she got there, it wouldn't cost much and Alice hadn't been to the seaside for years and a day out, on her own, would feel like a real adventure. You're sad, she thought to herself, if you think a day out at the beach is an adventure. But it was! Alice felt almost brave. There was an hourly bus to Woodly Bay from the bus station in the town centre and if she left now, she could have a good three or four hours there before catching the last bus back. Plenty of time for a walk on the beach, a bit of window-shopping, something to eat and then home. If that wasn't an adventure, she didn't know what was!

Although Woodly Bay was a bit 'kiss-me-quick', it was off-season and the weather wasn't warm enough yet to attract the day trippers. If she was lucky she might have the place to herself. Alice dressed warmly. Although there was no wind here in Smedley, Alice had vivid memories as a child of cold breezes blowing onto the beach, coming straight in off the North Sea, chilling her to the bone. So baggy jeans and a thick jumper were the order of the day. Sensible shoes. Alice didn't bother to look in the mirror; she didn't care what she looked like as long as she was warm. Her woollen coat had pretty much dried out from its soaking yesterday although it had now developed a really quite unpleasant, musty, stale smell. Still, as she always said, it would have to do. This time, however, Alice remembered her handbag and door keys. She left without saying goodbye to Frank and walked briskly into town.

As Alice turned into the bus station she could see that the Coasthugger Bus was already there, ready to go, its engine idling quietly. She handed the driver a ten pound note and noticed that there was only one passenger on the lower deck; a middle-aged man dressed for a summit attempt on the Eiger, with a bright red, thick down jacket, waterproof trousers and muddy leather walking boots. He had a folded map in a plastic wallet hanging round his neck and a collapsible walking stick and rucksack were wedged between his feet. He was sitting as close to the driver as he could and was regaling him with talk of yesterday's surprising win by the Witherby Wanderers, despite them being one man down, what with young dribbler being sent off for fouling. Alice cared little what sport he was talking about although no doubt Frank would have been able to tell her. She had to interrupt him in order to buy a ticket from the driver but the man hardly paused. The driver, a young man with ginger hair and freckles, looked at her with unbearable sadness in his eyes as he counted out her change. If the would-be mountaineer was going all the way to Woodly Bay it was going to be a long trip for everyone. Alice decided to sit upstairs and to her childish delight, found the front seats were all free. There were two other passengers, a couple of teenagers, a boy and a girl, dressed identically in black, who were sitting in the back row of the top deck, sharing headphones. Despite the fact that they were at the other end of the bus, Alice could feel rather than hear the throb of the music. Still, better than a mindless monologue about some short-staffed sports team which had problems fouling themselves. But it was a close-run thing. The bus left on time. A good omen, thought Alice.

The journey took just over an hour, passing first through the deserted, soulless town centre, then the suburbs, row upon row of terraced houses and here and there, a disused factory, empty shells now, abandoned and derelict, graffitied walls crumbling and broken. Alice was glad to leave Smedley behind, with its dull, uninspired buildings, its emptiness, its decay. It was a town living in the past; like her, she thought, it had no future. But the countryside was a different matter altogether. Rolling brown fields, neatly ploughed, hiding spring crops; hedgerows marking ancient boundaries; clumps of trees she couldn't name and random farm buildings. Cows and sheep enjoying the rare spring sun. A horse in a paddock, rugged up against the cold frosty nights. Now and then a village appeared, grey stone cottages with small windows and tidy gardens. Alice was thrilled with it all. She felt lighter. The bus stopped at a few of these neat villages and a handful of passengers got on. Time and again she wiped the inside of the window in front of her and the one to her right with the sleeve of her coat to get rid of the condensation which was distorting her view. Her sleeve got wetter and wetter and the musty smell returned with a vengeance but Alice didn't care. It was so long since she had done anything like this and nothing was going to spoil it, not even the boom, boom, boom of the incessant music, if that's what it was called, emanating from the conjoined duo at the back of the bus. She was loving every minute of it. The fact that she was on the move and that the scenery was changing before her eyes. The fact that she was going somewhere. Doing something. Wonderful! The gloom and despondency of yesterday had disappeared, for the time being at least. She was going to enjoy today. Tomorrow would come soon enough. Today there would be no thoughts of Frank or Bercow's, or Ronald even. Today is mine, she said to herself. It's a day for me and nobody, and nothing else, is going to get in the way.

Slowly, and with much noisy grinding of gears, the bus descended sharply into Woodly Bay. Alice peered out of the window, trying to see if she could recognise where she was. She couldn't remember the last time she'd come here. Her parents had brought her here often as a child and once they'd stayed a whole week in a bed and breakfast, the three of them sharing a room in a small house just up from the sea front. She'd thought it was the best time of her life, ever. And she'd come here once with Frank but that was a very long time ago too. They hadn't been married long and she felt so proud, showing him somewhere from her childhood, somewhere that meant so much to her. But he'd complained that the place stank of fish and was too noisy for him. Excitedly Alice shouldered her handbag and descended the stairs. What to do first?

She looked round the small bus station. This hadn't been here the last time she came. A green and black tourist signpost outside the main door pointed the way to the beach, the harbour, the twelfth century church which she could see up on the hill, the town museum, and the old fishermen's cottages, known as Herring Row. Very funny, she thought, only now after all these years understanding the joke. What else had she missed? Alice reckoned that by the time she'd had a walk along the beach she would be ready for some fish and chips in one of the many cafés that lined the harbour front. Then a brisk walk up to the church followed by a mooch amongst the touristy shops. A perfect day. She felt like a child again and couldn't help smiling. The beach was tucked in behind the south harbour wall as if it was sheltering from the wind and waves which always seemed to batter the ancient limestone ramparts. Even today, early spring, the sand was a golden yellow and the sea unusually blue, thanks to the watery sun. This bit of Woodly Bay looked so familiar, so re-assuring. It hadn't changed at all. But then it wouldn't, would it? Beaches don't change. Only people. Don't start, she thought, pushing the thought of Frank to the back of her mind. This is my day, she reminded herself. No unpleasant intrusions. The beach stretched away for just over a mile, ending under sandstone cliffs upon which was perched the tiny hamlet of Codling. A few people were walking their dogs but mostly the beach was empty. Access was by a seaweed-slippery concrete boat ramp and Alice clung tightly to the rusty metal handrail with both hands as she descended. At the bottom, she wiped her hands on her jeans then took a deep breath. My day. I'll walk as far as Codling and back. That'll be a good couple of miles. More exercise than I've had in years. Do me good, she thought. And give me an appetite. She strode out bravely, hands in pockets, taking in the clear bright light, the salty air. Everything seemed so sharp. So distinct. If only life were like that! Out to sea, the horizon was a flat line broken only by a cargo ship sailing south. Gentle waves rolled leisurely up and down the sand. Alice walked along the beach looking at the view and every now and again, bent down to examine the detritus left by high tides. Bits of sea-coal, pieces of wood from old fishing boxes, chunks of polystyrene, half a trainer and a plastic doll's leg. Now which is flotsam and which jetsam? she asked herself. She picked up a small interestingly coloured shell, pale yellow with brown stripes and examined it closely. Wouldn't it be wonderful if I could be transported to where this has come from? Somewhere far away and hot. Tahiti? Honolulu? Then she laughed. Knowing my luck, she thought, it's probably come from Grimsby! She was still peering at the shell and laughing when a voice stopped her dead.

"Alice?" She looked up. Oh no! "I thought it was you."

She could have died. Standing in front of her was Funeral Dog. Graham. He was smiling at her. Alice couldn't think of a thing to say.

"I thought it was you," he repeated. "What are you doing here?"

Automatically, Alice hid the shell behind her back, like a child caught stealing.

"Um, I, er, walking," she stammered. That was the best she could come up with at the moment. Bloody hell! This is *my* day and now it's ruined. You've gone and spoiled it.

Graham laughed. "I know this is going to sound awfully clichéd, but do you come here often?"

Alice laughed nervously. "To be honest, I haven't been here for years. I suddenly fancied a day out at the coast." She knew she was blushing. "And here I am," she added lamely. "What about you?"

"I was born here." He pointed vaguely in the direction of the town. "I like to come back when I can." He looked different. Alice realised that this was only the second time she had seen him without his overalls, the first time being at the Hackney Cabbage when she'd made such a fool of herself. His hairnet was gone, of course, and he was wearing normal clothes - a black waterproof jacket, jeans and sensible walking boots. For the first time she had a good look at his face. Out in the fresh sea-air, it had lost its factory pallor and he looked younger. Re-invigorated. A wide, intelligent forehead with deep-set dark brown eyes under thick black eye-brows. Graham's nose had a kink in it, like it had been broken at some stage and not set properly. And then there was the smile. It was the first time she had ever seen him smile. Really smile. An all-teeth smile. Suddenly she realised how dreadful she must look, in her old coat and baggy jeans. She was wishing now that she'd checked in the mirror before she'd left home. But never in a million years did she imagine she'd bump into someone she knew. Someone from work. And Funeral Dog, Graham, of all people. "Where are you heading?" he asked her.

Alice pointed to the far end of the beach. "I was going to walk to Codling and back." She felt an urgent need to explain to him why she was standing on a beach laughing for no apparent reason. It wasn't what normal people did. He must think her crazy. "But I got side-tracked." She produced the shell from behind her back and held it out to him in her open palm. "I found this and was wondering where it had come from." He took it from her and looked at it closely. "I thought maybe somewhere exotic. Tahiti or somewhere and then I thought, knowing me, it's more likely to come from Grimsby. Or Hartlepool." And that's why I was laughing, she wanted to say. It's not because I'm mad! Really!

"I don't think you're right about Tahiti," said Graham, holding the shell up to the light and turning it over and over. Well, I wouldn't be, would I? she thought. "But I think you've got the ocean right." I have? "It's definitely from the Pacific." It is? "My guess, and it's only a guess, is that it's a Tongan Torch Crab shell." Alice looked at him in amazement. He wasn't winding her up, was he? "Very definitely not from Grimsby." He smiled as he handed it back to her. "It's amazing how far some of this stuff travels." She put it in her pocket feeling very pleased with herself. The Pacific, eh? Graham turned to go. "Well, don't let me intrude any more. Enjoy the rest of your walk." And Alice watched, open-mouthed, as he headed back along the shore towards the town, striding out, straight-backed, hands thrust deep in his pockets. And was he whistling?

She gave up on the idea of walking to the end of the beach and back - the sun had disappeared and grey clouds were building and to be honest, Codling still looked an awfully long way off. It looked like rain too, and the wind was getting up again. Not a good idea to be caught out in the open in a downpour. She hurried back the way she'd come, up the slippery ramp and wandered along the harbour front. The waves were being funneled between the two piers and rocked the dozen or so gaudily painted fishing boats moored safely inside the harbour. She chose The Salty Sailor, one of the many cafés advertising fish and chips with a pot of tea and a plate of bread and butter. And all for £5.95! Eating out twice in one week, she thought. Luxury. The café was on the first floor and overlooked the harbour. From where she sat in the window, Alice could see that the wind was getting up and there were more and more whitecaps out at sea. A few brave folk were walking out to the lighthouse at the end of the south pier. She'd do that next time. Because there would be a next time, she was certain of that. She was coming back. As Alice ate her lunch, she thought about Graham. Dark horse or what? Was he kidding about the shell or did her really know what it was and where it came from? He must think her a right numpty. First, the incident at Indian, waving at him with the thong and now this. Standing on a beach laughing inanely at a shell. Still, in a few weeks time she'd never see him again so she could live with the embarrassment. And it would give the girls a laugh. Alice looked at her watch. She had just over an hour before the bus left. There was no sign of the rain yet so, wrapping the uneaten bread and butter in a paper serviette and slipping it into her handbag - waste not want not - she paid the waitress and decided to go and look at the shops. The main shopping area was pedestrianised - that was new - and was a mix of touristy shops selling sticks of Woodly Bay rock and other seaside goodies – garish plastic buckets and spades, flip flops, inflatable whales, all of which were stacked obtrusively on the pavement; mobile phone shops offering the latest smartphone with added GBData; a small off-licence called 'Brian's Boozer' with a sign in the window which read 'Cheap Tabs!'; a bakery, a butcher's and a grocery store. Realising she had nothing for dinner, Alice bought a piece of cheddar in the latter - she'd grate it over the bread and butter she'd kept from her lunch, grill it and call it Welsh Rarebit. That would have to do. Not only had it grown surprisingly dark in the few minutes she was in the shop, it had also started to drizzle so somewhere warm and dry was called for. The museum didn't appeal and the church was too far to walk to so the bus station was the next best place. Alice bought a newspaper and spent a pleasant hour reading it and people-watching. Since she was getting the last bus back, she wondered if Graham might be on it and kept an eye out for him. Not that she wanted to travel back with him or anything like that. She was just curious, that was all. But there was no sign of him. Maybe he drove here, she thought. Or took an earlier bus back. Whatever, as Alice travelled back to Smedley in the dark there were no rolling landscapes to be seen this time and, apart from the odd yellow light in an uncurtained window, there was little sign of life. The darkness only served to depress her. She was going home, somewhere she really didn't want to be. Her day at the seaside had been fun, despite the weather and even bumping into Graham like that hadn't spoiled it. Not really. And now she was heading back to Frank and back to Monday. Monday.

# CHAPTER 12

## SHEPHERDS PIE WITH PEAS

Monday. The day started out like any other. Grace and Bella were already in the staff room when Alice got there, changing into their overalls. Bella was prattling on about a dress she'd seen in Frocks but nobody was paying attention. Everybody had too much on their minds. Checking the rota Alice saw she was on Hazelnut Hearts this week - or however much of a working week there would be. Would she have a job at the end of the day? Would any of them? Alice stuffed her hair up into a hairnet then washed her hands at the sink. It was not going to be a good day.

Surprisingly, the first couple of hours passed by in a flash. The endless stream of small brown biscuits, about the same size and shape as a dog turd, she thought, not for the first time, passed quickly in front of her on the conveyor belt. Alice's job was to place a piece of broken hazelnut on the top of each one. Not a whole hazelnut - that reduced the profits. If the nut was too big, she had a small metal hammer on a tray next to her and carefully had to smash the nut into appropriately sized pieces. Not too hard or she'd end up with a pile of unusable nut crumbs. Not too big or she'd have to smash the nut again. The trick was to have a handful of correctly-sized nut pieces in each hand and to place them on a biscuit one at a time. A scanner detected if a biscuit was lacking its nut and automatically slowed the conveyor belt down until the operator, Alice in this case, put the vital nut piece in its proper place. Mindless and not difficult but she could never understand why someone hadn't designed a machine that could do all this, not just identify a missing nut. Still, it was a job, at least for the time being. She looked round the factory floor and saw Graham off in the distance talking to Shanti at her work station. Caramel Curls, was it? He looked just the same as he usually did. Round shouldered, pale, grim. It must be something about this place that made him the way he was, she thought. He'd been a different person altogether when she'd met him on the beach. Smiling. Pleasant. Normal. It has to be Bercow's. Probably has the same effect on all of us. Sucks all the lifeblood out of us. Chews up what little joie de vivre any of us may have and spits it out on the floor. That's Bercow's Biscuits for you! I wonder what Graham'll do with no job, Alice pondered. Same as the rest of us. Look for a new one or do something else altogether? Was Valerie right? she wondered. Would there be an announcement today? And if there was, would it be the day she told Frank? Frank. What was she going to do about him?

The rest of the morning passed with no announcement. Alice tried to concentrate on her biscuits and not to think about what the future might bring but it was difficult. It was occupying her every waking moment. Bercow's closing was going to change her life in every way imaginable. But since there'd been no announcement, maybe Valerie was wrong. Maybe a buyer *had* been found at the last minute and they could all sleep easy in their beds at night. No, that was not going to happen. I wasn't born under a lucky shooting star, or whatever the phrase was. The factory would close and that was that. Alice smashed a nut with uncharacteristic venom. It shattered into tiny pieces most of which shot off onto the floor.

"Everything alright?" It was Graham. Alice jumped. She hadn't heard him, what with noisy machines and her earplugs. Did he know something? Did he know he was about to be made redundant? Was that what he was coming to tell her?

"What?" she asked, removing both plugs. "Sorry, didn't hear what you said."

"I asked if everything was ok," Graham repeated, pointing to the hammer Alice still had in her hand

Alice nodded, embarrassed. Why was she always embarrassed when Graham was around? Perhaps it was because she did such idiotic things. If she wasn't waving thongs at him, she was standing on a beach laughing at nothing. What an imbecile! She swore at herself silently. "Fine. Just a bit heavy-handed," she said, waving the hammer. Graham automatically took a step back. "Oops, sorry. Don't know my own strength today."

"Ok, just take care, that's all."

Alice nodded and she put her earplugs back in as Graham moved off to the next work station. What a strange thing to say. To tell her to take care. He'd never done that before. She thought about it for a half a second before she realised that her un-nutted dog turds were piling up. Back to the important stuff.

"So have you worn your thong yet?" asked Iris, laughing.

This could be the last time we have lunch together in this canteen, thought Alice. You wouldn't be laughing if you knew what was about to happen. But then you probably would. You laugh whatever, don't you, Iris? One of life's sunbeams. And thank God for people like you. Alice shook her head. "No, not yet."

"Why not?" asked Shanti. "Not put it on for the old man?"

"*Frank*? Never in a million years!" exclaimed Alice.

"I didn't mean him. I meant your old man next door. Ron, isn't it? The one you look after. You'd look good in it."

Alice examined the sandwich in front of her. Tuna and sweetcorn, it said on the label. It was possible. Ever since Valerie had told her about Shanti, she found it hard to look her in the face. It wasn't because she was gay. Shanti was her friend and always would be. What did unsettle her was that Shanti could fancy her. That anyone could fancy her.

"Has he made you any more offers?" Grace asked.

"Just the usual."

"What's the usual," asked Iris.

"Show him my bosoms for £60."

"No!" exclaimed Bella.

"And have you?" asked Shanti.

Alice shook her head.

"Well, if you won't, I will!" offered iris. "£60 is £60. What I could do with £60!"

"Seriously, Iris, would you?" This was from Grace. "Would you show a man your breasts for £60?"

"Too right I would," she replied emphatically. "I mean, what's the harm in getting your knockers out? People do it all the time for free on those beaches. What do they call them? Naturalist beaches? What about you, Bella? Would you?"

"Too cold in Englan'. I not take my *coat* off on an Englan' beach! Even in summer!"

"No, Bella," Iris tried to explain. "I didn't mean on a beach. I meant anywhere. Would you show your whatever you call them in Spanish, for £60?"

"No," Bella was adamant. "I would be too embarrass'."

"Would you be too *embarrass'* for £100?" Shanti asked her.

Bella thought about it then shrugged her shoulders. "Maybe not so embarrass'."

96

"There you go, then. It's only a question of price, isn't it?" said Shanti. She sat back, unwrapping the Clingfilm from what she desperately hoped was chocolate cake. "What would you charge to sleep with someone?"

"Shanti!" Bella, Grace and Alice exploded in unison.

"Well, it's all a question of degree, isn't it?"

"What you mean? Degree" asked Bella. "I don' understan'. You have to have a degree to sleep with someone? You have to go to univers'?"

Shanti ignored her. "You charge him £60 to show him your tits, right?"

"No, I haven't!" cried Alice. "I haven't," she repeated lamely.

"Hypothetically. Although I reckon they're worth a lot more!" she added.

"That's what I said," said Valerie, pulling up a chair to join them.

Alice found her sandwich incredibly interesting.

"You charge him £60 to look at your tits," Shanti continued. "What would you charge to let him have a feel?"

"Shanti!" cried Alice. "That's gross!"

"You could have a scale of charges! Like, I don't know. £10 for a kiss? £20 for a cuddle? And so on." Shanti was enjoying this. "£100? £200 for a feel? But how much would you charge to sleep with him?"

"I never would!" said Alice, horrified. I don't even sleep with my husband, she thought. "I mean, I wouldn't. I couldn't. And he's in his eighties, for heaven's sake."

"Forget his age," said Shanti. "That's irrelevant. How much would you charge to sleep with him? Or anyone, for that matter?"

"I couldn't do it," repeated Alice. "Not with him or anyone. I couldn't charge someone for doing that!"

"I could," contributed Iris. "Maybe not for £100. Or even £200. But if the money was right, why not?"

"So as I said," repeated Shanti, "it's only a question of degree. You could have a price list and charge accordingly."

"I can't believe we're having this conversation," said Alice.

"Don't be such a prude," said Valerie. "You could get the chance to show off your thong!" She smiled at her friend. "And, anyway, what's the harm in it?"

"There's all sorts of harm in it," replied Alice.

"Like?" asked Shanti.

Alice tried to think. "Well," she started, "it would cheapen my friendship with Ron, for starters."

"Not if you regard it as a service," said Shanti. "You've got something he wants. He's buying a product. And you're selling." She looked round her. "Just like a packet of biscuits!"

Valerie roared with laughter. "Just make sure you don't give him the old broken ones!"

"This is not funny, Valerie," said Alice, her face grim.

"Loosen up, girl. I'm only joking."

"I'm not, though," said Shanti. "You're providing him with something he wants. And you are getting well paid in return. What's not to like?"

"And it would be tax-free," laughed Iris. "You couldn't declare *that* to the tax man!"

The klaxon sounded announcing the end of the meal break. Never had Alice been so glad to hear it.

All afternoon, Alice went over and over in her mind what Shanti had said. It was preposterous. Obscene. A price list for sex, that's what she was saying. Disgusting! But I also have a £189 electricity bill to pay. By Saturday. Or else we get cut off. And I'm just about to lose my job. Could it get any worse? Fine, she thought, irrationally. Let them cut us off. I'll move in next door with Ron and Frank can sit there in the cold and dark, all on his own. This was all his fault, anyway! If he hadn't turned into such a lazy bugger, such a sloth, and had a job, none of this would matter. My being made redundant would be grim but if Frank was working, it wouldn't be the end of the world. Which is pretty much what it felt like now. Alice had been so engrossed in reliving the lunchtime conversation with the girls and listing Frank's many, many shortfalls to herself, that she didn't hear the klaxon announcing the end of another day. It was only when the conveyor belt in front of her stopped moving and she looked around for the cause that she realised that people were packing up and getting ready to head home. No announcement then. What did it mean? Good news or bad? It had to be good, surely? Or was it, as she suspected, just a postponement of the inevitable. Alice changed quickly in the staff room, throwing her dirty overalls into the large laundry bin and with an unusual and inexplicable spring in her step, clocked out and pedalled for home.

"Good day at the office, dear?" Frank joked from his armchair as she walked in. Her good humour evaporated instantly. Strange how he had that effect on her. She hung her coat up behind the kitchen door. Frank suddenly materialised in the doorway like some ghastly overweight apparition. She didn't know he could move that quickly. "I got some mince," he announced proudly, as if he'd just reached the top of Annapurna. "I went out and got some mince. For our tea." Well, bully for you, she felt like saying. "I thought we might have some mince and potatoes. Or something. Shepherds pie, maybe?" Are you going to cook it? Do you know how? As tempting as it was to tell him where to put his shepherds pie, preferably while it was piping hot, she knew if she did, it would remain uncooked and Ronald would go hungry. She could never let that happen. Sighing, Alice found an onion in the vegetable basket and started peeling. Frank stayed in the safety of the doorway, watching her. "Aren't you going to talk to me?" he asked. She stopped what she was doing and looked at him.

"To be honest, Frank, I can't think of anything to say," she said simply. She turned her attention back to the onion. Frank watched her for a few moments longer then went back into the lounge and she heard the 'whumf', like the sound of an elephant farting, as all the air was expelled from his armchair as he dropped into it. Then the television went on and Alice sighed with relief. It was better than attempting conversation when nobody had anything to say. When the shepherds pie was in the oven, Alice sat at the kitchen table and thought about leaving him. Where could she go? The house was in joint names and even if they could sell it, and that was doubtful as no-one wanted to buy houses round here, it wouldn't be worth much. This was the old-fashioned part of town. Anyone with any money wanted one of the soulless breeze-block homes on the new estates which seemed to appear almost overnight on the edges of Smedley. Though why they were building them, she couldn't work out. There was little work here and the town wasn't exactly humming with opportunity. And whatever their house was worth, she'd only be entitled to half. Half of two thirds of bugger all, as her father used to say. It wouldn't amount to a pile of beans. No, she was stuck. Stuck with this house. Stuck with Frank. The thought of it filled her with such despondency. It was like a black thundercloud, following her every move. Wherever she went, whatever she did, it would be there. Just waiting to burst and cover her in its despair and futility. Alice hated being this negative but there seemed no end to any of her problems. Nothing was ever going to get better. The timer told her dinner was ready.

Alice plated up three servings and covered two of them with upturned plates to keep them warm "Yours is on the table," she said to her husband. "I'm going to eat next door. With Ronald."

Frank was so flabbergasted at this turn of events, he sat bolt upright. Or as near bolt upright as he could. Which wasn't very. "I didn't go and buy mince so you could feed him next door and then go and eat with the old sod," he snarled. "This was for us."

"Tough!" said Alice, leaving the front door wide open as she balanced the plates in her hands. She kicked on Ron's door and when he opened it and saw her there, his face lit up. He was always so pleased to see her. "I couldn't open the door," she explained, showing him both her hands were full. "Mind if I eat with you tonight?" Ronald held the door wide. He couldn't stop smiling. He was still smiling when he slurped up the last of the gravy.

"Delicious. Simply wonderful. I like your shepherds pie. One of my favourites." He wiped his mouth with the back of his hand and leaned back contentedly. "I never asked you if you had a nice birthday. Was it good?"

"The dinner out with my friends was." Alice laughed. "You never guess what one of my girlfriends got me."

"Go on. Tell me."

"A thong!"

"A thong?" repeated Ronald.

"A thong. For me. I mean, look at the size of me." Alice chuckled.

"I think that's a wonderful present," said Ronald, seriously. "Just right for you. Sexy!"

Alice looked at him in disbelief. "You are kidding, aren't you?"

"Absolutely not! Now," he said as he stood up. "I've got something for you too." He went over to the sideboard and retrieved his Coronation tin. He pulled two twenty pound notes from the roll and handed them to Alice.

"What's this for?" she asked, puzzled.

"For you. For the cuddle," explained Ronald.

"But you paid me already. I can't take this." And she tried to give him back the money.

"No," he said, refusing to take the money. "I paid you for the first cuddle, but not the second." Alice looked blank. "The other night.

When you were telling me all about Frank and I put my arms round you. I didn't pay you for that cuddle."

Alice laughed. "That wasn't a cuddle. That was just…you being nice."

"That was a cuddle in my book and I owe you for it. Take it! It's yours."

"No," Alice tried to argue, "that doesn't count. Here!" She tried to give him the money back but he was having none of it.

"It does in my book. My, but you're a feisty woman! I love it! What I wouldn't do to see more of your feistiness. And more of you!"

Alice sat and looked at him then at the £40 she was holding. That meant she only had another £149 to find to pay the bill. "Do you mean that, Ronald? Do you really mean that? You'd pay to see more of me?"

"What? Of course I do. When I said I'd pay to see your tits, of course I meant it! Why wouldn't I?"

Alice did a rapid calculation. Ronald had offered her £60 to show him her breasts. That would only leave another £89 to find. Perhaps the electricity people would take some money in part-payment. She'd work out how to get the rest of the money some other way. "Alright then!" She'd made her mind up.

"Alright what?"

"I will show you my bosoms for £60." Alice stood up. "But just this once!"

Ronald's smile could not have been wider. "Honest?" he whispered.

"Honest." I'm committed now, thought Alice. There's no going back.

"When?"

"Now?" she suggested. Strike while the iron's hot.

"Now?" Ronald could not believe his luck.

"Now." And with that, Alice unbuttoned her blouse and dropped it on a chair. With both hands, she reached behind her and unclasped her bra. With a flourish, it joined her discarded blouse. Ronald sat in his chair and stared, open-mouthed. Alice closed her eyes. All that could be heard was the buzz from the electric fire.

"Thank you, Alice," said Ronald, quietly. "That was lovely."

She opened her eyes. "Is that it?" she asked, reaching for her bra. It had been painless and strangely enough, she didn't feel at all awkward.

"Thank you," he repeated. "Wonderful. I'd forgotten what a beautiful woman could look like." He handed her the promised £60. "Worth every penny."

"It won't happen again," she reminded him. "It was a one-off."

"If you say so."

"What d'you mean, Ronald?"

He waved the roll of notes. "Plenty more where that came from. It's up to you. You want to do it again, I won't complain."

Alice tucked her blouse into her skirt. "It won't happen again, I can promise you that. For one thing, you haven't got that much money and what you do have, I can't keep taking it from you. It's yours. You need it."

"Yes, it's mine. And it's up to me how I spend it. I'll spend every penny of it on you if I want to."

"Ronald Sanders, you are incorrigible!" said Alice, bending down to give him a kiss on the cheek. She collected the dirty plates. "See you tomorrow."

"You bet! I'm not going anywhere!"

Alice quietly closed the door.

# CHAPTER 13

## TINNED RAVIOLI

It was another couple of days before the announcement was finally made and Bercow's employees learned their fate. Half way through the morning the klaxon sounded. Assuming it was a fire alarm, everyone stopped what they were doing. Those on the factory floor turned off their machines as they were instructed to do and looked round to see if everyone else was doing the same. The tannoy spoke; "Would all staff please report immediately to the staff canteen. I repeat, would all staff please go immediately to the staff canteen." Alice's heart sunk. This was it. Almost lovingly, she ran her fingers over the conveyor belt in front of her. These could be my last ever Hazelnut Hearts. "Oh, and this isn't a fire drill," the tannoy continued. "Just in case you thought it was." Alice stood, hands in pockets, as Shanti made her way over from Caramel Curls and joined her. "What's going on?" she asked. Together they headed to the staff canteen. "Do you know what this is all about?" Alice said nothing. She realised that she might be one of the few people in the factory who knew what was about to happen. Best say nothing.

The canteen was not designed to accommodate every single one of Bercow's workers at the same time, so it was an unpleasant, sweaty squash. It was standing room only. Although Shanti couldn't see Iris, she could hear her above the din - no-one had a voice like hers - so she followed the sound, elbowing her way through the crowd. Alice followed in her wake, apologising here and there for stepping on toes. They found Iris with Bella at the back of the room. Looking round, Alice noted that all of Bercow's Biscuit Biddies were here, as well as the S&M engineers; Graham and the other floor supervisor stood together next to one of the sandwich cabinets; the two catering staff were standing safely behind their counter; Jason from HR was here, even Kitty from Reception. There were a few people she didn't recognise. Must be from Marketing and the like, she thought. Everybody from every part of Bercow's was here. The entire workforce. The noise was deafening as everyone asked each other what was going on. Why they had all been summoned at such short notice? Had somebody died?

There was a commotion in the canteen doorway. Everyone turned.

"Quiet please! I said, quiet!" A disembodied male voice finally got what it wanted and the room fell silent. Presumably it was somebody from Management but Alice couldn't see who it was through the crush. "Mr Bercow wants to talk to you all. Quiet!" Immediately the noise erupted again. This was unprecedented. Bertram Bercow Junior himself wanted to talk to the workers? All of them? At the same time? Why? "Please, ladies and gentlemen," the man was almost crying now. "Please," he whimpered. The noise subsided. There was the sound of a throat being cleared. Alice stood on tiptoe, straining to see what was going on. Suddenly a giant appeared in the doorway, his head and shoulders rising above the assembled throng. There was a communal gasp. Like everybody else, Alice was confused until she realised it was BBJ himself, the factory owner, and that being a man of average height, he must have been standing on a box or something. Unless he had grown considerably since the one and only time she'd met him, when he'd presented her with her plaque and £100 for her Alouettes. How long ago was that! She recognised his barber-neat grey hair and trim matching moustache. His round black-framed designer glasses were perched on the end of his nose and as he peered through them, he appeared as if he were looking down on his workers. Which technically he was, as when there was a sudden gap in the crowd, Alice could see he was, indeed, standing on a chair. At the same time, she caught sight of Valerie standing next to him, holding on to his leg for support.

"Ladies and gentlemen," said BBJ, clearing his throat again. "Thank you all for coming here. I can't pretend it's going to be easy to tell you what I'm going to have to tell you." Shanti looked at Alice. What? "As you know, my grandfather started Bercow's Biscuits in the 1930s. For years we were a household name. Ask anyone what their favourite biscuit was and they would tell you...?" He paused as if expecting everyone in the room to shout out with one voice, BERCOW'S! There was silence. "That's right," he went on, as if they had. "Bercow's. Best biscuits in the world. And for over 70 years, 80 years, no, nearly 90 years, we've been the tops." Just get on with it, thought Alice. Silly old fart. She was certain everyone was thinking the same. "But sadly, no longer. We've lost our bite, you could say." He chuckled. Nobody else did. "I'll be brief," he continued. "This business is not what it was." None of us are, thought Alice. "We have tried over the years to become leaner." Haven't we all? "Where we can, we've made savings." Like no butter in the biscuits. "And we've all had to economise. Even me." Yes, those bespoke suits from Cross Bros are a snip, aren't they? "Competition has a lot to answer for." So has apathy and lack of investment. "We just can't compete on the world stage anymore." When did we ever? BBJ reached into his pocket to wipe his brow. It was hot in the room with so many people present and being as he was closer to the neon lights than anyone else, he was sweating profusely. He wobbled dangerously and half a dozen hands automatically reached out to steady him. BBJ smiled nervously. "Thank you. Anyway, what I was saying was that for a long time now, Bercow's has been struggling. But there's only so long you can go on." Unlike you, thought Alice irritably. Just spit it out and tell us the worst. "I'm afraid I have some bad news for you all." Here it comes. "Bercow's is closing down!" There was uproar in the canteen. Horror was written on every face. Disbelief. Despair. The lucky few who'd got to the canteen first and had been sitting at the tables, rose to their feet as one, pushing their chairs back and into those who were standing. It was pandemonium. There were cries of No! You can't do this to us! You must be joking! Get off my bloody foot! Shanti grabbed Alice's hand.

"Please, ladies and gentlemen, let me finish," shouted BBJ, trying to make himself heard above the clamour. He wobbled again. "Please!" The noise lessened slightly. He took his time looking at the sea of faces turned towards him. "I know this will come as a shock to all of you. It has to me. Bercow's is like one big family." I notice you didn't say 'happy' thought Alice. BBJ put his hand on his heart as if to show his workforce just what they meant to him. Either that or it was a touch of angina. "For weeks we have been trying to find a buyer to take over the business. But we haven't succeeded. So we've had no option but to call in the receivers." He made as if to wipe a tear from his eye. "Administration," he whispered, as if it was a dirty word. It certainly was to Bercow's workers.

"When do we close?" shouted a voice from Alice's right.

"What about our pay?" shouted another.

"And our pensions?"

"Yes, what about our pensions?" shouted several others together. This sparked even more outrage.

BBJ was clearly struggling to control his audience. "Jason here will answer all your questions," he said, pointing to a young man dressed in a grey hoodie, jeans and trainers, standing near the window. All heads turned toward him. Alice thought he hadn't changed a bit since she last saw him when he took her photo for the canteen wall. What was it? Five years ago? More? Same clothes, same spots. Jason bared his teeth in an attempted smile whilst looking as if he wished the ground would swallow him up and spit him out somewhere far, far away. "We're looking at redundancy packages and pensions and all that sort of thing. We are going to do everything we can for you," shouted BBJ. "We'll try and find you new jobs, help you with CVs…"

"How am I going to pay my rent?" cried a young girl from the other side of the room. Alice realised it was Grace. Tears were rolling down her face. "Where am I going to find another job in Smedley?"

Bertram Bercow Junior looked down at her with sadness. "We're going to do all we can," he repeated. He pointed again at Jason. "Our HR will leave no stone unturned." Jason looked as if he wanted a stone of his own. A very large one under which he could crawl. "Now because I know you're all quite upset by this news, I'm going to give you the afternoon off. I'm going to shut the factory. When I say 'shut' I mean just for the afternoon. Not permanently. Well, not yet anyway," he added hastily. "No, this is so you can all go home early today. Or you can stay and talk to Jason, if you'd rather." Go home, please, begged Jason silently. Don't talk to me! I don't want to talk to any of you! "And please, I know there will be press interest. Could I please ask you not to say anything to the media. Go home, have the afternoon off and we'll see you all again in the morning. Don't forget, we haven't closed yet." And with that he reached out to Valerie who helped him down from the chair and left the canteen as quickly as he could. There was a stunned silence. People looked at one another, total incredulity on their faces. This was the worst possible news. No-one left the canteen. They didn't know what to do or where to go.

"What are we going to do?" asked Bella, in a hushed voice. "I am mortify."

"Well, I never saw this coming?" said Shanti. She sighed. "Talk about a bolt out of the blue."

Valerie was pushing her way back though the crowd towards them. "Come on," she said, "let's get out of here. Let's go and grab a cuppa."

"I'm going home," said Bella.

"Me too," agreed Iris.

"I need to go and talk to Carol," said Shanti. "That's two wages we're not going to have." She smiled sadly at Alice. "Catch you later."

The canteen was starting to empty as most people realised there was nothing to be gained by staying there. A dozen or so had surrounded Jason and were firing questions at him; questions to which he had no answers. He'd either not been properly briefed, or, more likely, not briefed at all. He was almost as much in the dark as they were. "We're working on it," he kept saying over and over. "I'll have the answers for you next week."

"I don't envy him," said Valerie. "Poor bugger!"

"Poor bugger? He's young. He'll find another job. It's us I don't envy," replied Alice.

As they left the factory together, Alice wheeling her bike, there was a large white van parked just outside the gates. It had a satellite dish on the roof and a logo of two entwined 'N's painted on the side with Northern News written underneath. A line of staff queued up for their two minutes of fame. They were waiting to be interviewed by a tall, oddly handsome man with skin the colour of overripe oranges, dressed in an open-necked shirt with the same NN embroidered on the breast pocket. He wore no jacket, despite the weather, and his jeans had a crease down the front. His immaculate, unnaturally black hair stayed rigidly in place even though the wind was whipping up the skirt of the woman he was interviewing. A cameraman filmed the interviews. As they walked past, Alice heard the woman sob, a knuckle held to the corner of her mouth, "I've got four kids. Four kids! And no job! How am I going to feed them? We're all going to go hungry!" The interviewer nodded. It was a good sound byte.

"He didn't get his suntan here, that's for sure," commented Alice dryly.

"They were told not to talk to the press," said Valerie.

"What difference does it make?"

"I suppose you're right. Come on. Let's get go."

The Bottomless Cup was heaving with Bercow workers. A lot of them had obviously had the same idea. Not everyone wanted to go straight home. They wanted to commiserate with each other, derive some little comfort from their shared misfortune for a little bit longer. Before they had to break the dreadful news to their loved ones. Just how were they going to tell their husbands, wives, partners, children? Many of them were the sole breadwinners in their families - this was not going to be easy. Alice and Valerie could see how busy it was the café by the sheer amount of condensation fogging up the windows inside. There were even people queuing to get in.

"Pub?" suggested Valerie.

"Why not?" It would probably be the last time she would ever go to a pub. May as well enjoy a drink while she could still afford it.

Alice secured her bike to a lamppost outside The Amiable Dog, a dark, unattractive, dingy pub which still bore the nicotine-stained walls and ceiling of countless years of cigarettes. It was just as busy as the café with some Bercow employees deciding that rather than have a nice cup of tea, the answer was either to drown their sorrows or summon up some Dutch courage before they went home to break the grim news. Normally it had little trade, but today, it being the nearest pub to the factory, it was positively throbbing. The landlord could hardly believe his luck. An elderly couple, clearly not from Bercow's, frightened by the noisy influx of morose workers demanding alcohol, finished their drinks quickly and vacated their table near the toilets. Alice grabbed it quickly whilst Valerie got them a half a lager each from the bar.

"Cheers," said Alice, "here's to happier times." She swallowed half it in one gulp.

"Blimey, girl! Steady."

Alice put the glass down. "So what next?"

"Well, the administrators will see what assets there are in the factory, if any, and what money there is. They'll pay off any creditors, any outstanding bills and then see if there's enough for any sort of redundancy packages for the staff."

"No, that's not what I meant," said Alice. "What's next for us? I'm not going to be able to find another job. Not at my age. Not in Smedley. Even if there is any sort of package on the table, it's not going to be enough. It'll be a stopgap at best. What will we do?" Valerie said nothing. "And what about people like Grace. Her Ivan's lost his job and they can't even afford the rent. What are *they* going to do?" She finished off the rest of her drink and stood up. "My round." Alice came back with two pints.

"If we're having a session," said Valerie, I'm going to have to switch to wine. Or vodka. All this lager and I'll bloat."

"What will you do?" asked Alice. "Will you be ok?"

"Oh, I'll have to find another job." She played with the condensation on the outside of her glass. "I mean, I could just about manage but, well, to tell you the truth, Alice, I have a habit."

Alice stopped with her glass half way to her mouth. "A habit?" She put the glass back down on the table.

Valerie nodded. "I have a habit I need to feed."

"You've never mentioned this before, Val. Not in all the years I've known you." She squeezed her friend's hand. It just went to show. You think you know someone and then this. "I'm so sorry. What is it? Heroin?" she asked, whispering.

Valerie shook her head. "Worse."

What could be worse than heroin? "Cocaine?"

Valerie smiled. "Oh, much worse than that."

Alice couldn't think of any other drugs. "Well, it's not alcohol, is it?"

"No, not booze." And just to show Alice that she didn't have a problem with alcohol, Valerie took a large gulp of lager and burped quietly. "See what I mean?"

"So what is it?" asked Alice, intrigued.

"Do you really want to know?" Valerie was smiling broadly.

"Of course I do! I want to help."

This caused Valerie to burst out laughing. "You're so very sweet, Alice Coulter but I'm afraid you won't be able to help."

"I can try," said Alice, earnestly. "What is it? What's your habit?"

"Lingerie," replied Valerie and folded her arms.

"Lingerie? As in knickers and things? Underwear?" Alice could not believe what she was hearing. Her friend nodded. "How can you have a knicker habit?"

"It's just the same as any addiction. I have to buy - and wear, of course - nice, and usually very expensive, underwear."

"Like my thong? The one you got me for my birthday?"

"I have 56 at the last count."

"Thongs? No! What would you do with 56 thongs? You can only wear one at a time."

"And 135 pairs of knickers. All lace. And 27 teddies."

"27 teddies? I used to have *one*! I got it for my first birthday but a dog chewed the ears off and my mum threw it away. Why would you want 27?"

"Not teddy bears, you numpty. Teddies. You know, like little lacy corset things. With straps."

Alice didn't know. Teddies? Why would you wear such a thing? Must be like a vest. She thought about her motley collection of greying bras and large, off-white cotton knickers.

"And I won't even tell you about my bras!" grinned Valerie.

Alice looked at her in amazement. "Ok," she said, "you don't tell me about your bras and I won't tell you about mine."

"I'm serious. This is an addiction. It's cost me a fortune over the years. That's why my first husband left me. Cited 'unreasonable behaviour' in the divorce on the grounds of what he called my 'panty problem'! Fool! Anyway, it's what I spend my salary on, so I'm going to have to get another job."

"Or stop buying underwear," suggested Alice.

"Not sure I could do that."

"You could try. You may have to."

"Mmm. Want to split a bottle of wine?"

Alice shook her head. "Best not. I need a clear head. Lots of thinking to do."

"Sensible Alice, as always."

"I wish."

"What do you mean?" Valerie looked at Alice long and hard. "What have you done?" Alice said nothing. Then it dawned on her. "You haven't, have you?" she cried. "Your old man? You've done the deed?"

Alice nodded. "Sort of."

"Sort of? What do you mean?"

"A cuddle and a display of my er…parts."

"Way to go, girl! How much?"

"£100."

"£100? Fantastic!" Valerie stood up. "I think, in the circumstances, a bottle of wine is called for, and this one's on me!" And before Alice could argue, she barged her way to the bar.

"What're you going to do with it?" she asked, putting a bottle of Sauvignon Blanc and a couple of glasses on the table. "No Pinot, I'm afraid."

"Do with it? Why, pay the electricity bill, of course. At least, most of it."

"You're *what?*" Valerie was incredulous. She poured them each a glass. "This is your money. You earned it. Spend it on yourself!"

"If only. It's not that easy," said Alice and she spent the rest of the bottle telling Valerie about Frank's duplicity, about the threatening red electricity bill and about how desperation had driven her, in reality, into Ron's arms.

Valerie drained the last of her glass. "I had no idea. I thought you might do it for fun. You know, show him your bits for a laugh. But I had no idea money was so tight. Why didn't you come to me?" she asked. "I could have helped you out."

Alice nodded. "I know you would. I guess I was just too embarrassed. Didn't like to ask."

"For goodness' sake, Alice! How long have we known each other?" She upended the bottle over Alice's glass but it was well and truly empty. "Another one?"

"No! Absolutely not," said Alice, putting her coat on. She looked at her watch and grimaced. "I've had far too much anyway. And it's not even four o'clock. I'd best be getting home and tell Frank the good news. Not." She gave her friend a hug and hurried home, a bit more wobbly than usual on her bike.

"When were you going to tell me?" asked Frank. He was watching a news channel on the television as she walked in the door. This was a first. He never usually bothered himself with anything other than the sport channels. Bercow's imminent closure had made the national news. A red ticker-tape at the bottom of the screen shouted 'Breaking Story! Another British factory bites the dust. Tory government to blame. Another nail in the coffin for Smedley?" Alice recognised the woman being interviewed as the one she and Valerie had seen as they'd left the factory. The improbably handsome interviewer turned to the camera, microphone in hand, and promised an exclusive with Bertram Bercow Junior, the factory owner, next and later on, the local MP, John Lyreman, would be asked for his comments.

"I only just found out today," she said. Not quite the truth, but what did it matter when she knew. It made no difference to the outcome.

"What are we going to do?" asked Frank.

"I have no idea," she replied. She went into the kitchen to look for something to eat. The only thing Alice could find in the cupboards was a couple of tins of ravioli in tomato sauce. It would have to do.

"You'll have to get another job," he said, not bothering to get up from his armchair.

Sod you, she muttered under her breath. Alice poured the contents of the tins into a pan and turned the hob on. Stirring slowly, she stared out into the back yard. She could feel a headache building. Shouldn't have had all that wine. And lager. But what the hell! Why not? Probably be the last time she had some wine for a very, very long time. She wondered whether she should tell Frank about the £100 Ronald had given her for services rendered but decided against it. None of his business. She'd sort out the electricity bill and after that? Who knows? Alice divided the ravioli into three and gave one plate to her husband as he sat in front of the screen. As she opened the door, balancing the other two plates carefully in one hand, she turned to him.

"Oh, by the way, Frank, I'm leaving you."

She slammed the door shut behind her.

# CHAPTER 14

## FISH PIE

The weather matched Alice's mood as she got ready for work, her head throbbing. Foul. It was cold and miserable and even though it was dark, she could see even darker clouds scudding across the sky, tossed by the wind, threatening rain. She'd slept like a log, surprisingly, probably due to all that alcohol, or maybe it was because she'd finally made her mind up and told Frank she was leaving him. It was a momentous decision, no doubt about it. And now that she'd finally made her mind up, Alice felt as if a heavy weight had been lifted from her shoulders. This was to be a new beginning for her, a brave step into the big, wide world. If it hadn't been for her hangover, Alice would have felt almost happy.

Frank was already in bed when she'd got back from Ronald's and she hadn't been late. It was unusual for him to go to bed so early but she was glad he had. Now that she'd finally made the decision to go Alice needed to make plans. Like where would she go, for starters. And how she would live. Should she make a fresh start in a new town, one where there were jobs? Or stay in Smedley and hope that something turned up? What would she use as a deposit if she found a flat to rent? Frank had spent what little savings she had on that wretched television. Could she ask Valerie to help her out? Possibly not, after what she'd told her in the pub about her habit. Alice had never heard the like! Lingerie, for goodness' sake! Anyway, back to important things. Alice had major plans with no easy answers. In fact, no answers at all. As she cycled to work she wondered why she should be the one leaving. Why not tell Frank he had to go? Would he though? She doubted it. He had nowhere to go. He had nothing and no-one, apart from her. Alice could even see him ending up homeless. Sleeping in doorways. All his possessions in a supermarket trolley. Would the tv fit? No, she couldn't do that to him. Easier if she went. But where? Ronald had offered her a home but she didn't want to move in with him. She told herself she needed to buy a local newspaper on the way home and look at the Flats to Rent and Situations Vacant pages, although that would be what everybody else at Bercow's would be doing. Alice knew she didn't stand a chance.

She was surprised to see Jason from HR standing in the door at the staff entrance. He was dressed in the same clothes as yesterday and looked as if he'd slept in them.

"No home to go to?" joked Alice, immediately regretting what she'd just said. The way things were going, that might soon be the case for a lot of them. Wordlessly he handed her a piece of paper. "What's this?" she asked him.

"FAQS," he replied.

"No need to be like that," said Alice, tartly. "I only asked."

"No, FAQS. Frequently Asked Questions. You know, about the closure. We thought it would be a good idea to answer some of the questions. About wages and pensions and stuff. Save you having to ask me the same thing over and over."

Good idea, thought Alice, looking at the short list of questions;

When will Bercow's close?
Will I still get paid?
Will I still get my pension?
Will there be a redundancy package?
Will I still be able to buy broken biscuits?

Alice turned the paper over. There was nothing on the back.

"Haven't you forgotten something?" she asked.

Jason looked at her blankly. "Like what?"

"The answers, perhaps," she suggested. "Might be useful."

"Oh, that. That's WIP?"

"Whip? What are you talking about?"

"Work in Progress."

"Oh, WIP."

"It means we're still working on it."

"I know what it means," said Alice slowly, as if she was talking to a lower life form. She was. "Don't you think it would have been a good idea to wait until you had the answers to the questions before you went into print?"

"D'ya think so?" He picked at a spot on his chin. "I just thought it was a good idea to let everyone know that HR is thinking about the big issues."

I'm glad someone's thinking, thought Alice, just not sure who. By this time a small crowd had built up behind her, waiting to get in to the

114

building, out of the rain. Jason handed them each a piece of paper as they went in. Most of them read the single sheet quickly then crumpled it into a ball and threw it back at him. Jason looked as if he was about to cry.

"All my hard work," he moaned. "I was up all night doing that!"

God save us from the slow and dim, thought Alice. Brains of a coffee table. She left him to it and went to clock in. Wonder how many more times I'm going to be doing this?

If there hadn't been an announcement yesterday telling the Bercow workforce that the factory was going to close and that they were all going to lose their jobs, you wouldn't have known that anything was different. Apart from Jason's extraordinary and pointless appearance at the staff entrance the day was just like any other. Everyone had turned up for work, even the few who'd been off sick yesterday and had missed all the excitement. They'd heard the news by proxy or seen it on the tv and, like Lazarus, that had been enough to raise them up and struggle in. They reasoned that if they weren't at work, they might miss out on whatever there was to miss out on, if anything. Staff clocked in as usual; put clean overalls on over their own clothes as they normally did, stuffed their hair into unflattering hairnets as required, went to their respective biscuit machines as per the rota, and got on with making Bercow's biscuits as they did every day. Nobody spoke much but then they didn't usually, conversation being almost impossible over the noise of the machinery. Alice concentrated on her Hazelnut Hearts, carefully placing a shard of nut on the top of each biscuit prior to them being baked. They were probably the best-placed nuts she'd ever done. Like the rest of the Biddies she was working particularly carefully today as if to prove that, despite everything, Bercow's biscuits were still worth something, were still made with love and care and that the factory could still be viable and should not be written off. Fat chance.

It was in the staff canteen that the atmosphere of doom and gloom became apparent. An air of total dejection hit Alice like a wall as she looked round the room for her friends. Sombre faces, red eyes, downcast mouths everywhere. Conversation was muted, whispered almost, as if no-one wanted to raise any spectres by talking out loud. It's like a bloody morgue in here, she thought, as she made her way to a table where Shanti, Bella and Grace were sitting. A trio of misery, she thought. And I make four.

"Nobody eating?" she asked. Head shakes all round. "Come on, girls, you've got to eat."

"Not hungry," muttered Shanti. Alice had never seen her look so downcast. The sparkle seemed to have gone out of her and she looked pale and drawn.

"Well, I am," she said. She got up and selected a wrap from a sandwich cabinet. Mexican Chicken with Green Salsa Verde Sauce, it announced. Yeh. Right. Unwrapping it at the table she cut it in two and offered one half to her companions. There were no takers. Not surprising really.

"How did Ivan take the news?" she asked Grace.

"Not good. Now neither of us has a job." Her eyes were red and she looked as if she hadn't slept last night. "There was a cleaning job advertised in the newsagents. I rang them as soon as I got home yesterday. They said they'd had twenty-four applicants for the job. Twenty-four! For a cleaning job!" This news depressed them even more. If Grace couldn't even get a cleaning job, what hope was there?

"Same for us," said Shanti. "We're losing two wages. What about Frank, Alice? How did he take it?"

"Frank? Well, first off, he told me I'd have to find another job."

"What did you say?" asked Bella.

Alice looked at them in turn. "I told him I was leaving him."

"Talk about a double whammy," said Shanti. "You sure know how to sock it to someone when they're down."

"Serious?" asked Bella. "You serious about leavin' him?"

"Totally serious."

"Wow," said Grace. "That's a bit drastic. What will you do?"

"I have absolutely no idea."

"No idea about what?" asked Valerie, as she sat down with a hot drink from the vending machine. She wrinkled her face in disgust as she took a mouthful. "That's one thing I won't miss about his place."

"Alice is leaving Frank," said Shanti.

Valerie looked at her then at Alice. "Honestly?"

"Honestly."

"Well, good for you. Long overdue, if you ask me. Should have done it years ago. Where will you go?"

"I haven't thought that far ahead," said Alice. "I only told him yesterday."

"What did he say?" asked Shanti.

"Not a word. Sulking, I expect."

"It puts our problems into perspective," said the ever-generous Grace. "I mean, you'll have to find a new home as well as a new job." She thought about what she'd said. "But then I suppose Ivan and I will too. We can't pay the rent." Her shoulders slumped and she hung her head. Alice put her arm round her and gave her a squeeze.

"You can move in with me, Alice" offered Valerie. "Until you get yourself sorted, that is."

"I don't know what to say," stammered Alice. "That's so kind of you. Can I think about it?"

"Sure. Just let me know. I'd better get back," she said, standing up. "We've got the administrators going through the accounts. Bloody nightmare."

"How's it going up there?" asked Shanti.

Valerie looked around, not wanting to be overheard. "Not good. I shouldn't be telling you this but hey! What're they going to do? Sack me?" She laughed mirthlessly. "There's not much money left. Not after all the creditors have been paid. Don't go booking your Caribbean cruises just yet."

"What? You mean no redundancy?" asked Shanti.

"I think you'll be lucky to get the wages you're owed," replied Valerie. Shanti looked positively ill. "And even if you do, it won't be for a long time yet."

"Why do the creditors get first dibs?" asked Grace, close to tears. "It's so unfair. After all, we're the ones who've been making these bloody biscuits."

"That's the way of it, I'm afraid. That's the law for you. Gotta go."

Iris was coming into the canteen just as Valerie was leaving. They exchanged a few words then Iris joined the girls.

"Damned Marshmallow Moments," she said. "Could not get the mix right this morning. I'll be happy if I never see another one as long as I live. Now, what have I missed?" She sat down heavily. Before anyone could tell her about Valerie's grim financial forecast or Alice's earth-shattering domestic news, she pointed to the uneaten half Mexican Chicken wrap with Green Salsa Verde Sauce. "Anybody want that? No?" In two bites it was gone.

Alice bumped into Graham as she was walking back to her station. Her head was down, thinking about what Valerie had said, wondering how any of them were going to manage if they didn't get their wages. That would mean they wouldn't even have a breathing space, no matter how brief, to try and sort something else out. She was so wrapped up in this latest news and not paying attention to where she was going that she walked right into him.

"Ooh! Sorry," she said, instinctively putting her hands out to brace herself. They landed on his chest. Looking up, Alice blushed. Their faces were inches apart. "Sorry," she repeated, backing away.

"My fault. Not looking where I was going."

"Me neither. Mind on other things."

"Dreadful news," said Graham. "Will you be alright?"

"Have to be. No choice. What about you?"

"I'll look for another job but I'm not optimistic. Too old."

"You and me both!" agreed Alice. "Only good for the scrap heap. Anyway," she said, desperate to get away, "better get back to work. That floor supervisor, he can be a right bugger!"

Graham laughed, his brown eyes sparkled. "So I've heard." There it was again. That smile. The same one she'd seen on the beach. His whole face lit up and was transformed into something almost beatific.

"You look so much better without your hairnet on," she said suddenly. Idiot, she said to herself. Now why did I say that?

"So do you. They're not the most flattering things, are they?" He smiled at her again. "Still got your shell?" he asked her. Alice nodded. "See you around."

Alice stopped off on the High Street on the way home to pick up some coley from the fishmonger. Fish pie, she thought. Cheap, and one of Ron's favourites. She parked her bike in the shed but decided against going straight in. Alice knew she'd have to sort things out with Frank but not just yet. Later.

"How are you doing, Ron?"

As ever, he was delighted to see her. "I saw the news on the television," he said. "I'm sorry."

"Well, we knew it was going to happen."

"They said the factory will stay open for a bit. Is that right?"

"Yes. We've no idea when it'll close. But word is, there won't be much money left to pay the wages we're owed. And we probably won't get our pensions." Alice looked at the old man. "Still, I've got some good news! I'm going to leave Frank," she announced.

Ronald burst into laughter. "Now, that is good news! Come and live with me! I've said it once and I'll say it again. I'll look after you."

It was Alice's turn to laugh. "I know you will. Valerie, my friend from work, she's also offered but I haven't made my mind up yet. But thank you. You're very sweet." She gave him a quick peck on the cheek. He grabbed her hand.

"I've got some good news too!" He was clearly excited. "I was at the Day Centre today."

"I'd forgotten it was today," said Alice. Had another month gone by already? "What did they give you for lunch? I hope it wasn't fish pie?"

"No, it wasn't. But never mind about that. I spoke to a couple of my mates." She looked at him. What was he rabbiting on about? "You've forgotten, haven't you?"

Yes, she had. "Sorry, Ronald, had a lot on my mind recently. What have I forgotten?"

"I said that I would speak to some of my mates. The lonely ones? The ones who might be interested in a bit of a cuddle?" Ronald raised an eyebrow. "Remember now?"

Oh yes, now she remembered. Tell me they said they weren't interested. Please.

"Well, they're really keen!" Oh no! "Two of them, at least. One of the others said he'd think about it. What d'you think about that, then?" Alice didn't know what to say. "The only problem is neither lives close by. One of them lives at Meadowbank. Posh, eh? And the other's at Billyfields, the other side of the railway station. But you've got a bike. I got them to write down their addresses for you," he handed her a piece of paper, "and I told Arthur, the one at Meadowbank, that you'd be over this weekend. He said he'd be waiting for you. Now what d'you think of that?"

Alice looked at him, open-mouthed. "Oh, Ronald," she said, "I wish you hadn't."

"Why not? You need the money, now more than ever if what you say about the factory not paying your wages is true. And you've still got that electricity bill to pay, haven't you?" The bloody electricity bill. It would be the death of her.

"Yes, but this cuddle thing, and me showing you my…you know what's." Alice was suddenly very embarrassed. "Well, that was between us two. Private, you know. I mean, we're old friends. I've known you a very long time. It's our secret. I can't just go up to any Tom, Dick or Harry and show myself to them."

"Funny, I never thought to ask Tom and Harry if they were interested, but I know Dick is! I'll ask them next time."

"Ronald!"

"I'm joking," he said. "You don't have to do anything you don't want to. And I know for a fact that Arthur's loaded. I mean, Meadowbank."

Where Valerie lives, thought Alice. The expensive part of town. Maybe I could make a day of it and go and see Valerie the same day. Hang about! What am I saying? No, this was preposterous! Totally out of the question! I am not going to prostitute myself. Because that's what it is, isn't it? A form of prostitution. Bella was right. But then I've already done it, haven't I? Demeaned myself. Shown Ronald my body. Well, bits of it. But did it do me any harm? Really? It certainly made him very happy and I've got £100 to show for it. £100 towards that ruddy bill. Maybe I could do it just the once for Arthur. Pay the bill and then not do it again.

"Did you tell him what happened? This friend?" she asked Ronald tentatively. He nodded. "And what you paid?"

"Oh yes. Told him it was the best £100 I'd ever spent. Regarded it as an investment, I said."

"And what did he say?"

"Didn't bat an eyelid. £100 is nothing to him. Said he'd better go to the cash point." Ronald looked at her expectantly. "He's on his own too. Lonely, you know."

"Don't play on my heart strings, Ronald. It won't work. This is strictly financial. If it wasn't for this wretched bill I wouldn't be doing any of this."

"You don't convince me, Alice Coulter. You've got a heart the size of Yorkshire. You'd do it for free."

"I most certainly would not. And I don't even know if I'm going to do it at all with your friend. What's his name? Arthur?"

"You will, 'cos you're kind like that." He suddenly looked worried. "It won't spoil our arrangement, will it?"

"No, Ronald. Whatever I do, *if* I do it, it won't spoil what we've got," she promised.

Ronald stood up slowly. "You're one in a million," he said, opening his arms wide. Alice stepped into them. She squeezed his frail body gently, feeling every bone under his worn clothes.

"That one's on me!" she said. "Now, I've got your dinner to make."

Slowly he released her. "Oh, and by the way, Arthur's got a real sweet tooth. Loves biscuits. None of us get a look in at the Day Centre. But home-made ones are his favourites. You might want to take some with you. He'd be happy to buy a packet or two off you."

"Oh, so now you want me to make him biscuits as well. Is there anything I won't be doing for this man?" Alice asked sarcastically as she opened the door.

"You tell me," said Ronald, mischievously, as she left. "You tell me."

Frank ate his dinner in front of the television, Alice, hers at the kitchen table. He was engrossed in a darts match, of all things. Darts? Was that a sport? It was in Frank's eyes. She heard the audience roar with approval as the last dart was thrown and the commentator announced the winner to the apparent delight of everybody watching in the huge auditorium. Frank turned the television down and brought his plate through to the kitchen. He put it in the sink and looked at his wife.

"Can we talk?" he asked quietly.

"Not tonight, Frank. I'm too tired."

"You're always too tired."

"I think that's got something to do with the fact that I get up and go to work every day," she retorted.

"When then? When can we talk? You can't just drop a bombshell like that. Tell me you're leaving me and then not talk about it."

Alice sighed. She really didn't want to get into an argument now.

"If not now, when?" persisted Frank. "Tomorrow? Sunday? When?"

"I don't know."

"Did you mean it?" he asked her, sitting down opposite her. "Did you really mean what you said?"

Alice nodded her head. "Yes," she said simply.

Frank looked as if his world had fallen apart. To him it had. "If I get a job, will you stay?"

This was the first time Frank had ever mentioned work.

"But I don't love you anymore," said Alice.

"That doesn't matter, princess. It's not really important."

"It is to me," she replied.

"Whatever. If I get a job, will you stay?" he repeated. He was like a Labrador. Desperate to be loved. Desperate to have someone to play with.

"Not tonight, Frank. I really am tired."

"Tomorrow? Can we talk tomorrow?"

"For heaven's sake!" She was getting impatient. "Yes. Maybe. I don't know. I've got to go out tomorrow."

"Where? It's Saturday? Where are you going?"

"I've got things to do," she said, very conscious of the things she was going to be doing.

"When you get back? Can we talk then?"

Angrily, she stood up. "Frank, we'll talk when I'm good and ready." She realised she was being unfair to him but she did not want to start this now. "I'll sleep in the spare room tonight," she said.

"Spare room? It's no more than a cupboard," Frank pointed out.

"There's room enough for the camp bed if I shift some boxes." Alice noticed that Frank didn't offer to move out of their bedroom. He left her and went back to his television. As Alice went upstairs he was already engrossed in a programme on competitive fly-fishing. He didn't even notice she'd gone.

# CHAPTER 15

## SPAGHETTI HOOPS ON TOAST

Alice woke with a spring in her step. Or she would have done if she hadn't had such dreadful backache from a night spent on the narrow put-me-up which had a mattress the thickness of a butterfly's wing. The spare room had been airless and stale and she'd found sleep difficult at first. It was more a store-room than a second bedroom, used to hide the clutter they'd accumulated throughout the long years of their marriage. Spare bedroom? Nobody had ever come and stayed. Alice tried to imagine what Valerie's spare bedrooms would look like – not like this one, that's for sure. She'd had to stack a large number of boxes one on top of the other before she'd created enough space to unfold the camp bed. It was an old metal thing that folded into three. She couldn't remember how long they'd had it or even where they'd got it from. It was just one of those things that had always been there. Bit like Frank. It had taken all her strength and ingenuity to get the bed open and up. At one stage she thought she'd have to call Frank for help, but with a lot of swearing and sheer brute force she finally got it sorted. She made up the bed with sheets and a couple of old blankets, ignoring the moth holes. Alice had lain there, eying the precariously stacked boxes. If they were to fall on her, would anyone ever find her body? Death by detritus. The thin curtains did little to hide the full moon or to stop the draft. Cold and miserable, she curled up into a ball. This is what it's come to, she thought. Finally, despite everything, or maybe because of it, she fell asleep. And she woke feeling refreshed and relieved. But with backache.

The first thing Alice did even before she had breakfast was to write out a cheque for £189 to the electricity company and put it into an envelope. She'd post it on her way to Meadowbank. Because that's where she was going today. She'd made up her mind. If she could get another £100 today, she calculated, and pay it into my bank along with the £100 from Ronald, that would cover the bill. With £11 left over. Whoop de woo! £11! She smiled to herself. Well, that's one problem solved. Then all she had to do was leave her husband, find somewhere to live, find another job and start all over again. Easy!

The morning was spent making biscuits. If Arthur liked home-made biscuits as much as Ronald had said, and was prepared to pay for them, she would take him a selection. See what I can tempt him with, she giggled. A quick trip to the corner shop and she stocked up on all the ingredients, paying over the odds, she knew, but she'd figure that into the price. Her famous, but not quite life-changing, Apple and Almond Alouettes were the first out of the oven. Looking nothing like the mass-produced ones from Bercow's, hers having been made with real butter, these were pale brown, decorated liberally with toasted flaked almonds. Chocolate Cherry Cookies soon followed, the chewy, velvety richness enlivened with pieces of glacé cherry - one of her mother's favourites. Then a batch of Walnut and Coffee Cookies, crunchy and crisp. Alice couldn't decide whether to make a batch of Oatmeal Crumbles or Raspberry Sandwiches so she made both. She looked at the rows and rows of biscuits cooling on the wire racks with something akin to happiness and inhaled deeply. The kitchen smelled unbelievable. Just like when her mother used to bake. Now something to put them in. Alice hunted in the kitchen cupboards until she found a long-forgotten tin under a stack of plastic bowls. Once she'd washed it thoroughly she saw it was decorated with faded daffodils. Using the green tissue paper in which Valerie had wrapped her thong, Alice lined the tin then carefully arranged a selection of her biscuits. Very professional, she thought, if I do say so myself. A job well done.

Upstairs she could hear Frank moving. Quickly putting the remaining biscuits into a plastic container Alice ran upstairs and into the bathroom. She spent a long time in the shower, shampooing her hair three times. After all, she was about to meet a new gentleman and she wanted to look her best. Choosing a floral blouse and plain black skirt which ended mid-calf, she looked at herself from all angles with a hand-held mirror. Not too bad, she thought. Anyway, guess what? It would have to do. Frank came downstairs just as she was putting on her coat.

"Lovely smell," he said. "You been baking?"

"Just a few biscuits," said Alice.

"Off somewhere nice?" he asked, eyeing the daffodil tin she was holding.

"Going to Meadowbank." That was the truth. "To spend the day with Valerie." That was not.

"Have a nice time," he said. "You enjoy yourself."

Oh, I will, thought Alice. Her mind was made up. She was going to have a very nice time indeed.

Meadowbank was a very different world from the narrow street where she lived with its tiny two-up two-down Victorian terraced houses. This was posh. Seriously posh. Meadowbank was for the nobs; Greenfields, the riff-raff. It used to be on the edge of town, keeping the rich and their privileged families away from the soot and dirt of the factories they owned but gradually, over the years as urbanisation had spread and wrapped itself around this pocket of gentility, Meadowbank became just another part of Smedley, albeit still the best part. Handsome double-fronted, brick-built villas which once boasted servants' quarters tucked away up in the attics stood in their own grounds. Very grand indeed. And not cheap.

Alice pedalled along an avenue lined with beech trees and hornbeams, past large houses set well back from the road. Must be glorious in summer, she thought. It was pretty damn good now, in early spring. Valerie lived not far from here, though her house was not quite as grand as the one she found herself looking at. She double-checked the address on the piece of paper Ronald had given her. Yes, this was it. The house was hidden behind a tall privet hedge and she'd ridden past it a couple of times before she realised she was finally here. Alice's mouth dropped open. The place was huge, stretching over three floors, probably one of the grandest houses Alice had ever seen, with two large bay windows, one on either side of the front door and manicured lawns so perfect they looked as if they'd been trimmed with nail scissors. Alice leaned her bike up against the wall then stood on the doorstep and looked up. There must be what, five, six bedrooms at least? The front door was a bright yellow and looked as if it had been freshly painted. Taking the tin of biscuits from the basket on her bike, she straightened her skirt, tucked a stray wisp of hair behind her ear, breathed in deeply and rang the bell. A distant sound of the first few bars of the 1812 Overture. Beethoven? she pondered. Or was it Tchaikovsky? The door opened almost immediately as if someone had been waiting for her. Someone had. In front of Alice stood a tall man, grey hair with matching moustache, both neat and tidy. His chest was puffed out and he had an almost military bearing which was borne out by three medals pinned to the breast of his tweed jacket. Highly polished brown brogues shone from under his knife-edge creased yellow corduroys. And he wore a tie. This was the wrong house, surely?

"Alice Coulter?" he asked, somewhat peremptorily. It was all she could do to nod. "Enter!" He held the door open wide.

Did he always dress like this? she asked herself. Or was it just on special occasions? Did she count as a special occasion? She'd like to think so.

"Is my bike alright there?" she asked timidly, pointing.

"Of course," he barked. "Safe as houses. Wouldn't dare. Steal from me? Pah!"

She could well believe it. Alice stepped passed the man and into a large, airy hall. Looking around as he closed the door behind her, she took in the highly polished parquet floor, the four oak doors leading off in different directions and the large wooden sideboard on which dozens of silver-framed photographs were regimentally arranged on either side of a huge silver bowl. The only other piece of furniture was an elaborate grandfather clock, taller than Alice, which chimed the half hour as she looked at it. Everything was immaculate. There was an overpowering smell of furniture polish and sweet peas. Remembering where she was and what she'd come for, Alice turned to the man.

"Are you Arthur?" she asked. She thought she'd better check.

He shook her hand vigorously. She could feel her bones crunch together.

"Colonel Arthur Randolph Gnash (with a 'G'), retired. OBE, CME DSO and Bar. At your service!"

Should she curtsey? Should she call him 'sir' or would just 'Arthur' do? Alice was clearly in the presence of somebody great. He must be with all those letters after his name. She wasn't too sure what some of them meant but the fact that they were there impressed her. It was the first time Alice had met anyone with letters before. She looked round the hall again. Surely this man wasn't the same one that Ronald met up with once a month at the Evergreens Day Centre? What was a man like him doing in a place like that? He could do better than that. But then Ronald had said he was lonely. Maybe he just went for the company.

"Sorry," he said loudly. "Manners. Tea?"

Alice could think of nothing better. "I brought you these," she said shyly, handing him the daffodil tin. "Ronald said you like biscuits. Home-made ones. So I made you some."

Arthur took the lid off and looked at the contents. His face lit up like it was Christmas. He smiled at her.

"Bingo! Yummy!"

Alice couldn't help but laugh. He looked at her as if he found the sound strange.

"This way." She followed him through one of the doors into a large lounge with French windows through which she could see more immaculate lawns edged with neat flowerbeds. Two over-sized, pale cream chintz sofas, positioned precisely at right angles to one another, and on which matching cushions stood rigidly to attention, took up most of the space. Heavily pleated curtains on dark wooden poles matched the sofas. A log fire burned tidily in the grate. Alice looked at her reflection in the huge gilt-edged mirror which hung above the fireplace and promptly shut her mouth. Framed paintings of flowers adorned the walls. It was strangely feminine. "Sit!" he ordered. She sat. Arthur left her to admire the décor with its colour-co-ordination and orderliness, returning shortly with a tray on which were two matching cups and saucers, two silver teaspoons, a teapot, milk jug, sugar bowl, and a plate of her home-made biscuits, all of which sat neatly on a hand-embroidered tray cloth. Arthur sat down on the other sofa. "Wife's doing, all this," he said, gesticulating round the room. "Too fussy. Milk?"

"Sorry?"

"Milk. In your tea?"

"Please." Alice was slowly getting used to his staccato way of speaking and his one-word sentences. Arthur offered her one of her biscuits but she declined. She watched him as he stared at the plate for a full minute before taking a Walnut and Coffee Cookie. Carefully he nibbled round the edges, round and round, before putting the remaining centre in his mouth. Alice was spell-bound. "Outstanding!" He chose a Raspberry Sandwich next and ate it in exactly the same way. "Incredible." One by one, Arthur cleared the plate, eating each biscuit from the outside in. "Never tasted better," he said. "More!"

"Shall I get you some more from the kitchen?" she asked, confused.

"No. Bring more. Next time." It was an order. He clearly expected there to be a next time. "Better than Evergreens." Arthur wet his finger and dabbed at the few remaining crumbs on the plate, transferring them to his mouth, a look of sheer bliss on his face. "Delightful. Only Bercow's at Evergreens. Rubbish!"

Alice told him she worked there. Or did for the moment. He looked surprised.

"Wasted."

"Well, only now and again," she said. She didn't do it often and anyway, how did he know? It had been her birthday, after all.

"No. You. Wasted. At Bercow's." He pointed at the empty plate. "First rate! Best ever. Business opportunity here." Alice so wanted to give him some verbs. "Good money." Her ears pricked up. Maybe he had something there. But the mention of money reminded her why she was here. How should she broach the subject? Ronald had said he was lonely. Hadn't he said he was a widower? Maybe Arthur would like to talk about his wife?

Alice pointed round the room. "You wife must have put a lot of work into this. It's lovely. I bet you miss her."

"Bitch!"

"What? There's no call for that!"

"Not you! Her!"

"Your wife, you mean?"

Arthur stood up and stood with his back to the fire, hands clasped firmly behind him, rocking on his heels.

"Living in Owlford."

"I'm sorry. I thought she was dead." Isn't that what Ron had said?

"Left me."

"I am so sorry." Not a widower, then. Alice had put her foot in it.

"Not your fault," snapped Arthur. "Bloody captain from the Coldstream Guards." This was the longest sentence he'd spoken. Alice counted the words. Six. "Bastard!" One. "More tea." It wasn't a question. He poured her another cup.

Alice drank it quickly. "Would you like me to go?" she asked.

"Why?"

"Well, I thought I might have upset you. You know, talking about your wife?"

Arthur stared down at her until she felt positively uncomfortable. "Stay." So she did.

As she headed home, Alice had a smile on her face so broad and uninhibited that people stared as she cycled past. She had a lot to smile about. Not only had she had a lovely time with Arthur, who had treated her like a lady, but she had £120 in her pocket. £100 for services rendered and £20 for the biscuits. Except she hadn't rendered any services. All he had wanted to do was hold her hand. Other than that he hadn't asked her to do anything. Or to show him anything. They had spent a couple of hours sitting next to one another on the same sofa, holding hands, as Arthur recounted his life story. In short sentences, it was true, but his history nevertheless. How he joined the army after leaving school, worked his way diligently up through the ranks, met and married Amanda, (Bitch!), had children, (and grandchildren), served abroad, Middle East, Far East, came home, retired, wife left. He asked her about herself and she was almost ashamed to tell him, it seemed so tame in comparison. But Arthur insisted so she told him about her life, about Bercow's and her friends there, about its imminent closure. She glossed over Frank – that was always the best way to deal with him. It wasn't anywhere near as interesting or fulsome as the things he'd done but he'd seemed genuinely interested and listened intently.

They stopped, once, for a fresh pot of tea, Arthur picking up the tray and Alice following him into the kitchen. The size of it stopped her in her tracks. It was simply enormous, even larger than the lounge. This was the kitchen of her dreams. Bespoke wooden cabinets with brass handles, an enormous range, a stainless-steel double fridge, copper pots and pans hanging from the ceiling, a butler's sink; it even had an island. An island! Slap-bang in the middle of the room. With four stools arranged along one side.

"Arthur, this is to die for." And she meant it. What Alice wouldn't give to have a kitchen like this!

"Wife," he offered in explanation. Alice took it to mean it was his wife's, or rather ex-wife's, doing. She was getting used to interpreting what he said. Arthur filled the kettle.

"Here, let me," she said, taking it from him. Arthur looked surprised but was happy to let her do it.

"Don't cook," he said. "Can't cook."

"What do you eat, then?" Alice asked, alarmed.

"Eggs. Boiled. Fried. Can't do scrambled."

"All the time?"

"Mostly."

"Not good, Arthur. Not good." Now Alice was starting to talk like him.

She rinsed out the teapot carefully as he handed her the tea caddy. As the kettle boiled, Arthur replenished the plate with her biscuits. She carried the tray back into the lounge, thinking furiously. She fed Ron. Had done for ages. But that was easy because he lived next door. Could she feed Arthur too? God knows he needed it. How could anybody live on just eggs? She could feed him but she'd want to give him more than tinned ravioli and fish fingers and chips. But could she afford to, especially now she was about to lose her job? Alice didn't know how she would manage to keep feeding Ronald but she knew, no matter what, she would. Whatever it took. But what if Arthur was willing to pay? If he would pay for his food she could cook for him. Alice thought about her tiny, sad kitchen back at Greenfields. She couldn't cook there. Not easily. How would she get his food to him while it was still hot? But if he let her cook here? In this wonderful, clean, bright, fabulous kitchen. He would be doing *her* a favour. Food for thought.

Alice let go of Arthur's hand and stood up. "I'd better be going," she said, picking up the tray and carrying it through to the kitchen. She wanted another look at this wonderful room before she headed home.

Arthur followed her through. He took the few remaining biscuits out of her tin and handing it back to her, he smiled. "Thank you."

"For what?" she asked, as held her coat open for her. "I thought that you wanted to, you know, have a cuddle and things."

"Next time. Maybe. Good to hold hands. Good biscuits. Here."

Arthur took some money from his trouser pocket and handed it to her. She didn't think to count it. That would have been rude.

"Next week?" he asked her. Why not? "Saturday?"

"That would be lovely. I've really enjoyed today," she added.

"Good," he said, gruffly. "More biscuits?"

Alice nodded. "More biscuits."

Arthur closed the door. Her bike was still there, as he'd promised. Alice wheeled it down the path and out of the garden. When she was out of sight of the house, she took the wad of notes out of her pocket and counted it. £120. £120? For what? She couldn't take this. Racing back to Arthur's house, she knocked on the door.

"Not Saturday," he joked.

"Arthur, I can't take this," she said, showing him the roll of notes. He thrust his hands behind his back.

"£20 for the biscuits. The rest for you."

"But I didn't do anything," she said. "We didn't do anything. And those biscuits were not worth £20."

"Were to me. Best ever."

"But it's too much," she insisted.

"Good company," said Arthur. "Worth a lot."

Impulsively she stood on tiptoe and gave him a kiss on the cheek. "Thank you."

"Pleasure. All mine." He pumped her hand energetically and went back inside.

Alice now had £31 more than she'd bargained for. This was cause to celebrate. Tomorrow was Sunday. They'd have a roast! She stopped off at the supermarket and bought a chicken. Not free range - the celebration wouldn't extend to that. Potatoes, parsnips, carrots and broccoli. And rhubarb. For a crumble. Party time!

"You look pleased with yourself," said Ronald, the dismay very evident on his face as he looked sadly at his plate of spaghetti hoops on toast.

"Don't worry. Tomorrow we're having a roast. With all the bits," promised Alice.

Ronald immediately cheered up. "I love roasts. My favourite."

"Everything is your favourite," she said, smiling broadly.

"So why are you so happy? What you been up to? You look like the cat that got the cream."

"In a way, I did." Alice told him about her meeting with Arthur. "I thought you told me he was a widower," she said.

"He may as well be," replied Ronald. "All on his own. Doesn't see his children or his grandchildren. Like me. My son never visits." He sighed which turned into a racking cough.

"You alright?" she asked.

"Go on. What else?"

"That's about it. A real gentleman though. Don't find too many of those these days. And all he wanted to do was hold my hand."

"Are you going back?"

"Oh yes!" There was no doubt about it. "I'll take him some more biscuits. You were right about those. He ate nearly all of them while I was there."

"He recognises quality, that's what it is," said Ron, patting her hand.

"He knows what he likes, that's for sure."

"So do I," mumbled Ronald, looking at her from under his hooded eyelids.

"What? What did you say, Ronald?"

"I know what I like," he repeated.

"And what's that?"

"You."

"Well, we all know that, Ron." She watched him as he rubbed his hands together nervously. "You're after something, aren't you?"

"Is it that obvious?"

"Yes. What do you want?"

He spoke quietly. "You know that thong thing? The one you got for your birthday?"

"My thong thing?"

"Would you wear it for me tomorrow? When you bring me my dinner round? My roast? Would you?"

Alice was baffled and concerned. She didn't think it would fit, for starters. But it was a strange request. "Well, if you want. But you won't see it."

"I will if you don't wear anything else!"

"You are joking, aren't you?"

"I'll pay you. £100! Serve me my dinner dressed only in your thong and there's £100 in it for you."

This was getting silly. But £100 was £100. She did the sums. That would mean she would have made £220 this weekend. Not to be sniffed at. But dressed only in a thong? She blanched at the thought. But then again, why not? He'd already seen bits of her. What difference would this make? She wouldn't be naked. Well, not quite. No, she'd be wearing a thong. If she could fit into it. Alice shuddered at the thought. All that cellulite!

"I'll think about it," she said.

"Does that mean yes?"

"Ronald Sanders, you are the dirtiest old man I know! I said I'd think about it."

Even before she was out the door Alice knew she'd have to do it. Did she really have a choice?

# CHAPTER 16

## ROAST CHICKEN WITH ALL THE BITS

Alice lay on the camp bed looking up at the cracks in the ceiling. It was still early and she was savouring the fact that she didn't have to get up just yet. A Sunday morning lie-in. Mind you, when she lost her job, every day would be Sunday. Yet strangely, and very uncharacteristically for her, she felt smug. She had pocketed £220 this weekend. Not bad when she considered all she'd really done was bake a few biscuits and be friendly. If Arthur was going to give her £20 for every tin of biscuits she made, then Alice would be doing an awful lot of baking. It was a lot of money just for a few biscuits and she felt a bit guilty about taking it from him, but they were hand-made and he was clearly happy to pay over the odds. She liked Arthur. He was a true gentleman. If all he wanted to do was hold hands and eat her biscuits then that was fine by her. None of this having to expose herself, like she did for Ronald. Ronald. What a character. And now he wanted her to serve him his dinner dressed only in her thong. It was an unusual request, no doubt about it. But he was going to give her £100 if she did it. That would keep her going for a few more weeks. Alice wondered how the other girls were managing, Grace in particular. She was in dire financial straits and Alice worried about how long she would be able to keep going. Maybe Alice should lend her the £100 Ronald was going to give her for tonight's performance, just to tide her over for a bit. She'd think about it. And if she could persuade Arthur to let her cook for him? Alice would love to do it, especially if he let her use his glorious kitchen, and it would provide a bit of cash. And that other chap Ronald had mentioned. The one who lived over in Billyfields. Maybe he would be another Arthur. Loaded and a biscuit lover. Alice lay back, her hands behind her head, wondering where all this was going. Would it be all she had to rely on when she lost her job? Would it be how she earned her living? Looking after lonely old men, cooking for them and catering to their odd sexual proclivities? Who knows? Maybe she could get Grace to help out with some of it. The cooking side of things, at least. Give her some much-needed money. There were a lot of possibilities here. Hang on a minute, she told herself. Hold your horses! Just because you've got one man who's prepared to pay a lot of money for a few biscuits and a huge amount of money so he can sit and hold your hand, it doesn't mean you can start a franchise! Back to earth, girl. One step at a time.

Alice lay there, enjoying the peace and quiet. There was no sound of Frank across the landing. Far too early for him. He wouldn't be up till midday at the earliest. Good time to try on my thong, she thought. See if I can get into it. Can't serve Ronald his dinner if the thong doesn't fit. Alice retrieved it from the bottom of her handbag where she'd left it for safe-keeping the night of her birthday dinner. She held it up to the light. It was unbelievably flimsy and although she knew nothing about such things, it looked expensive. The finest black and red lace. Like gossamer. How decadent! But it also looked very small indeed. What on earth had Valerie been thinking? That Alice needed a bit of something to jazz up her sex life? Well, she was right, but not as far as her husband was concerned; this was going to be for Ronald. As quietly as she could she tiptoed into the bathroom where the light was better and she'd be able to get a better idea of what she looked like. Although Alice already knew. She would look foolish and fat. She let her dressing gown slip to the floor, took off her nightie and carefully stepped into the thong, one leg at a time. Alice pulled it up over her knees. So far so good. Her thighs and hips were a bit more problematic but the thong was forgiving; there was a lot of elastic in it. Finally it was on. The bathroom mirror was too high for Alice to see the lower half of her body so Alice held the small hand mirror as far away from her as she could, trying to get the whole picture. It's not good, she giggled. Not good at all. She put the mirror on the edge of the bath and angled it so she could see the principle area. The thong zone. Turning this way and that she saw thin wisps of lace digging painfully into her hips. Aren't these thong things meant to come up to your waist? They do in all the pictures I've seen. Or was that something else? Alice wondered why this one wouldn't come up any further. Must be too small. I wonder if they do extra large, she pondered. Maybe I could exchange it for an XXL. Whilst it covered her modesty at the front, the back left a great deal, a very great deal, to be desired. A strip of lace disappeared uncomfortably between the cheeks of her bottom. Why do people wear these things? I know Valerie meant well, but honestly! And all this cellulite. There was just so much of it. Alice grabbed a buttock in each hand as if to weigh up exactly how much there was. Just at that moment, the bathroom door opened and in walked Frank. She'd forgotten to lock the bloody door! There she stood in all her glory, clutching her buttocks, naked apart from the most pointless piece of underwear ever devised by man. And it had to be a man, didn't it? No rational woman would ever dream up such an excruciatingly uncomfortable piece of clothing. Frank's face was a picture. Of horror and disbelief, amazement and shock. Alice let go of her buttocks, quickly picked up her dressing gown from the floor and held it in front of her.

"What on earth are you doing, woman?"

Alice couldn't work out who was more embarrassed. Probably him. But it was a close-run thing. "I'm trying on a thong," she explained.

"A *thong?*" He made it sound something dirty. "Since when did you start wearing thongs?"

"Since Valerie got me one for my birthday."

"You should have more sense, woman. Look at you! You're far too old for that sort of thing."

If he'd said 'fat', she would have killed him there and then. Alice felt nothing but hate for the man standing in front of her. Pure blind hate. If she'd ever had any doubt about wearing the thong for Ronald tonight, it just went straight out the window. They stood there, not saying anything, like two Pit Bulls eyeing each other up.

"Can I use the bathroom please?" he said, crossly.

Alice didn't bother to answer but walked straight past him, head held high, slamming the bathroom door behind her.


"Here you are, Ronald. Roast chicken. Roast potatoes. Roast parsnips. Carrots. Broccoli. And rhubarb pie and custard for pudding. How's that?"

Alice had brought his dinner round dressed, like she usually did to all intents and purposes, in her baggy jeans and a jumper. It was only when she emerged from Ronald's kitchen with his meal on a tray that it was very evident she had done what he'd asked. There she stood, in all her glory, roast chicken in hand.

Ronald didn't know where to look first. Alice gave him the tray then put her hands on hips, totally naked except for the tiniest pair of knickers he'd ever seen. At least, he thought they were knickers. Or maybe that was the thong. He'd never really seen one close up before. There wasn't much to them, was there? Ronald was torn. Should he look at her? Or at this wonderful feast in front of him? A real roast dinner. With rhubarb pie to follow. And custard.

"I think I've died and gone to heaven," he said. Alice? Roast? Alice? Roast? Pie and custard? His head bobbed up and down like a nodding donkey.

Alice didn't quite know what to do next. Parade about for a bit? Rotate slowly for maximum viewing? Funnily enough, she didn't feel self-conscious at all. Why should I? she thought. This is what Ronald wants to see. He's not going to criticise and tell me I'm fat or anything like that. He wants to see me as I am. Look at the poor old dear. Bless! He doesn't know whether to gawp at me or eat his dinner.

"I'd get it while it's hot, if I were you," she told him, pointing at his plate. Ronald was still undecided. She gave a small, involuntary wriggle. Alice hoped he didn't think she was trying to be sexy - it was just the wretched thong kept disappearing further up where it ought not to go. She wriggled again, hoping to dislodge it. No joy. "Speaking of heat, Ronald, d'you mind if I turn the fire up? It's a bit cold in here." Alice turned the fire up to maximum then warmed her bottom on front of it. I wonder how strippers manage? she mused. They've got nowhere to warm their bums. Must be a nightmare. She sat down on one of the wooden seats but immediately stood up again. "Got a spare cushion, have you?" Ronald hadn't so she remained standing. Alice folded her arms, more for warmth than anything, and watched Ronald who continued to eat contentedly.

"You know I went to see Arthur, yesterday. Well, I've been thinking about him. All he eats are eggs, you know. Nothing else. I can't understand why he doesn't pay for meals to be delivered. He's obviously loaded. He could dine like a king if he wanted to."

"Like I do, you mean?" Ronald spooned up the gravy from his plate.

"Well, he could certainly do a lot better than he does now. Eggs, for goodness' sake."

"Eggs are good."

"Not for every meal, Ronald. Why doesn't he ask for Meals on Wheels? From Social Services? In fact, come to think of it, why have you never asked for them? I'm sure they're lovely."

"Arthur's proud. We both are, I suppose. But Arthur especially. It'd be like asking for charity. Anyway, you cook nicer stuff. You cook what I like." He tucked into his rhubarb pie. "Magic! Not too sweet. Just the way I like it. And you make the best custard in the world. You see what I mean. You cook the stuff I like."

Alice shivered. It was still cold in the lounge, notwithstanding the three bars of the electric fire. "D'you mind if I get dressed now?" she asked.

To be honest, Ronald had been so side-tracked by his pudding that he'd forgotten she was almost naked. He nodded, his mouth full. Alice slipped on her jeans and jumper. That was better.

"Yes, I was thinking about Arthur," she started again.

"What about him?"

"Whether I should offer to cook for him. Like I do for you. What d'you think?"

"Brilliant idea. I'm sure he'd love your cooking. I know I do." Ronald licked his spoon clean. "Any more custard?" he asked.

"So you think it's a good idea?"

"I do. But how are you going to get his meals to him? It's a long way to cycle to Meadowbank every night. The food would be cold by the time you get there."

"Yes, I know. I haven't thought it through fully yet," said Alice. "I just wanted to know if you thought it might work."

"As long as you don't forget me."

"I'd never do that," she promised.

"Thank you for that roast dinner, Alice. Wonderful. And the way you served it up! That was the thong, wasn't it? I thought at first it was just a tiny pair of knickers."

"I suppose that's all they are really. Very small knickers. I won't be wearing it again, I can tell you."

Ronald looked disappointed. "Not even for me?" he asked.

She smiled. "Only if you keep the fire turned up full," she said. "It's bloomin' cold with no clothes on."

He handed Alice £100. "It'll be three bars next time. I promise!"

"Hmm. We'll see."

Alice washed the dishes up, the kitchen door closed against the noise of the television. Frank was watching highlights of some football match. He hadn't even looked up as she came in, carrying Ronald's dirty plate and pudding bowl. Maybe Arthur *would* like her to cook for him. He couldn't be less appreciative than Frank. She'd ask him next time she saw him. After all, he could only say no. Alice finished tidying up and put the kettle on. A nice cup of tea and one of the biscuits she'd made yesterday. The plastic container was still where she'd left it but instead of finding it half full of biscuits, it was empty. Frank! The greedy old goat. He'd eaten the lot and there had been a fair few. Typical, she thought. Bloody typical. But d'you know, I don't care. Not any more. It's the way he is and he's not going to change. But that wouldn't stop her reminding him what a self-centred pig he could be. She took her mug of tea into the lounge and sat down opposite her husband.

With difficulty he tore himself away from a penalty shoot-out. "Lovely roast, by the way."

"Biscuit?" she asked.

"Oh, I couldn't eat another thing," replied Frank.

"I could. I could eat one of those biscuits I made yesterday."

Frank had the sense to look guilty. "Oh, those. Yes, sorry. They were delicious. I couldn't stop once I'd started."

"You didn't even leave me *one*!" Alice knew she was being petty but she couldn't stop herself. "You really are the most selfish, ignorant, lazy, good-for-nothing, idle, disgusting slob I have ever met." It was all coming out now.

Frank looked at her, amazed. Where had this come from all of a sudden? He'd only eaten a few biscuits. Honestly, she could be so touchy at times. "What is the matter with you, woman? What's got into you?"

"*What's the matter with me? What's the matter with me?*" She was shouting now, shouting to be heard above the noise of the television. Actually it was not so much shouting as screeching. "You're the matter with me! It's you!" She bet Ronald next door could hear every word. They could probably hear everything five doors down.

"Me? What have I done now?" asked Frank, indignant.

"Everything! Nothing!" Alice burst into tears with sheer frustration. She grabbed the remote control and switched the television off. She would not compete with over-sexed, tattooed morons who could hardly string a sentence together, had the IQ of a single book-end and who were paid obscene amounts of money to kick a ball around a football pitch.

Frank stared at his wife. "I was watching that! It's the final."

"And this is *our* final," said Alice.

"What do you mean?" he asked.

"You wanted to talk? We're talking!"

Frank looked decidedly uncomfortable. It wasn't quite what he'd had in mind.

"What d'you mean, this is our final?" he asked again.

"What I said. This is it!"

"It?" he repeated. "It?"

"It! I can't live with you any more. You're impossible. I'm going to leave you."

"You said that the other night," said Frank, trying to smile. It was not easy. "I thought you were joking," he added, foolishly optimistic.

"*Joking!*" she repeated, incredulously. Only Frank could think she would joke about something like this!

"It's why I didn't say anything. I thought you'd get over it."

"*Get over it?* Frank, which bit of 'I'm leaving you' don't you understand?" Alice blew her nose.

"Maybe we should talk about it?" suggested Frank. He tried to reach for her hand but she was having none of it. .

"We *are* talking about it. And anyway, it's all been said now. There's nothing to talk about. Not any more. We're finished Frank. I don't love you any more. I'm going to leave you."

"I don't want you to go," he whined.

"Tough!"

"Aw, Princess, don't be like that."

"Will you stop calling me your damned princess! I hate it! I AM NOT YOUR BLOODY PRINCESS! Get it?"

Frank seemed to shrink into his armchair. Maybe she wasn't joking after all.

"Why are you like this?" he asked. "Why have you changed?"

"Me changed? What about you? All you do all day long is sit and watch television. You won't look for a job…"

"I can't. You know I'm disabled," Frank interrupted her.

"You're not and you never have been. You're just lazy. That's all. You said you'd change and you haven't."

"Princess, I mean, Alice," he said quickly, "give me another chance."

"No," she said simply.

Frank looked at her, his eyes half closed. "It's Ronald, isn't it?"

"What?"

"You're in love with Ronald. That's why you're leaving me."

Alice burst out laughing. "No, Frank, I'm not. I'm not in love with him. I'm not in love with anybody."

"That's why you're always next door, isn't it?"

"I'm next door because he's a lonely old man. With no-one to look after him. That's why I cook for him. Take him his meals. Because he has no-one else."

"Neither do I," Frank pointed out. "You're all I've got."

"Well, you should have thought of that before you started taking me for granted."

"I should have done," he said quietly. Frank bit a yellowing thumbnail. "Can we talk about this?" he asked again. "I mean, really talk. Not shout. Please." Alice shook her head slowly. "What about counselling? There's that organisation. What's it called? Recant or something?"

"Relate."

"Yes, that's it. Relate. We could talk to them."

"I don't think so," said Alice, standing up. "It's too late for that."

Frank looked up at her from his seat. "You really mean it?"

"I do, Frank. I do. Once I know what's happening at Bercow's and I've got myself a new job, that'll be it. We'll probably have to sell the house, both of us find somewhere new."

"But what will I do?" asked Frank, whining like a small child. "Where will I go? Who's going to look after me?"

Alice shrugged her shoulders. "Frankly, my dear Frank, I don't give a damn." Now where had she heard that before?

Alice lay on the camp bed in the dark, still dressed in her clothes with her thong uncomfortably splitting her in two. She was playing back the evening over and over in her mind. Such a lovely time with Ronald, even if that was the last thing she'd expected and even if it had been a tad on the cold side. Then Frank. At his finest. She hadn't planned to let rip the way she'd done but once she'd started, she couldn't stop. And it needed to be said, Alice was in no doubt about that. And she felt better for getting it all out in the open. Now they both knew where they stood. Once she'd got a new job, that would be it. Time to make a new life for herself. Start again. She didn't want to move from Smedley – who would look after Ronald and Arthur? And there might be more, according to Ronald, more lonely old gentlemen who needed a bit of TLC. And then there were her girlfriends from Bercow's. Valerie. Shanti. Iris. Bella. And who would keep an eye on Grace? She didn't want to be making new friends, she was too old for that. But wasn't that what she'd just done? Arthur, for one? She counted him as a friend now. And then there would be this other friend of Ron's. From Billyfields. She would go and see him next weekend. And with the money she was making maybe she wouldn't have to leave Smedley even if she couldn't find another job nearby straightaway. Or ever? Alice smiled to herself. The future's not as bleak as it could be. There was definitely a light at the end of the tunnel and this time it wasn't the train coming. She could hang on for a bit longer. As long as the gods kept smiling on her, all was not yet lost. Alice finally fell asleep, despite the thong which continued to make its presence felt.

# CHAPTER 17

## BAKED COD WITH PARSLEY SAUCE

"How you doing, girl?" asked Shanti with a broad smile on her face. Alice grinned at her. They were all there in the canteen; Shanti, Grace, Iris, Bella. Even Valerie had managed to give the bean counters in the administration team the slip for half an hour. She sighed with relief as she sat down; it felt so good to take the weight off her feet.

"Worn your thong yet?" Trust Shanti to go straight for the kill.

"Funny you should ask that," replied Alice, unwrapping her sandwich. "It just so happens that I have!"

"For Frank?" asked Bella.

"Don't be daft."

"I only ask'," said Bella, miffed.

"Who did you wear it for then?" asked Valerie. "Not him next door. Old what's his name."

"His name is Ronald. And, yes, I did wear it for him since you ask."

"Go, girl, go!" sang Iris.

"And what's more, he gave me a generous financial reward for doing so."

"No! How much?" asked Grace.

"I don't know that I should tell you," said Alice, suddenly shy.

"Whyever not?" asked Valerie. "I just hope you got your money's worth. Or he did. Whichever."

"Well," began Alice, knotting her fingers in her lap. She felt so foolish. Telling the girls what she'd done would sound so tawdry. So unbelievably tacky. She really wished she hadn't started this conversation.

"Well?" prompted Shanti.

"Yes, go on," urged Grace. "We're all dying to hear."

"Ronald gave me £100 for wearing my thong!" There! She'd said it. There was silence round the table. Even Iris had stopped eating, her pork pie stranded in mid-air.

"And what else?" asked Shanti.

"What d'you mean, what else?"

"Come on, Alice. What else did you have to do?" asked Valerie.

"Nothing. I did nothing. He asked me to wear my thong and I did."

"You didn't have to do anything else?" Valerie asked again. "You sure?"

"Other than serve him his meal, no," replied Alice. She took a bite of her sandwich, checking on the label to see that it really was cheese and pickle. It was anybody's guess.

"Let me get this right," said Iris slowly. "You served him his dinner dressed in a thong."

Alice nodded, munching.

"Just a thong at twilight?" asked Valerie, laughing uproariously.

"I can't believe you said that," giggled Alice.

"And what else?" repeated Shanti. "I mean, what else were you dressed in? Not what else did you have to do."

"Nothing." Whatever it was, this was not cheese. Nor was it pickle, come to think of it. Alice gave up on the sandwich.

"Nothing?" cried Bella and Grace together.

"That's right."

"God, you can be so infuriating, Alice Coulter," said Valerie. "You're telling us that you served Ronald his dinner dressed only in the thong I got you for your birthday. And nothing else? There has to be more."

"Do you want the rest of that?" Alice asked Iris, pointing at the abandoned pork pie.

Iris took her eyes off Alice for a second and glanced at the pie. "Yes. Sorry." And she swallowed what was left without even chewing.

"So let's get this right. You were completely naked? Apart from the thong?" asked Shanti. "Wow!"

"And he gave you £100 to do it?" Grace asked her. "That's a lot of money."

"Yes, it is. And there's more."

"More what?" This from Iris. "More nudity?"

"More money," Alice tried to explain.

"Hang on a min'," said Bella. "Let me get this right. You took off all your cloth',"

"Except the thong," interrupted Shanti.

"You took off all your cloth' and stan' in fron' of a strange man for £100?"

"Yes, yes and yes," replied Alice impatiently. "Except he's not strange. Just lonely."

"Has he got a frien'?" Bella asked.

Iris nodded in agreement. "Yeh. Find one for me too! Or several. The more the merrier."

"And me," added Valerie. "I could do with some of that."

"Oh, no, Valerie" said Iris. "You would have to do the accounts! The rest of us'll do the business end."

"No," laughed Shanti. "Except Alice. She'll have to run the business; be our madam." The table erupted in giggles. "Valerie will be the accountant, Alice the madam and the rest of us will take our clothes off or whatever. Sounds like a plan."

"Could it work?" asked Iris, suddenly serious.

"Iris, I was joking," said Shanti. "We'd need dozens of men, maybe even hundreds, if it would stand any chance of paying."

"Ronald's got lots of friends," said Alice. "Maybe not hundreds but he must have dozens, I'm sure. That's what I keep trying to tell you. I made £220 this weekend. From Ronald and just one of his friends."

"You must have done more than just take your clothes off." Iris was sceptical.

Why would they not believe her? "No, I didn't! I didn't do anything other than serve Ronald his dinner dressed in my thong. That's all I did." Alice was getting fed up with having to explain herself. Why had she not kept her big mouth shut?

"You mentioned another friend of Ron's," said Shanti. "What about him?"

"I met him for the first time this weekend. Arthur. From Evergreens. You know, the old folk's day centre in town?. He gave me money for some biscuits I made and just to hold his hand."

"They must have been pretty damned good biscuits!" said Iris, winking obscenely.

"They were," laughed Alice. "*I* made them!"

"£220," repeated Grace. "That is a serious amount of money." She looked at her friend. "And all you did was hold his hand?"

"That's all. He's a lonely old man. Just like Ronald. Like most of the people he knows. They're old and lonely and all they want is a bit of companionship."

"Sounds as if you're giving them a bit more than companionship, if you ask me," said Iris, nudging Alice in the ribs.

"Just shut up, will you, Iris!" snapped Grace.

"Well, pardon me." But Iris did as she was told.

144

"They've got no family," explained Alice. "Or if they do, they never bother to come and see them. They live on their own and all they've got for company is television. Can you imagine that? Day in day out, staring at the tv all day long, no-one to talk to."

"Bit like your Frank, you mean?" interjected Valerie.

Alice ignored her and went on. "Don't you think that's so sad? And Arthur, the one who paid me for the biscuits, all he eats is eggs. Because that's all he can cook. Imagine that! Eggs!"

Iris tried to imagine a diet without her favourite pork pies. She couldn't.

"Awful," she whispered.

"All I'm doing is offering a bit of friendship. A bit of company. Someone to chat to. It's all I've ever done with Ronald. I've been keeping an eye on him for years. Cooking his dinner every night. And up till now, I've never taken a penny from him. It's only recently that he's offered me money for, well, extras. And if he wants to pay me for…things, well, that's fine by me. Especially since we may not have a job soon." There were murmurs of agreement round the table. "I'm only doing for Ronald what the council should be doing anyway. Social Services and such. Meals on Wheels, that sort of thing."

"I bet they don't provide extras," laughed Valerie.

"I don't think they provide very much at all at the moment," said Alice. "What with all the cuts and things. I know Ronald only goes to Evergreens once a month. Just imagine if that's your only contact with another human being. Once a month at a day centre." She shuddered at the thought of it.

"£220," repeated Grace again. She was fixated on the money as only someone who had none could be.

"And there are loads of people out there like Ronald and Arthur," continued Alice. "Lonely people. People who just want a friend. Someone to talk to. Someone who cares. I like to think I make a difference, that's all." Alice sat quietly. She'd expected her friends to greet her owning up to serving Ronald his dinner dressed only in a thong with derision. But none of them, except maybe Iris, thought it smutty at all. But then Iris thought everything was smutty. Grace was clearly overwhelmed by the amount of money Alice had made – and for not doing very much. Valerie thought it was a hoot, but then she would. Bella? Bella was difficult to read sometimes but maybe she meant it when she asked if Ronald had a friend. Maybe Alice should see if she could line up some of her friends with Ronald's lonely friends from Evergreens.

"But do you know what the saddest thing is?" She looked at each of her friends in turn. "Ronald nearly always says it. Every time I go. See you tomorrow? As if to check I'm coming back. And Arthur said it too. As if they're afraid I'll stop coming. I mean, how sad is that?" Nobody had an answer.

Alice grabbed Grace's sleeve as they headed back to the factory floor together.

"Here," she said, "this is for you." She handed Grace £100. "I've got more than plenty at the moment."

Grace looked at the money in her hand in astonishment. "I can't," she started to say. "I…"

"You can and you will," said Alice firmly. "Consider it a loan. Pay me back when you can."

Grace threw her arms round Alice and hugged her tight. "That'll put food on the table for a few weeks," she said, sniffing loudly.

"What about the rent?" Alice asked.

"The landlord's given us some breathing space. Because we've always been on time in the past. But only for a month. Something's going to have to turn up soon, though."

"I'm sure it will," said Alice. "Maybe they'll give us some wages."

"If only," agreed Grace. "Catch you later."

She turned and walked away but hadn't gone more than a few steps when she turned back. "Alice," she started, "you know this old friend of yours. Ronald, is it? Well, I meant it. If he does have any more friends or knows anyone who wants a bit of company, I wouldn't mind doing it. Not any of the other stuff. Like with the thong. Ivan wouldn't like it."

"Why would he know?"

"Oh, I'd have to tell him. I mean, haven't you told Frank?"

"No, and I have no intention of doing so. What I do is up to me and it's my money. I tell Frank as little as possible."

Grace thought about this. "Well, I'm still not sure. But I wouldn't mind being a friend to someone. For a little bit of cash. So if your friend does know anyone…"

"I'll see what I can do," she said. "But no promises."

Grace headed back to her Caramel Curls and for the first time in weeks she had a smile on her face.

As Alice kept an eye on the machinery churning out the Marshmallow Moments she was in a quandary. She was sure Ronald would know a huge number of people at Evergreens, men and women, who were lonely, isolated, and just wanted a bit of company. But were there enough to go round? After all, there were six of them; Shanti, Bella, Valerie, Iris, Grace and herself. How many 'gentlemen friends', as she was beginning to think of Ronald and Arthur, as they were both gentlemen and she thought of them as her friends, how many would she need to make a living when she lost her job? Alice hadn't given it any thought at all but maybe she should. And pretty damned quickly too. She didn't think she'd need as many as Grace who had a partner and a son to support as well as rent to find. After all, Alice didn't have a mortgage but she did have all the other bills to pay and she wanted to make a fresh start away from Frank. That would cost a lot of money. So maybe she would need the same number as Grace. Or more. Valerie wouldn't need as many because she had her own house too, but then she did have her lingerie habit to support. Then what about Iris? Divorced and back living with her mother? How many gentlemen friends did that equate to? And as for Bella, apart from the fact she had a boyfriend who'd infamously bought her an iron for her birthday, Alice didn't know a great deal about her. Things were starting to get complicated. It was like one of those mind-numbing mathematical puzzles at school that Alice could never work out; if it takes a man an hour to walk a mile at three miles an hour, how long would it take a one-legged man pushing a bicycle? or something like that. Far too difficult for her and maths had never been her strong point. Alice obviously wanted to share her good fortune with her girlfriends but how best to do it? If there were lots of gentlemen friends, should she divide them up equally? Would that be fair? It was getting complicated and Alice was beginning to wish she'd not said anything at all to anybody, not even Valerie. What had started out as a bit of a laugh, with Ronald making that ridiculous offer to see her breasts, was starting to go pear-shaped. Bit like my bosoms, Alice chuckled. It had been lucky for her when Ronald had told her about Arthur and, what with the two of them giving her a bit of much needed cash, she thought things were starting to look up. But was it luck? she asked herself. After all, she'd been feeding Ronald for a very long time, cooking him his dinner and generally keeping an eye on him. A bit of housework here and there. Sometimes a bit of washing. And although he'd sometimes given her a few quid towards the cost of his food, she'd never asked for a penny. Didn't she deserve something for all that? Maybe it was luck. Maybe it was a reward for all her efforts. Who knows? But whatever she called it Alice knew she couldn't make a new start if the money she got from her gentlemen wasn't enough. She wouldn't be able to save towards the Freedom From Frank Fund unless she got more money. I could easily add another 'F' in there! she thought. Five years from now, ten, twenty, Alice could still see herself living under the same roof as her worthless husband, sleeping on the camp bed in the spare room, with no prospect, ever, of escape. Her heart sank. Alice watched the Marshmallow Moments as they passed inexorably before her eyes. Each one identical. Dull, unappetising and all the same. Just like the days of her life.

Alice mashed the potatoes to go with the cod which was baking in the oven. Her parsley sauce had thickened nicely and dinner was nearly ready. She boiled some frozen peas in a pan then quickly served up.

"I could smell that cooking from in here," laughed Ronald, as she pushed his front door open with her hip. "I like a nice bit of fish." He proved it by polishing off the lot in a matter of minutes. "How's things going at the factory?" he asked. "Got a date for closing yet?"

"No," sighed Alice. "I'm not sure which is worse. Knowing or not knowing. We're still waiting to hear if we'll be paid any of our wages and there's no news yet about our pensions. I'm not optimistic though."

"Well, you've still got me," said Ronald. "And you've got Arthur too, now. You won't starve."

"I won't," agreed Alice. "But some of my friends might."

"What do you mean?"

"Well, when Bercow's closes, that's it for them. There's no jobs round here. Smedley's finished. Once upon a time if you didn't like working in one factory you could just go down the road and get another job in a different one. Now there's nothing. You either up sticks and move away or you starve." She laughed. "My girlfriends at work were even asking me if I had another Ronald. Or another Arthur."

"There's my mate at Billyfields. Malcolm."

"I'm going to go and see him this weekend. After I've been to see Arthur."

"I could ask around at Evergreens again if you like. Put the word round. Last time I only mentioned it to a couple of my mates. People I thought you might like. But I can ask more if you want. What d'you think?"

"I don't suppose it would do any harm, would it?"

"Perhaps," said Ronald mischievously, "you could do offers. Like they do in the corner shop sometimes. You know. Three for Two or Buy One Get One Free! Three cuddles for the price of two. Buy one thong dinner and get one free! You might get more takers that way. What d'you think?"

"I think you're a crazy old man, Ronald Sanders, that's what I think!" Where did he get his ideas from?

"Might just work, though. Tempt them in and then hit them hard."

"The only thing that's going to be hit hard is you if you keep coming up with such daft ideas!" Alice laughed.

"Well, it works for the big companies. Tesco and such. Sainsbury's. I know. I've seen it on the television."

"Ronald, I am not a big company. I'm a one-woman show."

"At the moment, yes. But what if all your friends get on board? Eh? You could find yourself in charge of a coalition. Or do I mean a consortium?"

"I have no idea what you mean, you daft old bugger!"

"And when you're rich and famous," he went on, "and running lots of cuddlers all over the country, you'll remember it all started here!"

"Cuddlers? That's a nice word."

"Yes, cuddlers. And it all began with me asking to see your tits! From little acorns…"

"I'm not sure you and Arthur are a consortium," smiled Alice. "I'll not order the Bentley just yet."

"You can mock, young lady. You'll be famous one day, I promise you that."

"Infamous, more like." Alice took Ronald's hand and held it. "But you do make me laugh," she said.

"Then I have done some good," he said, smiling at her.

"How could you doubt it? You're a good soul, Ronald. D'you know that? A good man."

Ronald's face shone. "I try," he said simply. "I try." Alice got ready to go. "See you tomorrow?" he asked.

"Tomorrow."

# CHAPTER 18

## BEEF STEW WITH DUMPLINGS

The weeks went by and Bercow's continued as usual. Like everyone else, Alice turned up for work, clocked in, made whichever biscuits the weekly rota dictated, clocked off and went home. She still met up with her friends in the canteen when she could but for the moment there was no more discussion about her gentlemen friends. This was because the talk focused on what was going to happen to the factory and more importantly, its staff. Rumours were suddenly rife; a Russian oligarch was going to buy the factory for his mistress just because she liked biscuits then he'd changed his mind – he was going to buy her a restaurant instead; a Chinese company was going to buy the premises and convert them into luxury apartments. In Smedley? That was never going to happen. Someone said the factory was going to be adapted to make soft furnishings and they'd all be re-trained. From biscuits to bolsters, went the rumour. Somebody else said that all the Bercow Biddies were going to have to move to Lithuania as that was where the future of biscuit manufacturing lay. The rumours went on and on, each more unrealistic and outlandish than the last. But there was still no announcement about whether wages owed would be paid or what would happen to their pensions and when Alice asked Valerie about it, her friend just shrugged her shoulders and said the accountants were still going through the books. Nobody failed to come to work - what else could they do? Every night Alice assiduously scoured the local paper for any jobs but like everyone else, she was chasing the same rainbow. Jobs in Smedley were as rare as rocking horse poo. She looked at the Rooms for Rent section too, but decided that would have to wait until, if, she found a new job. At the moment she wouldn't be able to afford the rent let alone the outrageous deposits being asked. At the very least, if the worst came to the worst and Frank became truly, truly unbearable, she could move out and take up either Valerie or Ronald on their offers of a spare room.

Every day after work Alice cycled home, cooked a meal for the three of them, invariably ate hers with Ronald next door, then spent the rest of the evening alone. If anyone had asked her why she was still cooking for her husband, bearing in mind she'd told him she intended to leave him, she couldn't have answered. Maybe it was because they were still living under the same roof. Maybe she felt some sort of reverse sympathy for him now that her attention was directed to looking after Ronald. Perhaps it was as Ron said, she had a heart the size of Yorkshire and she couldn't completely ignore him. But Ronald came first for Alice now; Frank, in her mind, was an afterthought but an afterthought which needed feeding. Being at home together was certainly strained and to say the atmosphere was awkward was an understatement, especially now he knew exactly what she thought of him. She tried to be civil to him but it wasn't easy. As far as Alice was concerned they no longer had anything in common and she'd told him so in no uncertain terms. She began to wonder if they ever had. Conversation was almost impossible and, for once, she was content to let him sit in front of his beloved television as it saved her from having to talk to him. Instead, she spent her evenings alone in the kitchen, looking at her recipe collection, or up in her cramped bedroom, sorting through the contents of all the cardboard boxes and several old, battered suitcases. There was nothing of value, either financial or sentimental. Some old clothes from a younger and thinner era; books about self-improvement – where did they come from? There were knitting patterns, a childishly embroidered place mat, a bald doll with a missing arm, an odd shoe. Who keeps this stuff? A lifetime's accumulation of rubbish went either to the charity shops in town or straight into the bin. Some of it must have been Frank's – the self-improvement books maybe? No. Not Frank's. Alice didn't bother asking him if he wanted to keep any of it as she was sure he'd want to keep it all. It was cathartic, getting rid of all this junk. She felt as if she was not only emptying the room of the sweepings of their lives but clearing a space in her mind too. Alice felt more relaxed. Freer, somehow. Yes, redundancy still hung over her, but she felt an inexplicable sense of relief. And now that the threat of being smothered at night by toppling boxes was gone she slept even better. But for Alice real happiness came at the weekends.

One week to the day after first meeting Arthur, Alice returned to Meadowbank. This time not only was she armed with the same daffodil tin full of her home-made assorted biscuits, but she had a large portion of beef stew with dumplings she'd made the night before. Arthur was delighted to see her.

"Not sure you'd come," he said, gruffly, standing in the doorway. He was still dressed very smartly in pressed trousers, jacket and tie but at least this time he'd not bothered to put his medals on.

"Whyever not?" she asked. "I said I would. I really enjoyed myself last time I was here and seeing how much you liked my biscuits, I made you some more." She handed him the tin. "And I brought you this." Arthur took the plastic container from her and looked at it from every angle.

"What is it?"

Alice took it from him and opened it. "Beef stew. With dumplings. I made it last night. It'll be good when it's been re-heated. These things are always better second time round."

Arthur buried his nose in the stew and inhaled deeply. "For me?"

Alice nodded.

"Now?"

"You can have it whenever you want," she replied, looking at her watch. It was only 11 o'clock but if he wanted to eat now, that was his choice. She headed into his kitchen and, selecting a pan from the overhead rack, she ladled the stew into it, careful to keep the dumplings on top. Arthur watched her intently. "Have you got any vegetables to go with it?" she asked. Arthur shook his head. "I stopped off on the way and got a few bits. Just in case. They're in my basket. On the bike." Arthur went to get them and came back with a plastic carrier bag. From it she took carrots, broccoli, potatoes and a bag of frozen peas. "For your freezer," she said, waving the latter.

Arthur sat on one of the stools and watched her as she started to peel a potato. She stopped what she was doing and looked at him.

"Do you know how to do this?" she asked him, in all seriousness.

"Hmmph," was the reply. Alice took that as a no.

"Watch me," she said.

Arthur followed her every move as if his life depended on it. Alice peeled a few potatoes and put them in a pan to boil then washed some carrots and broccoli. She was pretty certain he'd never seen a meal prepared before. Once the potatoes were boiling, Alice put the stew on a low heat and sliced the carrots into another pan. The broccoli and peas went on last.

"And that's all there is to it," she said.

In half an hour, during which time Arthur said not a word but didn't take his eyes off what she was doing, his meal was ready. He looked at the plate she put down in front of him.

"All for me?"

Alice nodded and pulling up a stool, she sat and watched him as he ate in silence until the plate was empty. Carefully he lined his knife and fork up, together, just touching. He shook his head.

"Didn't you like it?" asked Alice, alarmed. Ron had enjoyed *his* last night. Maybe Arthur just didn't like this sort of food.

"Like it? Loved it!" Alice breathed a sigh of relief. "Best meal ever!" He re-aligned his cutlery again. "Thank you. Better than eggs. Much!"

"There's enough left over to do tomorrow, Arthur. And vegetables too." She started to clear up.

"No. My job," Arthur insisted. "You sit." And he pointed her towards the lounge. "Tea and biscuits coming."

Alice waited as he tidied up, looking round the beautifully decorated room, wondering what it would be like to live somewhere like this. Posh. Luxurious. She leaned back into the sofa, listening to Arthur singing as he washed the dishes, imagining a completely different world. Before long he appeared with a tea tray and a plate of her biscuits. Once again, he devoured the lot, eating each one in the same way – nibbling round the edges then eating the middle in one bite. A creature of habit. When the plate was empty Arthur sat back and looked at her.

"Tomorrow?" he asked.

"Sorry," said Alice. "I've arranged to go and see Malcolm tomorrow. I was going to go this afternoon but tomorrow's best. I think you know him. Lives at Billyfields. Ronald said he could do with a visit."

"Shame."

"I've not met him before," she said. "What's he like?"

"Good chap. From Evergreens. No family. Old."

Sounds like all of you, thought Alice. Ronald, you, goodness knows how many others. "I bet he could do with a bit of company."

"We all could. Good for the soul."

"Arthur," asked Alice, intrigued, "what do you do all day?"

Arthur straightened the creases in his trousers. "Read. Television sometimes. Music. Mostly sit. Solitaire. Damned good at it. Never cheat."

Alice wouldn't doubt it for a minute. "Are you lonely?" she asked.

154

He nodded and stared into the distance. "Empty days. Silence. No-one."

"I don't mean to be rude," although Alice felt that was exactly what she was doing, "and tell me if it's none of my business, but you're not short of a bob or two, are you? I mean, look at this place. You could have meals delivered. And you could get out more. Join a club or something. What about going on holiday? A cruise maybe."

"Got Evergreens."

"Yes, but that's only once a month, isn't it? Can't you do something else?"

Arthur stared into his empty cup and sighed. "Ashamed," he said quietly, almost to himself.

"Of what?"

"Being lonely."

Alice could have wept. She went and sat down beside him. Taking his hand in hers she squeezed it gently. "You don't have to be ashamed of being lonely," she said. What could she do to help?

"Better now," he said, looking at her. "With you. Makes a difference."

That was the nicest thing anyone had said to her in a long time. Apart from Ronald, of course. He was always saying kind things. Oh, and Valerie. And Shanti. Grace too. They'd all said nice things to her. Alice slipped her shoes off and tucked her legs under her, making herself more comfortable.

"Arthur, I have a proposition."

"Fire away."

Alice had been mulling this over for a week, ever since the first day she'd met Arthur. Something that could work for both of them. And having seen his reaction to her beef stew, she had every confidence he would be up for it.

"I'll come here every Saturday and cook for you. Not just one meal, but all your meals. For the whole week. "

"Like Meals on Wheels?"

"That sort of thing. I'll cook and bake and fill your freezer. Then all you'll have to do is pop your meals in the microwave or the oven and you're sorted. I've showed you how to do some vegetables so you'll be able to manage those on your own. I'll do all your shopping. You just tell me what you like to eat and I'll cook it. What d'you think?" Was that a tear that fell onto the back of her hand? "You'll have to pay for the food, of course. And I would have to do all the cooking here. My kitchen's too small and anyway, I couldn't easily carry lots of food containers on my bike. What do you reckon?" Please say yes! Please say yes!

Arthur twisted her wedding ring round and round. "Marry me!" he said.

Alice laughed. "I'm already married, you know that. But what d'you think about my idea?"

"Beef Wellington?"

Alice nodded.

"Spotted dick and custard?"

She nodded again.

"Jam Roly Poly?"

"Arthur, it can be whatever you want," she said, smiling. And she'd be able to cook in his wonderful kitchen. Heaven! "Is that a yes?"

"No more eggs?" Arthur couldn't believe what he was hearing.

"Not unless you want them. Yes?"

Arthur's nodded his head vigorously. "Yes! Yes!"

"It's a deal," said Alice. "So all you need to do is to give me a list of the things you like to eat and I'll do all the shopping and then I'll come round next Saturday, tell you how much I've spent and then cook it all for you. How does that sound?"

"Good. But."

Alice wasn't expecting a 'but'. "But what?" she asked, tentatively.

"I have to pay you."

She had almost forgotten, so keen was she to get in that kitchen and do what she loved. "What about £50 a week? How does that sound?" she suggested tentatively.

Arthur's mouth dropped open. "£50 a week? No!"

Too much, thought Alice. I'm being greedy.

"£200 a week. For food. And everything. What you don't spend, it's yours."

Alice was gobsmacked. It was far too much. For £200 a week, she could feed him like a king and still have plenty left over. "Too much," she said. "Too generous."

"Nonsense! £200. Final offer!"

"Well, in that case, Colonel Arthur Randolph Gnash, with a 'G', OBE, KPMG, UFO and RSI, it's a deal!" Alice threw her arms round him.

156

"Good! Now. Down to business!"

Alice's heart dropped. There had been no mention of other 'services' and she was hoping he'd forgotten about that side of things. She'd much rather be cooking. Arthur picked up a notepad and pencil from the table next to him.

"No 1. Steak and kidney pie."

Alice had cycled home that day with £300 in her purse and Arthur's wish list; £200 for his shopping and her skills at turning it into a week's worth of tasty meals and £100 for today's beef stew with dumplings and the biscuits. And, apart from holding hands again, there was no mention of anything else required. Alice was elated. Not only did she have some money but she could continue to help Grace out too. And what's more, as long as Arthur continued to like her cooking and was happy to pay for it this could go on for the foreseeable future. Maybe long enough to tide her over until she found a new job. Alice was over the moon. When the inevitable happened and she was made redundant at least she now had a back-up plan. A safety net. And between Arthur and Ronald and who knew, maybe Malcolm too, a glimpse of independence was just poking its nose above the horizon.

As it happened, Malcolm was not in the same financial league as Arthur, nowhere near, but Alice hadn't really expected him to be. Billyfields was no Meadowbank. The area behind the railway station was one of the most run down areas in Smedley. Malcolm's road, Blossom Street, with not a tree or flower in sight, was grim with nearly every other house boarded up. Graffiti was everywhere. The whole area was depressed and cried poverty, neglect, abandonment. What chance for the poor few souls who still lived here? Alice's mood could not have been more different as she cycled up the road to Malcolm's house the following day. There would be no question of her leaving her bike outside in this street.

As if reading her mind, the first thing Malcolm said when he opened the door was that she'd better bring her bike inside if she wanted to be taking it home. The house was pretty much like hers but a bit more basic. A two-up two-down, small but spotlessly clean and welcoming, like the man himself. Malcolm could only be in his 70s, Alice guessed, but he was stooped and grey. His clothes, though old and worn, were neat and tidy. She looked round his compact lounge which was in complete contrast with the urban decay outside. Warm and cosy, homely and cared for, with a log fire burning in an open grate, the room was mostly taken up with two over-stuffed armchairs placed on either side of the fireplace. Malcolm sat down in one and pointed at Alice to sit in the other. This couldn't be more different from Arthur's luxurious, colour-coordinated house with its polished wooden floors and matching furnishings, but she immediately felt at home. Apart from the armchairs, there was a wooden table in the window covered in a floral plastic tablecloth, upon which a small radio and an old portable tv sat. Above the fireplace hung a large framed picture of a faded highland scene, misty mountains and an improbable castle. There was only one photograph, she noticed, in a plain black frame, hanging next to the light switch. Of a black Labrador. But there were no personal knick-knacks. No ornaments, none of the usual bric-a-brac that clutters up one's life. It was simple and modest, just like Malcolm. From where she was sitting, Alice could see through an open door into the kitchen. She knew it, too, would be spotlessly clean.

"This is a lovely home, Malcolm," she said, and she meant it.

"Aye."

Oh dear, thought Alice, not another man of very few words.

"Who's that?" she asked, pointing at the photo.

"That was Benji. Had him fifteen years," replied Malcolm. "I got him as a puppy the day I retired and he never left my side till the day he died."

Phew. A real sentence.

"You must miss him."

Malcolm nodded and taking out a white cotton hankie from his pocket, he dabbed his eyes.

Wrong thing to say. "Do you have any family?" she asked.

"No," replied Malcolm. "Just me. I never married. Couldn't find the right one. Except Benji, of course."

"Haven't you ever been tempted to get another dog?" she asked.

"Oh no! I couldn't replace Benji. He was a one-off. There'll only ever be one Benji." Malcolm blew his nose loudly. "I suppose it's like a good wife. If you find the right one, you can't replace them."

"I know people who've tried," laughed Alice. Actually, it wasn't that funny.

"And I'm getting on now," continued Malcolm. "I don't get out as much as I used to. It would be difficult for me to walk a dog, what with my legs. And there's nowhere to walk a dog round here, not any more. Nothing green, you'll have seen that."

"What do you do all day, Malcolm?" she asked.

"Well, I've got one or two mates who live nearby. I sometimes go and see them. But mostly I sit by the window and watch the world go by. Not that much of it goes by here. The pub's gone and most of the houses. There's nothing round here anymore. No reason for people to come. Council wants to pull it all down and start again but there's no money."

"I've heard that before," Alice agreed.

"I do a lot of thinking, too."

About what, Alice wanted to ask but didn't.

"And I like my television. And the radio. Sometimes I put the radio on, not to listen, just so I can hear the voices. It sounds like the house is full of people."

Thank goodness, Malcolm could talk. But Alice couldn't. She didn't know what to say. She couldn't imagine ever being so lonely that she'd have to put the radio on, just so she could pretend that somebody else was there. She wanted so much to be there for Malcolm. And Arthur. And Ronald. To stop them being lonely. To be a friend. But she wasn't having much success here. Whatever she said to Malcolm, it seemed to be the wrong thing. They sat there in silence. She looked round the room again, desperately seeking inspiration. Nothing came to mind. The silence continued. Was this a good move? she thought. Ronald had said Malcolm wanted a bit of company and here she was, at a loss for words. As much use as a chocolate teapot.

"Would you like a glass of sherry?" he asked suddenly.

Alice sat upright. "That would be lovely."

Malcolm went into the kitchen and came back with two large tumblers, almost full to the brim. He handed her one. "Cheers."

"Cheers," she replied, taking a sip. The nut-brown liquid was rich and deep and she could feel it burning as it went down, but in a sensuous, re-assuring way. "This is delicious. I don't think I've ever had sherry like this before."

Malcolm looked pleased. Alice took another sip. "Delightful," she murmured. The armchair seemed to wrap itself round her. She stretched her legs out, her feet almost in the fire. She warmed the tumbler in her hands, staring into the flames. This was heaven. Another sip. She felt soporific. Lazy. Alice closed her eyes. Why couldn't life always be this simple? A warm fire. A comfy chair. All my problems a million miles away.

Alice woke with a start. She looked round, confused. She sat upright, the empty glass falling to the floor

"Looks like you needed that sleep." It was Malcolm.

Alice looked at her watch. By her reckoning she had been asleep for at least an hour. An hour!

"I am *so* sorry," she said, picking up the glass. "I never do that. Fall asleep in the chair." She saw that Malcolm was smiling at her. "At least, not with people I've just met! You must think me so rude."

"No, I don't. I think you're tired. And that sherry was enough to send you off."

Alice looked ruefully at the glass in her hand. "You should patent this," she laughed. "Real knock-out stuff. Amazing!"

"Anyway, I enjoyed watching you sleep."

"I didn't snore or anything, did I?"

"Not too much," said Malcolm. "I only had to turn the radio up a little bit. It was the dribbling that got me!"

"No! I didn't, did I?" Alice was deeply embarrassed. She checked the front of her blouse.

Malcolm roared with laughter. "Got you there, didn't I!"

She smiled with relief. "Yes you did. I am sorry though," she said. "Ronald said you'd like a bit of company and what do I do? Fall asleep on you. That's unforgivable."

"No, it's not. You may have been asleep but you were still here. Like Benji." Oh no! Back to the bloody dead dog! "He wasn't a great conversationalist either." Alice wasn't sure how to take that. "But he was always there for me." Malcolm choked back a sob.

With some difficulty Alice stood up. The armchair was far too comfortable and the room too warm.

"Another sherry?" he asked.

"Best not," she said. "I can see me drunk in charge of a bicycle! I'd better get going."

"Will you come back?" he asked her.

"If you want me to."

"I do. Even if you do fall asleep! Here." He passed her two £10 notes. "For your company." She thanked him. "It'll be even more if you manage to stay awake next time!"

"I'll do my best," she promised. "But £20 is far too much." Alice handed him back £10. She wasn't going to take £20 for doing nothing and anyway, it was clear that Malcolm wasn't anything like as well off as Arthur. He pocketed the money gratefully. And she was more than happy with a tenner. He hadn't mentioned wanting anything else and that was fine by her. No cuddles or hand-holding. Or showing him her assets.

"I've got a mate two doors down. Jack. He's on his own too. Loads of family but they never come to see him. I think he'd like a bit of company too. Would you go and see him next time you come? As well as me?"

"Of course I will."

"He'd like that."

This is growing like topsy, thought Alice. Jack will make four. Four lonely old men to visit. At this rate, I'm soon not going to have enough time to go to work. This could turn into my new full-time job. Cooking, companionship and what? Cuddles? Yes, that was it. Cooking, companionship and cuddles. I could set up my own business, Shanti was right. And once I'd got a lot more gentlemen friends on my books, I could start sharing them out amongst the girls. It'd be like creating jobs for them. What a wonderful thought.

Alice fell asleep that night with something close to contentment.

## CHAPTER 19

## BACON AND POTATO GRATIN

Finally it happened. The news they were all dreading. An announcement was made over the tannoy on a Monday afternoon. "Would all staff please report to the canteen. Again. Quick as you like!" The same announcer as before. And no-one was in any doubt what they were about to be told. Crunch time, thought Alice. Actually, that's not a bad name for a new biscuit.

This morning when she'd clocked in there had been no intimation that today would be the day. It started just like any other. Checking the rota, Alice was pleased, as she always was, to see that she was on Apple and Almond Alouettes this week, as she took great personal pride in the fact that these were *her* biscuits and they were one of the most successful that came off Bercow's production line. It wasn't that she paid any more attention to these biscuits than she did to any of the others - she didn't have the time - but she did feel that a little piece of her soul was in each and every one she made. Nonsense of course, but nobody else she knew had the accolade of having their name still appear on 10,000 packets every week. Alice's Apple and Almond Alouettes. She spent a relatively pleasant morning mixing the various components in the right amounts; dehydrated yellow biscuit mix; violently green emulsion from an overhead container which provided, amongst other things, the flavouring and preservatives; dried apple; ground almonds, and finally flaked almonds for the decoration. No butter. Once combined, the mixture was dolloped in biscuit-sized pieces from a machine with a dozen metal nozzles which Alice thought looked like some high-tech space-age udder, onto a conveyor belt. At this juncture, it was a bit like Hazelnut Hearts as she placed a nut, a flaked almond this time, in the centre of each pile then watched as her handiwork disappeared into a heat machine which resembled a horizontal toaster on wheels. This wasn't so much an oven, more a mini blast-furnace, the plan being that the biscuit would not dry out completely but still retain a slightly gooey centre, vaguely reminiscent of apples. But this was never more than wishful thinking as sometimes it worked, sometimes it didn't. The heat machine was old before its time and desperately temperamental, more so than any other piece of machinery on the factory floor and it needed constant tweaking. Sometimes it got excited and spewed out biscuits which were bone dry and burst into a cloud of fine crumbs when you bit into one. On other occasions the biscuits were barely cooked and the mixture behaved like chewing gum in every respect, although there was a faint taste of apple. Whichever way the biscuits turned out they were still packaged, boxed, dispatched and sold. Occasionally a customer wrote in to complain about the lack of consistency; once a woman from Didcot submitted a dental bill for £150 to repair a chipped tooth sustained while eating one of the drier versions of the Alouettes. She was sent a box of Bercow's assorted biscuits by return of post and was never heard from again. The wags in Customer Services joked that a box of Bercow's assorted was enough to see anyone off!

The morning passed quickly and Alice was, unusually, enjoying her work, her mind elsewhere. She was thinking about the strange path her life had taken recently. Such highs and lows. And in such a short space of time. Arthur and Ronald? Highs, definitely. Frank? You couldn't get much lower than Frank. Bercow's closing? A low for sure. Getting paid for what she loved doing, cooking and baking? Oh, that was a high. And being someone's friend? Their companion? That was the biggest high of all.

Valerie and Grace had already started their lunch break and were in the canteen by the time Alice got there.

"Any news?" she asked Valerie.

"Any time now," replied Valerie. "The money men have been through the books with a fine tooth comb. It's not looking good. Apart from the actual building itself, there are no real assets worth selling. The machinery is so worn out and obsolete it's not worth anything."

"So that's really it?" asked Grace.

"I'm afraid so."

"And what about our wages? And pensions?" asked Alice. "Will we get anything at all?"

"That's what they're finalising now," said Valerie.

"So it's goodbye Chocolate Dropsies? Farewell Shortbread Sweeties?" asked Grace sadly.

"'Fraid so."

"And that's another factory to close in Smedley. This town is dying bit by bit. There's nothing round here any more. It's the kids I feel sorry for. What future have they got? " complained Alice.

"They can always move away," said Grace. "It's us who haven't got any choice. We're stuck here."

"Yes, but if there's no jobs anywhere else, then they're in the same boat as us."

The three women sat silently, eating their lunch. Iris waved at them from the canteen door.

"Why the glum faces?" she asked as she sat down heavily on one of the plastic seats. It groaned under her weight. "You look like you've lost a penny and found a pound. Or is it the other way round?"

"Just thinking about the future," said Grace quietly.

"Well, I've got some news for you." They looked at her expectantly. "And it's good news too. And it's all thanks to you, Alice."

"Me? What have I done?"

"Well, you know how we were talking about you and your gentlemen. The ones you look after and...service?"

"Iris! That sounds awful! You make it sound like I'm providing a stud service or something. Like I go round and have sex with them! I don't!"

"Sorry. Bad choice of words!" She smiled. "But you know what I mean. The men you look after. Hold hands and cuddles and things."

"And feed too. There's a bit more to it than that," Alice reminded her.

"Well, anyway," continued Iris. "There's this old geezer lives next to my mam. Moved there some years ago after his wife died. Called Vincent. He's called Vincent, not his wife. Lovely old man. Anyway, after what you'd said and how much money you were getting, Alice, I decided to bite on the bullet. Give it a go."

"You didn't!" exclaimed Grace. "What did you do?"

"I rang on his doorbell, told him who I was. Except he already knew that what with him living next door to my mam and such. Remembers me from before I was married. But he hadn't seen me for years. Not until I got divorced and moved back in with mother."

"Cut to the chase, Iris," said Valerie. "Some of us have to get back to work. Tell us what happened?"

"Well, I knew he lived on his own so I told him I could offer him a bit of companionship, for a small fee, if he was interested."

"And was he?" asked Alice.

"Was he? He practically bit my hand off! Said he didn't get out much and didn't have any friends or anyone to visit him. I asked him if he

164

wanted me to cook for him. And he does! Not that my cooking's much to write home about. Not like yours, Alice. But he did say he liked pork pies! So what do you think?" Iris sat back in her chair and folded her arms, looking very pleased with herself.

"Pork pies?" said Valerie. "A marriage made in heaven!"

Iris ignored her.

"I think it's brilliant," said Alice. "For both of you. Well done!"

"I couldn't have done it without you," said Iris. "If it hadn't been for you, I'd never have thought of doing it. And probably wouldn't have had the courage either. So thank you, Alice Coulter."

"What about 'extras'?" asked Valerie. "Have you offered him anything else?"

Iris grinned. "That's for me to know and you to find out," she replied, tapping the side of her nose with her forefinger, trying to be enigmatic. Iris being Iris, it didn't quite work.

"Go on," said Grace. "Have you?"

"All I'm going to say is that it's up for discussion. He hasn't got a lot of money but he's quite happy to spend what little he has on me."

"So it's win-win all round?" Alice asked.

"I think so," agreed Iris. "I'm happy and so is he. And what's even better, he says he's got loads of mates who are in the same boat as him. On their own. No-one to talk to. You've really started something here, Alice. You should give it a go, Grace. There's loads of them out there. Just waiting for you."

Grace had been thinking about it. A lot. She needed money, simple as that. "Did you really just go up and knock on his door?" she asked. "I don't think I could do that."

"Couldn't do what?" asked Shanti, joining them. "Bloody Marshmallow Moments playing up again. Couldn't do what?" she asked again.

"Iris has gone and got herself a gentlemen friend, Vincent, like Alice," explained Valerie.

"Why, that's great news," said Shanti, clearly delighted. "What's he like?"

"A bit like Alice's men," replied Iris. "Old and lonely."

"Well done you!" Shanti patted her on the back.

"And I was just saying that Grace should give it a go. It's so easy."

"What's easy?" asked Bella, collapsing onto a chair. She was out of breath. "Damn' Hazel Hearts. Machine not workin' proper'."

"All the machines are on the blink," explained Valerie. "They're letting them run down. No point maintaining them if we're going to close."

"I suppose that makes sense," said Alice, "but it doesn't make it any easier for us if they expect us to keep turning biscuits out."

"I don't think that's going to happen for too much longer," said Valerie.

"D'you know," said Shanti, "I think we're all missing a trick here."

"What? With the machine?" asked Bella.

"No. Forget the machines. With Alice's gentlemen."

"What d'you mean?" asked Grace.

"Well, we're concentrating on men. I mean, Alice has Ronald and Arthur…"

"And Malcolm now. And then there's Jack," Alice added.

"You didn't mention those," said Iris. "Since when? You dark horse!"

"And you've got, Vincent was it, Iris?" asked Shanti. Iris nodded. "But what about all the women out there? There must be loads of them who are all on their own. Men don't have the monopoly on loneliness. Who's to say they wouldn't want a cuddle? Or someone to keep them company?"

"Ronald said that," said Alice. "He told me that there were lots of lonely women as well as men at Evergreens."

"Well, there you go then. And, don't forget, what about the ones who don't go to Evergreens? There must be hundreds of them. We could make a difference to them too. Or to some of them at least."

"I don't know that I could have sex with a woman," said Iris. "I mean, I've got nothing against it, it's just not for me. I'm a man's woman, if you know what I mean. Or do I mean a woman's man?"

"Shanti is right," said Alice. "We *are* forgetting the women. And nobody's asking you to have sex with them, Iris. It's more a question of being a friend. A companion. Talking to them. Listening. "

"Yes," said Shanti. "Sex is optional."

"Now there's someone I wouldn't want to have sex with," said Iris, nodding her head in the direction of the canteen entrance. "Funeral Dog. He's a right misery. I like a man that can make me laugh!"

He made me laugh once, thought Alice. And he's certainly made me smile a few times too.

"Oh, hang on, he's heading this way," said Grace.

166

Alice watched Graham as he walked towards their table, dressed, as usual, in overalls and a hairnet. There was something about your work clothes that don't do you any favours at all, she thought. But then who am I to talk?

"Sorry to interrupt, ladies," he said, "but I'm afraid you're wanted back upstairs, Valerie."

"Not Mr Bercow this time? I haven't seen him all week."

"No. It's one of the administration men asking for you."

Valerie left them to it. Graham stood awkwardly as one by one the women drifted back to work until only Alice remained.

"Is it true, Graham?" Alice asked as she got up to go. "That's there's to be no more maintenance on any of the machines? Because we're about to close?"

"That's right. We've been told not to bother and just keep things going as best we can."

"So it's imminent, is it?"

"I reckon so."

"It's not looking good, is it?" she asked.

Graham shook his head. "Got anything else lined up yet?" he asked her.

"You must be joking. There's nothing round here. You?"

"Same. What will you do? Sign on?"

Alice hadn't thought about it. "I suppose I'll have to but I don't like the idea. I've worked all my life. Never signed on before. What about you? What will you do?"

Graham shrugged his shoulders. "I don't know. I'm trying to be positive about all of this. I've got a little bit tucked away so I won't starve. Maybe I'll do some travelling. Always wanted to travel."

Me too, thought Alice. Even if it was just the Scottish Borders.

"Well, whatever. Good luck," she said. And she meant it. "I hope something turns up for you."

"Thank you," Graham replied. "You too."

"And I hope you'll be happy." Now why on earth did I say that? she cursed herself. What a fool he must think me.

He smiled at her. "Yes," he said. "And you. I hope it all works out for both of us. I mean…" he stammered, "for you and me. No, that's not what I mean. I…"

Alice laughed. "I know what you mean. And thank you. Best get back to work."

Graham stood aside to let her pass.

The women had just got back to their work stations after the lunch break and turned on the machines when the announcement came for all staff to report to the canteen. Alice turned off the Alouettes machine and put her ear plugs in her overall pocket. This can only mean one thing, she thought. This is it. How appropriate that I finish at Bercow's on my very own prize-winning biscuits. There's something right and proper about that. Unusually, she picked up a biscuit from the conveyor belt and popped it into her mouth. One of the better ones. The centre was still slightly soft and there was an unmistakable tang of apple. Sighing, she joined the procession of glum faces from all over the factory heading to the canteen.

Once again it was packed. Alice squeezed her way in until she was standing just inside the doorway. She found herself next to Grace and Bella. Jason from HR could clearly be seen as he was standing on one of the tables in front of the window, a piece of paper in his hand. He was sweating heavily, clearly uncomfortable and every few minutes he wiped the palms of his hands on his jeans. Two sombre men dressed in black suits stood on the floor behind him, one with a goatee beard, the other clean-shaven. They've got to be the money men, thought Alice. She looked for Valerie but couldn't see her in the throng. Graham caught her eye as she looked round the crowded room. He looked serious but then again so did everyone else. He gave her a half smile then turned his attention back to Jason.

"Ladies and gentlemen," began the youth from HR. "I've got some important news for you." He consulted the paper in his hand. "As you know," he read, "Bercow's has gone bankrupt. Mr Bercow himself told you a few weeks ago that the factory was to close."

"Where is Bercow?" shouted a voice from the back. "Where's the man himself? Why's he not talking to us today?"

"I'm afraid Mr Bercow is unavoidably unavailable."

"Why?" shouted someone else. "Where is he?"

Jason coughed several times.

"What? What did you say?" demanded one of the Bercow Biddies.

"He's re-grouping," muttered Jason.

"What does that mean? Regrouping? How can he re-group when there's only one of him?"

"Where's he re-grouping?" shouted Grace. Alice looked at her with surprise.

"Bahamas," Jason coughed into his hand.

"*Bahamas?*" There was uproar. And boos. Lots of boos.

"How can he be in the Bahamas when his factory's going to the dogs?" shouted a man close to Alice. She recognised him as one of the S&M guys.

"Dogs? What dogs?" Bella asked her.

Jason looked at the angry faces in front of him. "Don't blame me," he said, almost crying. "I'm only the messenger." The uproar continued with people shouting and swearing.

"SShh!" said one or two voices. "Let him speak. It's not his fault." Gradually the noise abated a little. Alice noted that the money men's faces remained expressionless and they did nothing to help poor Jason.

"The f...factory will close today," stammered Jason.

"No!" shouted the whole room as one. There was much shaking of heads and Alice could hear several women close by crying.

The sheet of paper trembled in Jason's hands as he continued to read from it. "The factory will close today and you will all be paid all the wages owing to you. Including any overtime." There was a collective sigh of relief. "The Job Centre on Coley Street has arranged to hold special sessions for Bercow's staff every afternoon for the next two weeks from 2pm until 4pm. They'll tell you about signing on, filling in job application forms, making CVs and anything else you need to know."

"Like where to find another bloody job, for one thing," shouted one of the canteen workers.

"Yeh! And how to pay my bills!"

"And feed my kids!"

"Weren't you supposed to do that, Jason?" shouted one of the canteen workers "Help us with CVs and all that sort of stuff. You said you were going to."

There were several cries of "Yes, that's right. Why didn't you?"

"What's the point in filling in a job application when there are no soddin' jobs in Smedley?" shouted an angry woman standing next to one of the money men. He took a step back, certain he was going to be thumped.

Jason took a deep breath. "As for your pensions," he said, "I'm sorry to have to tell you that no decision has been made yet." He wiped his brow with his sleeve.

This was greeted with the pandemonium he'd expected.

"That's our money!"

"We earned that!"

"You can't do that!"

"What am I going to live on in my old age?"

"You thieving bastard!"

Jason promptly burst into tears. "It's not my fault," he wailed. But no-one was listening. One of the men in suits, the little-bearded one, clambered up onto the table next to him.

"Ladies and gentlemen," he said. Nobody paid him any attention either. "LADIES AND GENTLEMEN," he shouted at the top of his voice. This worked. "You will each get a letter once the business has been wound up. That will tell you what will happen to your pension."

"When? When will we know?"

"It could be as soon as a few weeks but I wouldn't expect to hear for a few months."

"A few months?"

"I'm sorry," said the bearded one. "These things take time."

"And in the meantime, what do we do?" Shanti shouted.

"You pack up your things and you go home."

"Just like that?"

"I'm afraid so," he replied, nervously tugging the tuft on his chin. "I'm sorry," he added.

"You and me both!" said Shanti. And she turned her back on him. Others, seeing what she had done followed suit. In no time at all every single Bercow employee present had his or her back to Jason and the money man. Realising there was nothing further to be gained by remaining on the table, man and boy climbed down. They made their way, joined by the clean shaven man who was frightened to be left on his own, out of the canteen, jostled and shoved every inch of the way by the newly unemployed.

"We've got to keep in touch," said Shanti. "It's very important."

The ladies' staff room was busy as women stripped off their overalls and hairnets for the last time and emptied their lockers.

"Absolutely," agreed Alice. "You've all got my phone number, haven't you?"

"Why don't we meet up once a week? For a coffee somewhere?" suggested Iris.

"Not sure I'll be able to afford a coffee," said Grace, despondently.

"Then I'll treat you," said Alice. "I think that's a brilliant idea, Iris. How about the Bottomless Cup?"

"Good for me," said Shanti. "I'm game."

"Me too," Bella said, as she removed numerous photos of kittens from the inside of her locker.

"How about every Thursday?" suggested Alice. "3pm?" There were nods all round. "Sounds like a plan. I'll let Valerie know." Alice looked at a small ball of grey fur Iris had found in her locker and was holding at arm's length. "What you got there? Is it dead?"

"I do hope so," said Iris. "I was wondering where that'd got to." She dropped it in the rubbish bin.

"What was it?" Grace asked.

"Old pork pie!"

"You're kidding!" said Shanti. "Fancy you leaving half a pork pie! Well, I never!"

A burst of laughter filled the room. The only moment of levity on such a grim day.

"Yes," agreed Iris. "I can hardly believe it myself!"

There were hugs and kisses and tears as each of the women said their goodbyes.

"Not goodbyes," Alice reminded them. "Au revoirs. We'll see each other on Thursday."

Grace watched as Iris and Bella left arm in arm then sat down and burst into tears. She felt as if she'd been crying forever. "I don't know how I'm going to manage," she wept. "I really don't."

Alice put her arm round her. "It'll be alright."

"Promise?" sniffed Grace, looking up into her friend's face.

"I promise," said Alice. Shanti looked at them both and raised her eyebrows.

"I promise," repeated Alice. "It'll all work out. Just you wait and see."

"I just hope you're right," whispered Shanti. "Boy, do I hope you're right."

Despite Alice's promises to Grace she was not convinced things were going to work out. In fact, she didn't see how they could. Not for all of them. She was so absorbed in thinking about what the future might hold for her and her friends that as she extracted her bike from the racks for the last time and pedalled home, she was completely oblivious to the traffic, the rain, everything. And it was only when she wheeled her bike into the back yard that she realised that she'd meant to stop off on the way home and get some bits for dinner. Too late now. She wasn't in the mood. Alice found an old onion in the bottom of the vegetable basket along with some rubbery potatoes, and a couple of rashers of streaky bacon and a bit of cheddar in the fridge. The cheese was a bit green but it could be revitalised once she'd scraped the mould off. That would have to do. Bacon and cheese gratin. Improvisation. That's what they all needed. Make it up as you go along, she thought. It's the only way.

# CHAPTER 20

## MEATBALLS

Alice spent the next few days in a state of shock, still trying to come to terms with the fact that the worst had really happened and her life and everything in it had been turned upside down. Chaos reigned. She was confused and didn't know how to feel. Bercow's had been more than just a job and she felt as if a huge chapter in her life had just come to a very unsatisfactory end. And it wasn't just her job that she'd lost. Her income was gone and she felt that any stab at independence might have just trotted off into the distance. Her opportunity of getting away from Frank might be as remote now as her winning the Grand National on a three-legged incontinent donkey. The chance was gone; had ever really been there in the first place? Everything was about to change and she wasn't convinced it would necessarily be for the better. But maybe it would. Despite the confusion, sometimes she felt strangely upbeat, even happy. Alice couldn't work it out.

The last few weeks had been manic for Alice but oddly enough, she thought she had never been more content. After a long week at Bercow's, on Saturday mornings she cycled to the Co-op where she spent a good hour buying the food in order to fulfil Arthur's wish list. Then it was off to Meadowbank, bike groaning under the weight of several plastic bags draped over each of the handlebars and her basket overflowing with his shopping. Alice spent the rest of the day cooking food for the following week for him, loading his freezer with tasty meals that even he could easily reheat when she wasn't there. She'd baked cakes, biscuits too, his favourite sorts. And while she worked non-stop in Arthur's wonderful kitchen, he sat on one of the stools and chatted away, his sentences growing with his familiarity. These days were a delight for them both. And because Saturdays were now fully occupied, Alice now visited both Malcolm and Jack on Sundays, always going armed with some treat or other, usually her home-made biscuits. Alice intended to ask them if they wanted her to cook for them too. She wasn't sure how she'd physically manage it if they said yes, which she was sure they would. Maybe Arthur would let her cook for them in his kitchen as well. Then at the end of every day, she'd return to Greenfields Road and cook for the three of them; Frank,

Ronald and herself. Alice was working non-stop and she was utterly exhausted but she had never felt more satisfied. She had no time for herself but she didn't mind. Each night she fell onto her camp bed, asleep before her head touched the pillow. And though she woke every morning with her usual backache, she could not have felt more contented. Apart from Frank everything was going swimmingly and, ever the optimist, although she knew it couldn't go on forever, Alice had hoped it would carry on for a good while yet. But she still had nagging doubts - the rug had well and truly been pulled out from under her feet and she'd lost her job. All she had was her gentlemen friends. Sometimes she wasn't convinced it would be enough.

It wasn't just the future that was concerning Alice. She was worried about Ronald too. Now that she didn't have to go to Bercow's each day she found herself popping round more than usual to see how he was. He looked tired and distracted. There'd been no request for a repeat of the thong display and she was glad of that but he hadn't even asked for another cuddle. Ronald was now content simply to sit and hold her hand. She told him about the Bercow's closing and how she and her friends planned to meet up once a week so they could all keep in touch. Friends are important, Ronald had muttered. She told him about Iris and her pork-pie-loving neighbour. Ronald managed a tight smile. She told him about her mammoth weekly cooking sessions at Arthur's in his designer kitchen and how he was happily paying a small fortune for her biscuits. I told you so, Ronald had said. Biscuit mad, that man. And Alice told him about Malcolm and Jack and how they had introduced her to Eddie and George, friends of theirs, who also lived on the same street.

"Don't know them," he said quietly. "They don't go to Evergreens."

"They're lovely men, both of them. And Eddie, he says he knows a lady who could do with a bit of a chat now and then. Carol. Lives in one of the posh retirement flats near the old cinema." Alice shook her head in dismay. "You'd think living somewhere like that she'd have lots of friends. But Jack says she doesn't. Awful, isn't it? I'll pop round and see her in the next few days."

"You're doing a wonderful job, you know," said Ronald. "You're making a real difference."

"Well, it's doing me a favour too, I can't deny it. Providing me with a bit of money."

"What will you do with it all?"

Alice laughed. "At the moment I'm barely keeping my head above water."

"And Frank? How's things?"

"Frank is Frank. Unfortunately."

"Still planning on leaving him?"

"One day," said Alice.

Ronald shivered and she pulled the blanket up higher. "Want another bar on the fire?" she asked. He shook his head. Alice looked at him closely. Was it her imagination or had he lost weight? Heaven knows, he could ill afford to. "Are you alright, Ronald? You're awfully quiet these days." His eyes welled up. "Ronald! What is it? What's the matter?" She found a clean tissue in the bottom of her handbag and gave it to him.

"They want me to go into a home," he sniffed.

"Who do?"

"Them. The council."

"What are you talking about?" she asked, concern written all over her face.

"They say I can't cope any more."

"Hang on a minute, Ronald. Start at the beginning. When did this all come about?"

Ronald told her. On his last visit to Evergreens he'd been approached by people from the Council. There were two of them there, a young girl who looked no more than fourteen with a ring in her nose, just like a bull.

"Now why would someone do that?" he asked. "Looked like a giant snot from a distance." He wrinkled his nose in disgust. "And green hair. Never seen anyone with green hair before. And the other one was no better. Bloke. Middle-aged. Sandals. Socks. Never trust a man who wears sandals and socks. Going round everybody asking about how they manage at home. The girl asked me why I didn't use Meals on Wheels. How I washed, that sort of thing. Lots of personal questions. So I told her."

"Told her what?"

"Told her to mind her own bloody business, that's what."

"Not good," said Alice. "Now why did you do that?"

"Because it *is* none of her business," said Ronald petulantly. "I don't ask her how she washes. Mind you, by the smell of her, I don't think she does. Armpits like a dead dog."

Alice smiled grimly. "Go on. What happened next?"

Ronald told her how the girl had got all miffy and said that a home visit would be necessary as she had concerns for his welfare.

"Concerns for my welfare, my arse! Just a busybody, that's all she was! Anyway, she said she thought I wasn't eating properly so I told her about you and my meals. Speaking of which, what are we having tonight?"

"Meatballs."

Ronald cheered up slightly. "One of my favourites. Used to call them faggots as a kid. You can't say that any more. Not PG or whatever they call it. Faggots with gravy. Cracking! And we always had peas with them. You had to have peas to mop up the gravy. But you had to mash them. That was best."

"Ronald," Alice said impatiently, "just tell me what she said."

"The green-haired one was concerned that if you didn't turn up with a meal for me, if you forgot, then I'd go hungry. Told her you never forgot. Never had. Not even with all those other things you had to do. Nevertheless, she'd said. Notwithstanding, and other big words like that. Said she would arrange a home visit. And the day before yesterday they came round." Ronald was clearly distressed.

"Why didn't you tell me all this before?" asked Alice. "Why didn't you say something?"

"Didn't want to worry you. You've had a lot on your plate recently. Lots of things going on. I didn't want to add to your troubles."

"Ronald, that's why I'm here. To help you. Honestly, you should know that by now." Alice couldn't be angry with him for long. "You should have said something." she said, more gently this time. "What happened? When they came round?"

"It was her again. The green-haired child and another man this time. Beard. And one of those silly moustaches that curl up at the ends. With a clipboard. Went round the house ticking things off it looked like."

"And what did they say?"

Ronald burst into tears. She reached for his hand. "Said I should move. For my own good. Into a home. I told them I'd lived here all my life. This is my home." He looked round the room. "I know it's nothing special but it's mine. I don't want to live in a home. Full of lots of old people. I want to stay here." He sobbed louder. "They just want my money, that's what it is. Sell my house and put me in a home. Why should I move, Alice? I can manage."

"No, Ronald, *we* can manage."

"We can, can't we?" He looked at her hopefully. "And you're not going anywhere, are you?"

Not any more I'm not, she thought. Not now Bercow's has gone. Ronald's face broke into a grin.

"I'll ring the council tomorrow," she said. "Or go and see someone about this. We'll sort it out. They can't force you to move if you don't want to, I'm sure."

"Oh, thank you, Alice. Thank you so much. I've been worried sick."

"Ronald, you should have told me. You're not on your own you know."

Ronald looked abashed. "I know," he said. "Thank you."


Alice was furious! How dare they treat an old man like this! Bullying him into doing something he didn't want to do. Frightening him like that! Making him ill! It was not on. She'd give them a piece of her mind! It may well be for his own good but she didn't like the way they were going about it. If he didn't want to go into a home that was his choice, surely? Why, she'd adopt him if it meant he didn't have to move. Alice didn't know if that was possible but she'd give it a damned good try. Perhaps she could put up Frank for adoption at the same time. Now that was worth thinking about. Nah! Who'd have him?

The following morning she got up early and dressed in a blue skirt with a pale blue jumper. Smart but serious. Alice was in battle-mode. She cycled to the Council Offices close to the bus station and tied her bike to nearby railings. Standing on the steps leading up to the building, Alice thought how depressing and uninviting it was. Maybe that was the intention. It was awful, built in the '60s, concrete and glass. No doubt it had won some prestigious award for architecture or drains or something. In all her years of living in Smedley she'd never once had to cross over its threshold and she wasn't thrilled with the idea now. The glass doors opened automatically and Alice approached Reception, a glass cubicle inhabited by a young girl dressed entirely in black, down to her dyed hair and matching eye-shadow and nail varnish. The effect was alarming. She looked as if she had two black eyes, which to all intents and purposes she did. But her smile was warm and welcoming.

"Help you?" she asked.

Alice explained that she wanted to talk to someone about her neighbour and the visit he'd had from council workers threatening to put him in a home.

"I didn't think we did that," said the girl, "but let me see if I can find someone for you to talk to." She consulted her computer. "Housing," she announced proudly. "Take a seat while I see if there's anyone available."

Alice did so. There was a small waiting area with two rows of purple plastic seats, a few of which were occupied. Rather than sit, Alice walked over to a bright notice board entitled Smedley Council Community Initiatives. She scanned the notices attached; Beekeeping for Beginners; Grow your own Pots (someone had rubbed out the 's'). Alice smiled. The attractions continued. Tango for Teens; My Life with Moles - a slide show by Johnny Norman. This Thursday in the Town Hall. Alice wasn't sure whether that was a gardening presentation or something to do with health. She wasn't tempted either way. But one notice did get her attention. Smedley Market - every Wednesday. Stalls for £5. She read it again. A market stall for £5? That was nothing. £5? Alice wondered. Could she sell some biscuits at the market? There was a telephone number to ring to book a stall. Alice wrote the number on the back of her hand.

"Lady wanting Housing?" shouted the receptionist. Alice walked over to her.

"Sorry that took so long. I've been in touch with Housing. They said you can only make an appointment if you're family. Are you family?"

"No, I'm not," said Alice. "I'm the next best thing, though. He's got a son but he never comes round. I'm a neighbour. I look after him."

"I'm sorry," said the girl. "But rules are rules. Unless you're family, you can't help, I'm afraid."

"But that's ridiculous. He's got no-one else. Just me." Alice was aware that she was getting louder as she got angrier and that everyone in the waiting room was enjoying every moment of her discomposure.

"Isn't there someone I can talk to? I mean, he's terrified he's going to be put into an old people's home."

"I'm sorry," repeated the girl and she looked as if she meant it. "You're a third party. Either your neighbour makes his own case or his family do it for him."

Alice realised she was going to get no further.

"Thank you," she muttered, not meaning it. She went and sat down, close to tears. How could she tell Ronald?

"Never mind, luv," said a huge man dressed in a stained England football shirt and tracksuit bottoms. "I was third party once. Not nice."

Alice looked at him as if he were an idiot, which he was. "Fool," she spat and rushed out of the building. She was so livid, so incandescent that she wouldn't be able to help Ronald that she didn't watch where she was going. Alice missed her footing on the top step and plunged forward, tumbling down the half dozen or so steps and ended up sitting at the bottom. She struggled to get to her feet.

"Here. Let me help you." The voice sounded familiar. Alice looked up.

"Graham!" With his help she struggled to her feet. Not again! Why did she keep bumping into him, sometimes literally, when she was being a prat?

"Alice? Are you alright?" he asked solicitously, holding her by the elbow.

Alice nodded. "Just a severe case of embarrassment," she replied.

"Nothing broken?" he asked anxiously.

"My pride's been dented but nothing worse than that. More haste less speed, as my mother used to say."

"Wise words. You sure you're ok?"

"I'm fine, thank you. Just not watching where I was going. "

"As long as you're not hurt."

Graham turned to go. He got to the top of the steps and turned round. Alice was still there, straightening her skirt.

"Alice," he said. She looked up at him. "I don't suppose, I mean, would you…"

"Would I what?" she asked.

"Would you like to go for a coffee or something? I've just got to drop this letter off." Graham pulled a letter out of his pocket and waved it in the air. "I've got nothing else to do. Not to worry if you can't. Just an idea."

"That's very kind, Graham but I really must be getting along. Thank you anyway."

"Fine." Graham's face fell. "No problem. See you around." He disappeared inside the building.

Idiot! Alice chastised herself. You are a rude, thoughtless, insensitive idiot. What harm would a coffee do? He's been nothing but nice to you all the years you've worked together. Why not go and have a coffee with him. Alice decided to wait for Graham and as there was nowhere to sit she plonked herself down on the top step. He emerged a few minutes later, letterless, and when he saw her sitting there he smiled broadly.

"I changed my mind," she said. "About the coffee. If that's alright?"

"Yes," he said. "I think it is."

"No broken bones?" he asked.

They were the only customers in a small café round the back of the council offices. It was called Don Giovanni's and professed to sell the best Italian coffee in Smedley, according to a sign in the window. It was run by a large, hearty woman with mischievous black eyes and thick plaited hair who could easily have passed for Italian except she'd never been further south than Margate in all her life. She put two lattes on the table in front of them and retired behind the counter to re-arrange her cupcakes.

"I'm fine, honestly," she said. "How are you doing? Got used to not going to work yet?"

"It's not been easy, I must admit," said Graham. "I feel as if something is missing."

"Me too. Like I'm missing a limb or something. What about your travel plans? Got anything booked yet?"

"No. I'm not sure what to do at the moment." He took a sip of coffee. "What about you?"

Alice didn't think it a good idea to tell Graham about her sideline in gentlemen. She wasn't too sure he'd understand. "Nothing much," she said. "Oh, but there is this." She showed him her hand with the telephone number written on it. He took it in both of his and looked at her quizzically. She could feel herself blushing. "It's the telephone number of someone in the council where you can book a stall on the market for £5. I was thinking of making some biscuits and selling them. After all, it's only a fiver. What have I got to lose?" She took her hand back. "And I know some people who are happy to pay a pretty penny for my biscuits."

"Really? Go for it then. Sounds like a good idea. Why not? After all you won the biscuit prize, didn't you? For the Alouettes."

"Oh, don't remind me of that, please. That awful photo of me in the canteen. Dreadful!"

180

"I thought it was rather nice," he said. "And they were our best-selling biscuits," he added. "Or were." Alice didn't know what to say. "But it's a good idea."

"I have got some lovely recipes," she said.

"With butter?" he laughed.

"Some of them. People love home-made biscuits, don't they?"

"Got to be worth a go. Let me know if I can help." Alice looked at him, puzzled. "Oh. I've got lots of skills you don't know about," he said, mischievously.

"Like identifying shells?" she smiled.

"One of my many talents. But seriously, if I can help at all, just give me a ring." He took her unnumbered hand in his and wrote his telephone number on her palm. "There," he said, "a number for each hand. Don't muddle them up!"

Alice looked at each hand in turn. Two phone numbers.

"Thanks," she said. "And thanks for the coffee. But I'd better be going."

They left the café together and Graham waited while she untied her bike from a lamppost.

"Don't forget," he reminded her. "If I can help, I will."

Alice gave him a little wave and pedalled home.


Alice could see that Frank was in his usual place in front of the television as she came in the back door, but she ignored him. After all, what was there left to say? They tolerated each other's presence, exchanged the odd words. And she still fed him. But that was about it. Not much to show after goodness knows how many years of marriage. Alice was delighted that her new-found interest took her out of the house at weekends and increasingly on weekdays as well. One of her real fears about being made redundant was that she and Frank would be thrown together more. That was something not worth thinking about. Now she might have a plan to get her out of the house even more. If she could get this market stall business off the ground and Arthur was happy to let her bake at his house, she'd hardly be at home at all. Alice picked up the phone and dialled the number on the back of her hand. A pleasant man at the council who answered explained that the scheme was proving extremely popular and that the first available date for a stall was in three weeks time. Three weeks? Alice was impatient to get started but there was nothing she could do about it and, anyway, it would give her time to get herself organised. She wrote the date in her diary. Yes, plenty of time to plan. Alice was excited. She started to make a list of the biscuits she intended to make and began a shopping list. Could Graham help? She doubted it but you never knew. Maybe there was something he could do. At least she could give him a ring and tell him that she'd got a stall. Yes, that wouldn't do any harm and it would actually be nice to talk to him again. She'd enjoyed her time with him in the café. He was a different man outside of Bercow's. Alice looked at her palm. Damn and blast! His number was a black smudge. Her sweaty palms on the handlebars must have caused the ink to run as she cycled home. She had no way of getting in touch with him. Another opportunity lost. Alice cursed again. Even if Graham had been able to help the chance was lost now. And she still had to break the bad news to Ronald that she wouldn't be able to help him after all. The day had started well enough but, boy, had it gone down the pan.

# CHAPTER 21

## GRILLED SALMON WITH DILL

It was on the second ladies' get-together at The Bottomless Cup that Alice told them of her plan to sell biscuits on Smedley market the following Wednesday.

"Gentlemen not enough for you?" asked Valerie.

"Plenty," replied Alice, "but I quite fancy giving this a go."

"How many have you got now?" asked Iris. "You know, men?"

Alice started counting. "Ronald, Arthur, Malcolm and Jack. George and Eddie. Then there's Carol and Dee. That makes eight."

"You've branched out into women too?" asked Shanti. "An equal opportunities companion. Good for you!"

"Yes, and I'm cooking for most of them too. Arthur lets me use his kitchen every Saturday and I spend the whole day making freezer meals. Sunday, Monday and Friday I do my visiting. Apart from Ronald. I go round to see him every night. He's worrying me, though. He's not at all well. Not after the visit from the council. I tried to help but I'm not allowed to do anything."

"What's the problem?" asked Grace.

"There's talk of him going into a home. They think he can't look after himself any more."

"Wouldn't that be better for him?" asked Valerie. "He'd have lots of company and he'd be well looked after, I'm sure."

"He doesn't want to. He wants to stay in his own home. I tried to talk to the council but because I'm not family they're not allowed to discuss it with me. Poor Ronald. He was heart-broken when I told him I couldn't help. He's so worried, it's making him ill. And he's lost all interest in everything. Even his food. Off his grub. "

Several of the girls clucked in sympathy.

"At least you don't have to do any more thong displays," said Grace.

"There is that, but to be honest, I could do with the money."

"Know what you mean," said Bella.

"Anyway, that's why I thought I'd give this market thing a go. Arthur's happy for me to use his kitchen on Tuesdays as well as Saturdays so I can bake biscuits there and sell them the following day at the market. What d'you think?"

"Sounds like a plan," said Iris.

"That's what Graham said."

"Graham? Funeral Dog? You been seeing Funeral Dog?" asked Iris.

"Once. And only for a coffee," replied Alice. "How many people have you got on your books, Iris?" she asked, rapidly changing the subject.

"Three so far. With another two waiting in the wings. But Vincent! He's the best. Do you know what he likes to do?"

"Not sure I want to hear this," said Valerie.

"He likes to shave my legs!"

"What! Now that's pervy!" cried Grace.

"I don't think so," said Iris, haughtily. "I'm rubbish at shaving, so it's brilliant. And anyway, I don't bend."

"You can't bend!" Valerie pointed out unkindly.

"I choose not too, that's all. Bending is for other people. And anyway, Vincent likes to do it for me. Just that. Nothing else."

"Gross!" said Bella. "Yeuch!"

"What about your Arthur?" Valerie asked Alice. "How's he doing?"

"Oh, he's fine. Asks me to marry him every time I go round!"

"He's kid', right?" asked Bella.

"Not sure," said Alice with a smile.

"Tempted?" asked Shanti.

"For his kitchen alone!"

The women laughed.

"And Frank?" asked Valerie.

"Still Frank."

"Never mind," said Shanti. "The way your business is growing, you'll soon be able to retire."

"If only. Speaking of which, has anybody heard anything about our pensions yet?"

Everyone shook their heads.

"I got my wage'," said Bella. "An' the Job Centre help me with a CD."

"Going to start a career in singing, are you?" laughed Shanti.

"No," said Bella, perplexed. "Why singin'?"

"CV," corrected Iris. "It's a CV, not a CD."

"I had an interview for a cleaning job at the Job Centre," laughed Grace bitterly. "No joy. Inside job, I bet."

"How are things?" asked Alice. Grace shrugged her shoulders. "Want to give me a hand on Tuesday?" she asked impulsively. "At Arthur's? Making biscuits? That's if you've got nothing else on."

"May as well. I'm going stir crazy in that house. Once Shawn goes to school it's just me and Ivan. He's driving me round the bend. Be nice to get out and do something different."

Alice gave her directions to Arthur's.

The day of the market started fine. It was cold with a biting north wind but at least it was dry. Alice walked her bike into town, not trusting her ability to ride it safely with so many carrier bags draped over the handlebars. Grace was bringing another half dozen bags, all packed with the biscuits they'd made the day before.

And what a day it had been! Grace had turned up promptly at 8 o'clock at Arthur's, arriving just before Alice. She'd waited on the pavement outside his house, too shy to knock on the door of one of Alice's gentlemen friends without her. But she needn't have worried. Arthur greeted her like a long-lost daughter, insisting on making her a cup of tea and showing her round the house. Grace was smitten.

"He's lovely," she whispered to Alice as Arthur got in the way in the kitchen.

"What did you expect?"

"I don't know. I thought maybe he'd be, you know, a pervert or something."

"Why? Just because he wants a bit of company?"

"More tea, Grace?" Arthur asked.

"I'd better not," she said, smiling at him. He smiled back, a happy man. Two ladies in his kitchen. Heaven!

"Arthur, could you help me unpack these bags?" Alice pointed at the bulging carrier bags she had brought with her; yesterday's shopping. He was thrilled to be part of this – his kitchen had never seen so much action. Carefully he arranged bags of flour, sugar, (castor, icing, Muscovado and Demerara), tubs of butter and margarine, jars of spices, cooking chocolate, desiccated coconut, ground almonds, whole nuts, baking powder and dried fruit of every description and colour in an orderly fashion on one of the counter tops. He stood back to admire his handiwork. "Ready?" Alice asked him.

"Ready," he answered, saluting smartly.

"Right, let's make some biscuits."

At the end of the day, with only a brief stop for a quick sandwich at lunchtime, Alice and Grace, with a little help from Arthur, had made over five hundred biscuits, all from Alice's or her mother's recipes. There were Choc'n'Rock Cookies, Ginger Crowns, Ramjam Bodgers, Nutty Discos, Desperately Digestives, Fruity Fancies and the newly invented Crunch Time. They surveyed their efforts.

"Wow," said Grace, looking at the biscuits cooling on wire racks.

"Indeed. Splendid," agreed Arthur.

"What are we going to put them in?" asked Grace.

Alice's heart sank. She'd been so focused on baking the wretched biscuits that she'd forgotten about anything to put them in.

"Plastic bags," said Arthur. It would have to do. It wouldn't look very professional, especially if she was hoping to sell them at a premium. And how would she label the bag so customers would know what was in them? Alice cursed her stupidity. I bet Graham would have thought of this. What an idiot she'd been to spoil his telephone number. Never mind. She'd get it right next time.

Arthur produced rolls of small plastic bags, including roasting bags, and the three of them bagged the biscuits and sealed them with nylon ties. Hardly the top-end look Alice had been hoping for. There was also the problem of how to get them to the market. If she took them home on her bike a lot of the biscuits would be broken by the time she got there, and even more would be broken when she took them from home to the market the next day. They'd be better off in tins or storage containers, neither of which Arthur had. After a long discussion with Grace they decided to leave the biscuits at Arthur's overnight and collect them very early in the morning. It would mean a much earlier start than they'd intended but hopefully would mean fewer biscuits broken in transit. There was obviously more to baking biscuits than just baking biscuits.

Smedley market was located right in the town centre and had taken place every Monday, Wednesday and Saturday ever since the town was a small farming village and before coal had been discovered in the nearby Stapleton Hills. It used to sell only fresh produce; fruit and vegetables from the local farms; fish caught in the North Sea during the night and brought to Smedley still alive and flapping; meat butchered locally. But in the last ten years, the market struggled to compete with the out-of-town supermarkets and business dropped off slowly. Even though prices were lower, the variety and convenience wasn't there so the market was curtailed to Wednesdays only. And this had an unforeseen and unwelcome knock-on effect. With the reduction in market days coupled with the closing of so many factories, the town, and the town centre, started to die. Shops closed and people started to go elsewhere for the things they needed; food, entertainment; even, for the lucky ones, jobs. The town lost its soul. So the council, in a desperate attempt to bring people back into the town, had started an initiative to encourage anyone to rent a stall for a day, selling pretty much anything they wanted to. And it was this initiative, advertised in the council offices, was the reason Alice was here on this cold, clear day.

She wheeled her bike carefully among the stalls. Even though it was still early the place was alive with stall-holders setting up their goods. She found her pitch sandwiched between one selling fortune-telling crystals and lucky pebbles and one selling home-made knitting products, most of which seemed to comprise toilet roll-holders vaguely resembling either pink poodles or ladies in yellow crinoline frocks. She nodded a good morning to her neighbours, thinking how they suited their wares – the crystal-seller was a young man with blue dreadlocks and an array of piercings in his ears, nose, eyebrows and lips. How on earth do you blow your nose? thought Alice. Or clean your teeth? He was dressed in a grey hoodie and enormously baggy camouflage trousers the crotch of which hung down between his knees. Poor thing, she thought. Incontinent. Probably has to wear them like that to hide those incontinence pads you see advertised or extra large absorbent knickers. Such a shame for someone so young. After all, there couldn't be any other reason for it, could there? Mrs Toilet-Roll Holders was older, grey, dressed in a thick black coat with a hand-knitted red bobble-hat with matching scarf and fingerless gloves. She spent the entire day crocheting or knitting furiously, breaking off only to sip hot tea from a thermos she kept in a basket under her stall.

Alice was unpacking the biscuits, noticing with increasing dismay just how many were broken. I can't charge much for these, she thought. People aren't going to spend good money on broken biscuits, no matter how good they taste. Grace arrived, heavily laden with carrier bags in each hand. I hope yours aren't as broken as mine, Alice thought. Otherwise this is going to be a disaster.

"I bought a tablecloth," Grace announced proudly, unfolding a white linen cloth and draping it over the table. Now why didn't I think of that? Alice berated herself. I'm really not very good at this.

The two of them arranged the plastic bags containing biscuits on the tablecloth. Alice didn't like the way they looked so she re-arranged them. It was no better.

"Doesn't look very exciting, does it?" said Grace.

Alice could only agree. Her plans of selling high-end, home-made biscuits for a handsome profit were disappearing fast. And, what was worse, they had nowhere to sit. Looking round at the other stall-holders she saw that they all had foldable camp chairs and flasks full of hot tea or coffee. Alice thrust her hands deep into her coat pockets. This was all going horribly wrong. A young couple walked past, hand in hand. The girl stopped and picked up a bag.

"What are they?" she asked.

That just about says it all, thought Alice dejectedly. If people can't recognise what I'm selling, what hope is there?

"Home-made biscuits," replied Alice.

"Really?" said the girl, turning the bag over and over in her hands. "What sort?"

Good question. Alice took the bag from her and looked at them. "Fruity Fancies."

"Are they meant to be broken like that?"

"No," said Grace quickly. "That's why we've reduced them in price. They're only £1 a bag now, as opposed to £3." Alice was impressed. She hadn't given any thought as to how much to sell them for.

"In that case we'll try a bag, won't we, Prince?"

Prince counted out £1 in change and they walked off. Alice and Grace high-fived.

"Our first sale!" beamed Grace.

"Only thanks to you," said Alice. She realised that not only had she not given any thought as to how much to charge for the biscuits, she hadn't taken into account how much they'd cost to make, nor how much profit she was hoping to get. This whole thing was falling apart before it had even started. Looking across to the perforated man on the stall next to her she was disheartened to see that his lucky pebbles were selling like hot-cakes. No sooner did he get another box out from under the table than crowds seemed to appear out of nowhere and couldn't buy them fast enough. Mostly youngsters, Alice had to admit.

Some of who looked a tad unwashed. But at least he was selling which was more than Alice and Grace were doing. They had a lot to learn. "I'm going for a look around, Grace," she said. "See what other people are doing."

Alice wandered among the stalls. Every one was occupied and there were a lot of people milling about, some shopping, some just browsing. There were several fruit and vegetable stalls, one even selling fresh herbs. There were two meat stalls, one selling nothing but sausages, and a fish stall where Alice bought three small salmon fillets for dinner. One stall displayed gaudy cotton shirts imported from India and there was what Alice called a 'useful stall', selling cheap rolls of clingfilm and tin foil, dishcloths and pan scrubbers. Two stalls sold 'antiques' which mostly comprised chipped china cups and old embroidered tablecloths hung up like sails in the wind. Alice stopped to look at a shoe stall specialising in 'comfi-fit' shoes for the wider foot ('We're thinking of your bunions', a handwritten sign announced solicitously), but wasn't tempted by the one next to it which sold fleecy ankle-length nighties and large beige knickers. Near the public toilets, a hugely overweight man with bright red cheeks and a cloth cap was praising the efficacy of his totally natural aphrodisiac.

"Made it myself from genuine wildflowers," he boasted. "Turns your Lesser Periwinkle into a Greater Periwinkle, if you know what I mean, arf! arf! I'll turn your Common Chickweed into a Springbeauty. Want to try some love?" Alice declined, smiling. "Go on," he urged. "For your husband? It'll make his Tufted Forget-me-Not into a Butcher's-Broom." Alice walked on, laughing. Finally, there was a burger van at the edge of the market where she bought two coffees.

"Here you go, Grace," she said. "Keep you warm."

Grace took the coffee from her and wrapped her hands round the cardboard cup.

"Hello Alice. Grace."

Alice turned quickly, nearly spilling her coffee. "Graham!" she exclaimed, flustered. "What are you doing here?"

"I've come here to see how you're doing. Been coming every Wednesday since I saw you," he said. "Just to see if you'd managed it. You know. To get a stall going. How's it going?"

"Not very well, I'm afraid," said Alice, gesturing at the dozens of small plastic bags lying uninvitingly on the table. "We've only sold one bag and that was thanks to Grace's quick thinking." Graham picked up a bag and examined the contents. "A lot are broken I'm afraid. From bringing them here on my bike," she added, by way of explanation.

"I can see that." He turned the bag over and over. "Shame." He put the bag down. "I thought you might have rung," he said quietly.

Did he mean 'shame' that the biscuits were broken or 'shame' that I hadn't rung? pondered Alice.

"Er, I've just seen some really nice turnips on a stall over there," said Grace diplomatically. "Won't be long." And she hurried away.

Alice felt a fool. "I wanted to. I wanted to ring you. I know you're probably not going to believe this but the number you wrote on my hand? On my palm? By the time I'd got home it was all smudged." She held her palm out to him as if to add credence to her explanation. "I couldn't make it out. You've no idea how stupid I felt."

Graham smiled. "Honestly?"

"Honestly. I felt such a fool. And we could have done with all the help we could get. Look at it." She pointed again at the unsold bags of biscuits. "It's been an absolute disaster."

"I wouldn't say that," said Graham. "You've sold one bag!"

Alice laughed. "It's better than none, I suppose."

"I like the tablecloth. That's a nice touch. Makes it look more homemade."

"That's Grace again." She could see Grace out the corner of her eye, hovering near one of the fruit and vegetable stalls and waved for her to come over. "But I didn't think about packaging or labelling or transport or storage or how much to charge or anything. All I thought about was baking biscuits. And I'm probably going to have to throw this lot away."

"No, you're not," said Grace, joining them. "We just sell them off cheap. Like we did the first bag."

"That's right," agreed Graham. "And we get it right next time."

"*We?*" said Alice and Grace together.

"If you want," said Graham.

"I'm not sure I want there to be a next time," said Alice, morosely.

"I do," said Grace. "I've really enjoyed myself."

"Well, there you go then. I have a van you could use. And some proper airtight containers. Where do you do your baking?"

Alice and Grace looked at each other. Best not to tell him the truth about Arthur.

"I have a friend in Meadowbank with a pretty amazing kitchen. We bake them there," said Alice. "But it's quite a long way on a bike."

"Hence the need for my van," said Graham. He looked at the two women. "This can work. It's a brilliant idea. It just needs a bit of fine tuning. What d'you think?" he asked them.

"It's your plan, Alice," said Grace. "It's up to you. I only came along to get me out the house. Your call." She looked at her friend hopefully. "But I think we should give it another go. What have we got to lose?"

Alice thought about it. What *had* they got to lose? "Yes please, Graham" she said. "That would be great."

"Good." Graham was smiling. "Now what we need to do is get rid of this lot then sit down and make some plans," he said.

"Home-made biscuits for sale!" shouted Grace, at full volume. Alice looked at her. Where had that come from? The shy, reserved Grace never ceased to surprise her. "Get 'em while you can. One week only. Best biscuits in town! Hand-crafted and full of flavour! Unrepeatable offer! Chance of a lifetime!" Gradually one or two shoppers headed towards their stall, attracted by the pretty young girl shouting about cheap biscuits. What's not to like?

"I think we'll leave you to it," said Alice. "You're good at this."

"Another bag, sir? You won't regret it! Come back next week, they'll be three times the price."

Graham took Alice by the arm and led her away. They wandered through the market.

"Look at the stalls that are busy," he said. "They look good. Makes people want to buy. We've got to do the same. It's no good just having something that tastes good. We've got to make it look good too."

Alice stopped and stared at him. "Where did you get all this know-how from? Not at Bercow's that's for sure."

"I've done other things apart from being a supervisor in a biscuit factory," he said. "I told you I had a lot of talents you knew nothing about."

"I'm beginning to believe it," said Alice. "You're a bit of a dark horse, aren't you?"

"I have my moments."

"Do you really think we can make it work?" she asked him.

"I do. I know it'll work."

And he was right. It did.

# CHAPTER 22

## LAMB STEW WITH VEGETABLES

The following Wednesday could not have been more different.. On Graham's advice, she'd rung the council first thing the following morning and booked a stall for the next four Wednesdays.

"That'll give us a fair crack at it," said Graham. "If we can't make it work in that time, we never will." That seemed sensible to her. "The next thing we need is a timetable." That too, was sensible. She had a pretty good system before but now Alice was going to have to factor in Graham. Arthur was happy, more than happy, for her to come and bake at his house every Tuesday as well as Saturdays, but now Graham would need to come to Meadowbank to help her and Grace with the packaging and storage and then taking the biscuits to market on the Wednesday. She would have to introduce Graham to Arthur and she wasn't sure how they'd get on. Furthermore, she'd have to introduce Graham to Frank, as Graham had suggested that he pick her up at Greenfields Road on Tuesday morning in his van so that they could go shopping together. That would save her having to carry everything on her bike up to Meadowbank. Alice was not looking forward to either introduction.

As it happened she needn't have worried because when Graham turned up early on Tuesday, Frank was still in his usual place, in bed. Alice was waiting for him when he pulled up in his small white van which he parked outside her house, the engine running.

"Good to go?" he asked her.

She pulled the front door shut and thanked him as he held the van door open for her. When did someone last do that?

It had been agreed that Alice and Grace would make the same biscuits that they had last time and that Graham would leave them to it. He would return to Meadowbank at the end of the day to help them package and label the biscuits before storing them in airtight plastic containers in his van overnight. On the Wednesday morning, he would collect Alice and take her and the biscuits to the market. Grace would meet them there.

"What d'you think?" he asked them.

"Sounds good to me," said Grace.

"Me too," agreed Alice, delighted that she would no longer have to cycle everywhere.

Grace was already at Arthur's when Alice and Graham arrived with the shopping. Alice introduced Arthur to Graham, and as she expected, it did not go well. She'd told Graham that Arthur was an old friend and that she cooked his meals for him on a Saturday; she didn't feel she needed to tell him anything more. He didn't need to know about Ronald or Eddie or George, Malcolm and Jack. Or her ladies. They were her secret. Alice introduced Graham to Arthur as an ex-colleague from Bercow's and a friend who was helping her get her biscuit business off the ground. Arthur took an immediate dislike to him. He shook hands with him on his doorstep but only reluctantly stood aside to let him in. Graham followed Alice into the kitchen, laden with shopping bags.

"Morning Grace," said Alice.

"Hiya."

"Tea?" barked Arthur.

"Ooh, yes please," she said, giving him a peck on the cheek. This seemed to mollify him a bit.

"Tea?" he snapped at Graham.

"I'm ok, thanks."

Graham thought it best to leave Alice and Grace to it. Arthur thawed a bit when he'd gone.

"Friend?" he asked Alice

Alice nodded.

"Sure?"

"Yes Arthur, I'm sure. He's helping us get going with the biscuits. That's all." Alice looked to Grace for help.

"That's right," said Grace. "He used to work at Bercow's with us and what he doesn't know about biscuit making you could write on a pinhead."

"Hmm!"

"Why don't you like him, Arthur?" Alice asked as she started to weigh flour into a bowl.

"Biscuits."

"What? What do you mean?"

"This biscuit thing. If it works, you'll stop coming." Ah, that was it.

"No, I won't. Even if I can make a go of it selling my biscuits, I would never stop coming here."

"Promise?" he asked plaintively, like a child wanting a guarantee that the night monsters would never get him.

"I promise. I will never stop coming here. I am never going to stop looking after any of my friends. Ever. No matter how well the biscuit business does. Happy? Good. Now, would you chop these walnuts for me?"

By 5 o'clock hundreds of biscuits were baked and cooling. Alice had made some of her Apple and Almond Alouettes this time. Since they were so successful when Bercow's made them maybe they would be equally successful for them at the market. Alice and Grace were exhausted.

"If we sell this lot I can give you a bit more money," said Alice. Last Wednesday she'd insisted that Grace take all the money from the biscuits they'd sold. It wasn't anything like as much as she'd hoped but maybe tomorrow would be better. It would have to be. She couldn't go on spending many tens of pounds on ingredients and getting pennies back.

"Fingers crossed," agreed Grace. "I didn't want to take that money," she reminded Alice.

"I know, but you were the one who sold all the biscuits. I didn't know you had it in you," she said, referring to Grace's many talents at attracting customers.

"Me neither. But wasn't it fun!" The doorbell rang. "That'll be Graham."

This time it was all very different. For one thing, the weather was warmer with a real hint of spring in the air. The sun shone and Alice was sure that would bring people out in their hordes. It wouldn't do their business any harm at all. And their stall looked very different from last Wednesday too. Grace had brought her tablecloth again but Graham had gone one better by buying some yellow and red bunting which he'd draped round the edge of the awning and across the front of the table. Alice clapped her hands with delight.

"It was only cheap," he promised her.

But it was how the biscuits looked that really thrilled her. Graham had bought an industrial amount of paper bags, red and yellow striped, with a cellophane window so you could see the contents. "Not particularly cheap but look upon it as an investment," he'd said last

194

night, as they bagged the biscuits. "We want them to look good, don't we?" Grace had then carefully hand-written a stick-on label for each bag, identifying the contents. Now, displayed on the table, the bags matching the bunting, the stall looked interesting, tantalising. And, what's more, Alice could see through the cellophane that none of the biscuits were broken. This was thanks to careful packing in Graham's many plastic boxes which were delicately placed in the back of his van and driven to Greenfields and from there to the market the following day, with love and considerable care. Several of the other stall-holders wandered over to have a look.

"What're these, then?" asked a bearded man in a duffel coat. Alice recognised him from last week. He had one of the antique stalls.

"Home-made biscuits," said Alice proudly.

"How much?"

"£3 a bag."

"£3! That's bloody expensive for a bag of biscuits," he exclaimed.

"They are homemade," Grace reminded him.

"Aye, go on then. What you got?"

"Well, there's Crunch Time." Grace held a bag aloft. "Or these. Nutty Discos. Or we have a bag of assorted."

"I'll take those," he said. "Assorted." He handed over his £3 and opened the bag. "Smell good." He put an entire Fruit Fancy in his mouth and chewed noisily. "Taste good too." Alice beamed.

"I almost forgot," announced Graham, as their first customer wandered off. "La pièce de résistance!" And with a flourish, he drew two straw boaters out of a holdall. The women gasped. Round each was an entwined red and yellow ribbon. "Found them in a junk shop and tarted them up a bit. What d'you think?"

"They're brilliant!" cried Alice, delighted. She put one on at a rakish angle.

"Wow," said Grace, reaching for hers. "How do I look?"

"Foxy!" This was from Graham. "And finally, this." From the same holdall he produced a long thin banner which he tied just beneath the bunting. On it was written a single word. 'Alice's'.

Alice could not speak, she was so choked up.

"I thought we'd keep it simple. Do you like it?" he asked.

"Like it? I love it!" And she threw her arms round him. Graham and Grace didn't know what to do with themselves. "Thank you so much, Graham. What a difference. It looks so…so professional." She stood back to take it all in. Her stall. After all, it said so. 'Alice's'. With its red and yellow bunting and its home-baked biscuits in matching bags. "What d'you think, Grace?"

"Fantastic!" She touched the rim of her boater with her finger. "Thanks to you, Graham."

"'Ere love, you servin' or what?"

Alice turned round. Three customers were standing there, waiting.

"I'll leave you ladies to it," said Graham. "Good luck!"

It wasn't until 11 o'clock that they stopped to draw breath. Alice looked under the table.

"Only two boxes left," she said, delighted.

"Really? No!" Grace checked for herself. "I can't believe how different it is from last week."

"And all down to Graham."

"Not completely. I mean, it's your gorgeous biscuits we're selling."

"Yes, but it was him who showed us how to sell them," said Alice. "That's what's made the difference."

"He's nice, isn't he?" said Grace simply. "Totally different from how he was at Bercow's. He's not a Funeral Dog at all. I like him."

"So do I," agreed Alice.

"Must be the hairnet that did it," smiled Grace. "Not his best feature." They sold a few more bags of biscuits. "Who'd have thought, eh? Not so long ago we were all doom and gloom. And now look at us."

Yes, thought Alice. Now look at us. She really believed they could make a go of this. And it was largely down to Graham. She owed him.

By 2.30 they were sold out. Completely. Alice could not believe it. Every single bag of biscuits had gone.

"Any more of them assorted ones?" asked the antiques man. He was back.

"None of any, I'm afraid," she replied. "They're all gone. Sold out." She couldn't help smiling. Never in her wildest dreams did she imagine she'd ever be able to say that. Sold out!

"You coming back next week?"

"We're planning on it," said Grace.

"Good. Well save me another bag of them assorted. Bloody marvellous they were. Ate the whole lot, I did. Best biscuits ever. Oh, and like yer 'ats, by the way. Classy."

Alice counted the takings while Grace packed everything up, carefully rolling up the bunting. They'd taken over £300. This was as good as looking after her gentlemen – and lady – friends. She handed Grace £100.

"This is far too much," said Grace, "I can't take it. And I still owe you loads."

"That can wait," Alice said. "And anyway, you helped make it a success. When I take off the money for the ingredients and the cost of the stall, give some to Graham, I'll still be quids in."

"It's almost like being paid to have fun, isn't it?"

"That's the best description yet, Grace. Want to do it again?"

"Oh, I'll say! Look! Here's Graham."

He walked towards the stall, arms open wide. "Where've they all gone?" he asked.

"Sold them," Alice told him. "Every last bag."

"Well done both of you. That's amazing."

"Well done all of us," Alice corrected him. "We couldn't have done it without you." She took the money out her handbag. "Here," she said, peeling off several twenty pound notes.

"What's this for?" he asked.

"For the bunting. And the bags and hats. And your petrol. And your time, too."

"No," he said. "Have it on me. Think of it as a gift. When you're rich and famous and have factories all over the country making Alice's biscuits, then you can give it to me." Alice put the money away. "And anyway, I enjoyed it. Same again next week, ladies?"

"Wouldn't miss it for the world," said Grace. "Never had so much fun."

"Me neither," agreed Alice. "It *was* fun, wasn't it?"

"You get off home, Grace. Alice and I can finish off here."

"Sure?" she asked Alice.

"We're fine. There's not much to do. See you next Tuesday." Alice watched Grace walk through the market. She could have sworn there was a bounce in her step that hadn't been there before.

They loaded up the boxes into Graham's van. "Home?" he asked.

"Yes please." Alice didn't realise how tired she was. The early start combined with being on her feet all day. And she still had a meal to cook. "Give me a minute, will you." She dashed to one of the meat stalls and grabbed some diced lamb. "Dinner," she explained to Graham. "Lamb stew."

"Sounds good. Ready?"

She was. He dropped her off at her front door and she watched him drive away. Was this the start of something? Something that could change her future? The biscuit business, of course. What else could she possibly mean?

"You look like the cat that got the cream," commented Frank snidely, as she walked in. Alice was taken aback. She and Frank hadn't exchanged more than a few words in the last couple of days. Why the sudden need for conversation? "What have you been doing all day?" Should she tell him? Was it any of his business? "I saw you get into that white van with that man." Ah! "Who is he?" Alice didn't know whether she was more surprised at the question or the fact that Frank had actually been up and out of bed at that hour of the morning. After all, she'd left the house as quietly as she could. Was he spying on her? "Where did you go? Is he your lover?" Frank's face looked like a smacked bottom. Alice thought he was about to burst into tears. "Are you having an affair?"

Is it an affair if your marriage is over? Alice pondered. Not that she and Graham were having an affair. Or anything at all, for that matter. "He's a friend, that's all." She didn't have to explain but felt she had to say something. "From work."

"D'you like him?" he asked her.

Alice thought about it. Yes, I do. He treats me like a lady. Like you used to. When she didn't answer him Frank went back to his television. Tennis. She watched as his head followed the ball, back and forth. Back and forth. Nothing you say or do is going to make any difference. I had a good day today. Special. For lots of reasons. Not least because I may be able to see a future for myself. One which definitely doesn't include you. It may include biscuits, but that's not necessarily a bad thing. She smiled to herself and she kept smiling while she cooked the dinner.

Her good mood evaporated when she saw Ronald. He looked thinner and more tired. "Here you go, Ronald. Lamb stew with vegetables." She put the plate down on the table. "How're you doing?"

"I'm ok," he replied, struggling more than usual to get up out of his chair. "That looks nice." He speared a piece of carrot and chewed it slowly. "Lovely."

It took him a good half hour to eat his food. Alice sat and watched him.

"You're not yourself, are you?" she asked. "What's the matter? Still worried about the council?" He nodded slowly. "Have you heard anything else from them?"

"Not a thing. But I know they're plotting."

"No, they're not, Ronald. You're imagining it. I'm sure they can't turn you out of your home and put you into a care home unless you agree to it. Has your son been in touch at all? Ricky, isn't it?"

"Not a peep. But then I wouldn't expect it. Not been in touch for more years than I care to remember. I don't exist as far as he's concerned."

"I'm sure he's just busy," said Alice, although she had no idea why she was defending Ronald's absentee son. Maybe it was just to try and make him feel better.

"Too busy to come and see his old man? He only lives the other side of Smedley. Hardly a million miles away. But you can guarantee, once I'm dead, he'll be down here like a swarm of locusts. Just you wait and see."

"Don't talk like that, Ronald. You're not going anywhere. You're just a bit down in the dumps." Ronald definitely needed cheering up. "I know. Would you like to see my bosoms?" she offered, thinking it might cheer him up.

"It's kind of you," he said, "but I'm not in the mood."

"No charge? A quick flash?" Alice prepared to undo her blouse.

"No thanks."

"Not even a glimpse of thong. Although I would have to go home and put it on."

"No, really."

"It's no bother, honest."

He shook his head. Alice was at a loss. Ronald was becoming more and more despondent. He'd lost his sparkle. "What would you like for tea tomorrow night?"

"Oh, whatever's easy."

"Would you like to hear about the biscuit stall? In the market?"

He showed some signs of interest so Alice told him about her wonderful day.

"D'you know, I'm doing something I love. Cooking and baking. And I might be able to make a go of it. This is small-scale, I know. But it's a start. You can always think big, can't you?"

Ronald agreed. "Go for it, girl. You're a cracking cook. You deserve to do well."

Alice yawned and stood up. "I'm shattered after today. I'd best be off. Will you be okay?"

"I'll be fine," he reassured her. "See you tomorrow?"

She patted his shoulder. "Tomorrow."

# CHAPTER 23

## EMPIRE PIE

The next three Wednesdays were just as good. Alice and Grace sold every biscuit they made and could have sold more. The man on the antiques stall, the one in the duffel coat, proved a loyal and greedy customer, buying three bags of assorted every week.

"If everybody was like you," said Alice, "I could retire tomorrow!"

"Aye, well. I really like them appley ones. Quality is quality. Recognise it when I see it."

That's strange, thought Alice, considering the tat you sell on your stall.

Their Tuesday routine continued like clockwork; Graham picked up Alice early in the morning and they shopped together for the ingredients at the Co-op; he then dropped her and all the bags off at Arthur's and left her and Grace to spend the day baking. Arthur was still cool towards Graham, seeing him as a threat despite Alice's promise. Late in the day Graham returned to help them bag and label the biscuits and he stored them overnight prior to delivering them the following day, with Alice, to Smedley market. Alice and Grace dressed the stall then donned their boaters and by lunchtime, they were sold out. Alice was having the time of her life but one thing was rapidly becoming clear. She was exhausted. Every Saturday was spent at Arthur's cooking meals for him and her growing number of ladies and gentlemen – word had spread and she now catered, in various senses of the word, for a total of eight gentlemen, including Ronald, and a further two ladies in addition to the two she already visited, increasing her clientele to twelve. Alice had to do an extra couple of trips on the bike each Saturday between Meadowbank and her home as even Arthur's freezer was too small for all the additional meals she was now having to cook and the only place she could put them was her freezer, small as it was. Arthur had offered to buy her another freezer – heaven knows, he had the space – but transporting and delivering the meals to their various locations was proving to be a problem. And now, because of her recent new additions, when she wasn't at Arthur's cooking freezer meals or baking biscuits, or at Smedley market, every day was now taken up with visiting. Something would have to give and Alice didn't know what. She loved what she was doing. Being a companion could be emotionally exhausting; all of the twelve were lonely, which was why they'd turned to her in the first place. Most were widows or widowers; some had family who never visited; one had family who visited occasionally but not enough. She didn't mind being a friend - Alice was naturally warm-hearted and sympathetic and she was a good listener. It broke her heart to hear them tell her their sorrows. She didn't even mind the odd cuddle or squeeze although she was happy that, apart from Ronald and the thong, nobody had yet asked for anything more. She loved cooking for the ones who'd asked her but that was putting a strain on Arthur's kitchen and it was a struggle to prepare so many meals in just one day. Thank goodness not all of them had asked her to cook; she simply wouldn't have been able to manage. Three of the ladies and several of the gentlemen were fiercely independent and were more than capable of fending for themselves. They would never dream of asking for help. But they were more than happy to sit and hold her hand and talk for hours on end. And happy to pay for it too. Then there was her market stall. She was proud of the fact that people were willing to pay good money for her home-made biscuits. But she couldn't go on like this. At least at Bercow's she had weekends off. Now it was full-on, seven days a week, non-stop, flat-out. Even finding time for a couple of hours with the girls at The Bottomless Cup on a Thursday afternoon was now proving increasingly difficult. Yes, something would have to give.

Crunch time for Alice came when, at the end of one market day when she and Graham were loading the empty plastic containers into his van, he suggested a day at the beach together, at Woodly Bay. Just the two of them. A walk on the beach. Fish and chips. A drink before they got the bus home. Or they could even go in his van? Alice realised she would love nothing more. After all, it wasn't like it was a date or anything. It was just a day out with Graham. A day at the sea-side. She so wanted to do it but how could she fit it in? She didn't have a single free day and she couldn't tell him why. What would he think of her if he knew what she got up to when she wasn't making biscuits? But Alice wanted a day off. Desperately. And she wanted a day off with Graham. The more time she spent with him, the more she liked his company. He was good fun; he made her laugh. And, she made no bones about it, it was mostly down to him that her biscuit-baking business was doing so well. It would be a small way of showing him her appreciation for all he'd done. It was the very least she could do.

Alice discussed it with Grace while they baked at Arthur's. He was sitting at the dining room table writing labels but she still spoke in a whisper.

"He's asked me to go to the beach for the day."

"Who? Graham?" asked Grace. Alice nodded. "Why, that's great. What's the problem."

"I don't have the time."

"What d'you mean?"

"I'm working seven days a week. Either with the market or looking after my people. I've got a dozen of them now. And I cook for most of them."

"I didn't realise you had so many oldies. How come?"

"Word of mouth. Someone knows someone else. I can't say no."

"Well, you're going to have to. Either that or stop the market."

"I don't want to stop either. I love the market and I love my oldies, as you call them."

"I'd be really sorry if we stopped the biscuits," said Grace. "It's giving me an income." And it was. Not a huge amount, she'd be the first to admit, but enough to keep things ticking over. "And I enjoy it. Ivan said I got all moody and depressed when Bercow's closed. He says I'm a different woman now."

I know I am, thought Alice.

"Why don't you give a couple of your people to one of the others?" suggested Grace. "Iris maybe? She's really into it. Then you could still keep most of them but give yourself a day off."

Alice thought about Grace's suggestion. It was either that or bring someone else in to help with the biscuits. Or maybe both? Would one of the other girls be interested? Bella? Shanti? Maybe even Valerie. Alice would have to think long and hard about what to do.

Alice sipped her latte and took a bite out of her prawn and egg mayonnaise sandwich. At least here in The Bottomless Cup the sandwiches and their contents were recognisable. And almost edible. The café was quiet and, apart from the one large table the six of them shared, only two other tables were occupied.

"Did everybody else get a letter about their pension?" asked Valerie.

"I got mine this morning but I don't understand it," said Alice. "I thought we weren't going to get anything."

"Me too," said Grace. "I thought that after we were paid our wages by Bercow's there was nothing left."

"There wasn't, technically," said Valerie. "This is some sort of government safety net. Some sort of fund. We won't get everything we should, but it's better than nothing."

"But I'll still have to wait until I'm 65 'till I get it, won't I?" asked Iris.

"Not long to go then, is it, Iris?" quipped Shanti.

Iris gave her a black look. "Funny!"

"How're things going in the world of private entrepreneurs, then, Alice?" Valerie asked. "Made your first million yet?"

Alice updated the girls on her biscuit venture. Up to now she'd been a bit coy when they'd asked her how she was doing. She so desperately wanted to show them she could do it. Make a success of it. They were all delighted to hear she and Grace were doing so well. What had started as a simple idea had clearly taken off and, what's more, it was paying.

"I can't take all the credit," she said. "Graham has helped enormously."

"Funeral Dog?" exclaimed Iris. "Since when?"

"Since our first day on the market failed miserably and we virtually had to give the biscuits away," explained Grace. "And anyway, he's not Funeral Dog. He's Graham."

"Well I never!" said Valerie. "So how did he get involved?"

"He came up with some suggestions about packaging and how to make the stall look appealing," said Alice, not quite answering the question. She wasn't ready to tell them what she felt about Graham yet. Mainly because she didn't know herself. Yes, she did. He was a friend. That's what he was. Nothing more. Just a good friend.

"And he made us wear boaters," added Grace.

"Boats?" asked Bella, confused. "Why you wear boats?"

"Boaters," explained Alice. "They're like a straw hat. And he even decorated them with ribbons which match the bunting he got for the stall."

"Who'd have thought it," said Shanti. "Funeral Dog has a feminine side."

"You'll have to come and see it. It looks good and it works. In fact, it's going so well, I need some help."

Several ears pricked up.

"Wow!" said Shanti, clearly impressed. "I'm impressed. What sort of help d'you need?"

"Well I've now got twelve people to look after and I feed most of them. What with them and the biscuits, even with Grace's help…"

"And Graham's," added Grace.

"Even with Grace's and Graham's help, it's still too much for me. I'm working flat out and my couple of hours with you girls here on a Thursday is the only time I have free. I'm shattered, to be honest. And it's only going to get busier. Only last night I had a phone call from one of my new men, Paddy, with another three names of people who'd like a visit. That would take it to fifteen. It's growing like crazy. I never thought it would take off like this."

"You've done well," said Valerie. "Really well."

"When I got made redundant I thought this would provide me with a bit of money to tide me over until I found something else. I didn't really take it seriously. Now I've got Grace on board…"

"And Graham," Grace reminded her.

"Yes, thank you, Grace. And Graham."

"So what are you thinking?" asked Shanti.

"How are you doing Iris?" Alice asked.

"Pretty well. I've got six to visit at the moment. Why?"

"I was thinking of asking you if you would like to take on Paddy and the three new ones."

"For real?"

"Oh yes. You'd be doing me a favour. Paddy is lovely. I don't know anything about the other three but I hate turning anyone away. After all, they come to us for a reason. I'd have to ask Paddy, of course. But I'm sure he won't mind. What do you think?" asked Alice.

"I wouldn't mind at all. I'm loving it. Has Paddy got any, er, peculiarities?"

"Well, he's not a Vincent, if that's what you mean. He's not mentioned shaving at all. He does like his feet rubbed though. Oh, and anything with cheese."

"Cheese I can do!" said Iris. "Consider them mine."

"Brilliant. Thank you, Iris. I'll call you when I've spoken to him. I know you'll get on with him famously. Now I'm looking for someone to help out with the stall every Wednesday. Anyone interested? Shanti?"

"Actually, Alice, I was going to tell you all today. Carol's got a job up in Edinburgh. We're going to be moving at the end of the month."

"No!" "You can't go!" "You can't leave us!" came a chorus of disappointment and sadness.

"Needs must, ladies. I don't want to go. I was born in Smedley. Lived here all my life. But it's a good job for Carol and it pays well. And I stand more chance of getting a job up there than I do here. So count me out, Alice. Sorry. It sounds like a lot of fun."

"We'll miss you," said Alice sincerely. "We all will." There much nodding of heads. "Valerie? Bella?"

"Sorry, Alice," said Valerie. "I've been offered a job as a sales rep for Ursula's Undies."

"No!" Alice smiled. "Why, that's right up your street."

"I know! Can you believe it! It doesn't pay brilliantly but I get discounted lingerie. What's not to like!"

"I am so pleased for you," said Alice.

"And I get to go round the big department stores. Try to persuade them to sell Ursula's underwear."

"You could always have a stall on the market," suggested Grace. "There's a chap there already selling giant-sized cotton knickers that could house a family of five and bras you could sail the Atlantic in. You'd fit right in!"

"Thanks Grace! I'll think about that one!"

"You won't have to move, will you?" asked Alice, desperate not to lose another friend.

"Nope. I'll have to travel a lot but Smedley will be my home base."

Alice breathed a sigh of relief. "So Bella. What about you? Want to help out on the market?"

"Will I have to wear a boat'?" she asked.

"Only on Wednesdays," laughed Alice.

"Ok, then. I wear a boat'."

Alice cycled home very pleased with herself. She was sad that Shanti was going to move to Scotland. She'd been a good friend and she would miss her. But Edinburgh wasn't the other side of the world. It was a different country, for sure, and Alice had never been. The closest she'd ever come was almost going on that coach trip to the Borders but Frank had put paid to that. Maybe now she'd go and have a real holiday there. But, on the plus side, not only had she got Iris to take on

Paddy and the three new oldies, it meant she hadn't had to turn them down. After all, they'd gone to Paddy because they wanted company and someone to spend some time with them. How would they feel if she'd said no? Too busy. Sorry. No, she couldn't have done it. Somehow she would have managed. Exhausted as she was, she would have added them to her growing clientele. But this way was great. Iris would be good for them, no doubt about that. She was larger than life with a heart to match. Alice wasn't quite sure what Iris offered her menfolk but that was between her and them. Good luck to her, thought Alice, whatever. She felt really pleased with herself. That was a good day's work and now Bella was on board too. She was going to help Grace out with the market. Okay, Alice would have to pay her too but that wasn't a problem. What with the money from the biscuits and the cooking side of things, not to mention the little extra services she occasionally delivered, Alice was doing very nicely. She would have been happier if she could get Graham to accept even a small payment for his time, his petrol, his advice. But he wouldn't budge. "When you're the CEO of your own company, then you can pay me," he said, over and over. And, speaking of Graham, now that Iris had agreed to take a chunk of work away from her and the fact that she wouldn't have to go to Smedley market every Wednesday, Alice could finally have a day off with Graham and go to the beach.

She sang to herself as she stirred some curry powder into the remains of last night's lamb stew and mashed some potatoes to put on top. Alice had some notion that this might be called Empire Pie, a throwback to the days of the Raj, but she didn't really know. She knew Ronald liked it. That was all that mattered. When it was ready, she plated it up into three as usual, left one on the kitchen table for Frank and carefully carried two plates next door.

"Here we are, Ronald, Sahib. A little touch of the Empire. Your Mem Sahib has brought you a little bit of India to dull old Smedley," Alice announced in a sing-song accent which she thought sounded vaguely Indian, but resembled Welsh more than anything. She put the plates down on the table and went into the kitchen to get some cutlery. "I'm sorry it's lamb two days running but things have been pretty hectic. And anyway, I know you like this. I've got some good news to tell you." Ronald was quieter than usual. It was most unlike him. "Do you want a glass of water with that, Ronald? Ronald?"

Alice filled two glasses with tap water and put them on the table next to the rapidly cooling dinner.

"Shall I turn the fire on? It's quite cold in here. You're very quiet, Ronald. Are you alright?"

Ronald didn't answer. Alice stood in front of him then dropped to the floor. Ronald was sitting there in his armchair, his tartan blanket across his knees, his hands together in his lap. He looked old, worn out. He looked dead. Alice checked to see he wasn't just sleeping. He wasn't.

"Oh, Ronald," she cried, reaching up to feel his cheek. Stone cold. "Oh, Ronald," she said again, wiping away a tear which rolled down her cheek. "All alone. I'm so sorry I wasn't here." Alice straightened his blanket. "I am so going to miss you." The tears fell thick and fast. "At least you died in your own home," she sobbed. "That's good. It's what you would have wanted." She rested her head on his bony knees. "I just wish I'd been here so you weren't on your own." She sat up and looked at him. "That was the whole point, wasn't it," she said quietly. "All you wanted was a bit of company. Someone to be with you. Someone to talk to now and again." She straightened his sparse grey hair. "I just hope I made a bit of a difference." Alice clambered to her feet and kissed him on the cheek then went home to ring for an ambulance. She sat with Ronald until it arrived, holding his hands and crying softly.

# CHAPTER 24

## STEAK AND CHIPS

The day of Ronald's funeral was bright and sunny but still cold with a slight breeze. Alice stood outside the crematorium stamping her feet to keep warm, her coat buttoned up, hands deep in pockets. It was too early to go inside and anyway, she wanted to see who else would turn up. The crematorium was on the outskirts of Smedley and it had taken her a good half hour to cycle there. It was an unprepossessing building, grey breeze blocks with a red-brick chimney. The gardens were pretty though; formal, well-tended beds of spring flowers, daffodils and narcissus, even the odd snowdrop still lingered. Here and there floral tributes to loved ones lay on the lawns, hot-house flowers adding bright, almost unreal colours to the sombre setting. Alice didn't expect many people would come. Arthur had promised he would and he'd told her that several others Ronald had known from Evergreens would be coming too, as well as a few of the care assistants and the mini-bus driver who, once a month, had picked him up, taken him to the day care centre then delivered him home safely at the end of the day. But Ronald only had a handful of friends so Alice didn't expect a lot of mourners. Even Frank wasn't going to attend. Don't like funerals, he'd said. Who does? she thought. We don't go to them because they're a barrel of laughs. We go because we should. To pay our respects. Show we cared. But there was no point arguing with him. And anyway, I hardly knew the man, her husband had told her. No you didn't, despite the fact you lived next door to him for nearly twenty-five years. A quarter of a century. Basically you couldn't be arsed, she thought bitterly. Like everything else it was too much bother. Alice shook her head in disgust. But one person who would be coming, the one person she did want to see was Ricky. Ronald's son. The one who'd never visited. She wanted to see what a man who didn't care about his father looked like.

The ambulance crew had turned up fifteen minutes after Alice had dialled 999 to report Ronald's death. There were two of them, an older man, greying at the temples and a young girl with startling blue eyes. They'd been lovely, both of them. Sympathetic and respectful. They'd seen it all before but that didn't stop them being kind and gentle. They confirmed Ronald was dead and asked her if she was next of kin. She told them she was just a neighbour, someone who gave him his dinner every night, pointing to the table where the plates of cold Empire Pie sat untouched. Looks like you were more than just a neighbour, the man had said kindly. That was the nicest thing anybody could have said. She could have kissed him. I hope I was, she thought. I tried to be. They'd asked about family and she told them Ronald had a son. It would help if you had a contact number for him, the young girl had told her. He needs to know. Alice said she didn't but she'd look. The ambulance crew told her the Police would be involved – routine in the circumstances – but if she could let his next of kin know that would help enormously.

After they'd taken Ronald away, Alice sat for a few minutes in his armchair. The house felt suddenly empty. It wasn't just Ronald that had physically gone. Something else had gone too. She shivered, cold. And it had nothing to do with the fire not being on. Looking round the room, a room where she'd spent so much time with him, trying to make a difference, Alice felt a weariness come over her. It was just a shell, this house, but it had been Ronald's shell. Just like his body, she thought. It had served its purpose. Alice had searched high and low in all the obvious places for a contact number for Ricky; the sideboard in the lounge where Ronald had kept his Coronation tin full of money – empty now; in the cupboards and drawers in the kitchen; his bedside cabinet; but it was in a shoebox on top of the wardrobe that she finally found Ricky's telephone number written on the back of an old envelope. She slipped it into her pocket, collected the uneaten dinners and closed Ronald's door behind her.

"Old bugger not hungry?" asked Frank, spying the uneaten meals. "I'll eat it if he doesn't want it."

Alice looked at him with complete and utter loathing. You obviously were so engrossed with your bloody television that you didn't hear me ring 999 earlier, did you? thought Alice. What was it? What did you find so riveting on the television? Boxing for vegetarians? Kazakhstani ten pin bowling? Synchronised swimming with natterjack toads? What was it that kept you so transfixed that you didn't notice me come into the house, pick up the phone and tell the person on the other end that Ronald was dead? How come you only noticed when I brought his dinner back in? But she said nothing. What was the point? Nervously she rang the number on the envelope. A female voice answered and

Alice asked to speak to Ricky Sanders. Who's calling? the woman had asked. I was a friend of his father's, Alice explained. There was a pause as the woman digested the past tense, realising the implication of what Alice had just said. I'll get him for you.

Alice smiled as she saw Arthur getting out of a taxi with Malcolm and a very small woman dressed in a purple skirt and jacket with matching gloves. Alice had never seen her before. Must be from Evergreens. The woman dabbed at her eyes with a large pink handkerchief and blew her nose repeatedly.

"Bloody shame," said Arthur, putting his arm round Alice and giving her a comforting squeeze. "Fine man."

Alice could only agree. She looked at her watch. "Shall we go in?"

She slipped her arm through his and together, followed by Malcolm and the purple lady, they walked into a large, sombre, wood-lined room where a lonely coffin stood on a dais tucked away in one corner, almost as an afterthought. A solitary wreath lay on top. Red and yellow roses from Alice. Electric candles in wrought-iron holders on the walls did nothing to dispel the gloom and unidentifiable piped music added to the air of despondency. There were a dozen or so rows of hard wooden benches, clearly not designed to tempt you to linger. The four of them took a seat in the back row. Two women in smart white uniforms (from the day centre, Arthur whispered in her ear), sat a few rows in front of them along with a man in a bright green jacket with 'Evergreens' emblazoned on the back. The only other person present was a man in the very front row, his back to them. Alice could not take her eyes off him. Ricky.

She remembered little about the service; some woman in a blue suit appeared out of nowhere and talked about what a wonderful life Ronald had had. Where did you get that from? Alice was perplexed. Doesn't the fact that there are only eight people here to say goodbye to him, to mourn him, to acknowledge his death, tell you something about his life? Eight people? You know nothing. You don't know how his wife died in childbirth, the daughter she was giving birth to dying too. You know nothing about his only son who never visited him, even though he's standing in front of you. You know nothing about Ronald's loneliness. His isolation. How he craved company. You don't know how he relied on me, a neighbour, the only real friend he had, to provide that tiny bit of companionship. A little bit of human contact in

211

his lonely world. Your words are empty. Meaningless. You think something needs to be said. But they're inane. Trite. Wouldn't it be nicer just to sit here in silence? To remember Ronald just as he was. Alice couldn't remember ever feeling this empty. This bitter. And to make matters worse, the purple woman sitting next to her would not stop sniffing. Alice wanted so much to smack her. To smack the woman in the blue suit. To smack Ricky.

There were no hymns. No songs. Just more piped music as the service ended and Ricky went up to nod at the coffin before following the woman out of the room by a side door. The care assistants snuck out the back door, eager to be away and back to work. Arthur took Alice's hand and together they stood in front of Ronald's coffin, heads bowed.

"Bloody damned shame," muttered Arthur.

They filed out and walked round to the front of the crematorium, standing in the weakening afternoon sunshine with Malcolm and the sniffer waiting for Arthur's taxi.

"How are you getting home?" Malcolm asked her.

"I've got my bike parked round the back," said Alice. She hugged both men as a minicab pulled into the car park. "See you soon." She watched them climb in, gave a little wave and sighing heavily, went to get her bike. As she unlocked it from a convenient drainpipe, a voice startled her.

"Are you Alice?" It was Ricky.

Alice stood up and took a good long look at the man in front of her. Tall and thin. Elegant was the word that sprang to mind. He was clean-shaven and dressed in a well-cut grey suit with a black tie. She didn't know much about tailoring but Alice knew that this screamed money. She'd seen models in magazines wearing suits like this. Except she'd bet her bottom dollar *they* visited their parents.

"I am." Alice found it incredibly difficult to be civil to this man. How could he not even visit his own father? Except when he was dead.

"I know what you were doing."

"What d'you mean?" she asked. "What are you talking about?"

"Shagging my father!"

"*What*?"

"Making him pay for sex! You're a disgusting old woman!"

Alice was incandescent. "I did not take money from your father for sex," she said through gritted teeth. She could feel her face flushing with anger and she clenched her fists hard. "I was a friend to him. Someone who was there when you weren't." She stared at him. "And I'm not old," she added, almost in tears.

"You are old," Ricky shouted at her. "You're..."

"Can I help?" asked a calm voice. "Are you alright Alice?" It was Graham.

She nodded, shocked. What was he doing here? How much had he heard of what Ricky had said? Graham walked over and took her bike from her.

"Have some respect, young man," said Graham. "This lady has just said goodbye to a very dear friend today. I'll thank you to let her grieve in peace."

Ricky stood there, open-mouthed. Before he could say anything, Graham turned his back on the man and, with one hand wheeling the bike and the other on Alice's elbow, he led her away and out of the crematorium, across the road to a small park. There was a wooden bench overlooking a pond where a few moorhens pecked at litter floating in the grey water. Graham sat her down and Alice immediately burst into tears. He let her cry. Eventually she ran out of tears.

"I'm sorry," she said.

"For what?" asked Graham.

"I don't know," she replied. "I really don't know. I'm just sorry, that's all." She wiped her eyes with a tissue and blew her nose loudly. I must look a sight, she thought. "What are you doing here?"

"Grace told me where you were. I thought you might be able to use some moral support."

"Thank you, Graham." She dreaded asking the next question but Alice had no option. "How much did you hear?"

"About what Ricky said?" No use pretending. "All of it."

Alice groaned. "It's not true. I didn't sleep with Ronald. He was a friend, that's all. A lonely old man who wanted someone to talk to." And then she found some more tears she didn't know she had. When she finally stopped crying she looked at Graham. "What now?" she asked him.

"Have you eaten?" She shook her head. Graham looked at his watch. "Well, I suggest we find the nearest decent pub and have something to eat. What d'you reckon?"

Alice realised she was unexpectedly hungry. "That would be good. Thank you."

"For what?" he asked.

"For back there." She nodded towards the crematorium over the road. "Thank you for coming." She smiled. "For the moral support."

"You're welcome," he replied. "Now, I don't know about you but I could eat a scabby horse."

"Make mine with chips," she said, smiling.

Over steak and chips (Alice was pretty sure it was beef and not horse) and several halves of lager in the Stumbling Parrot she told Graham everything. Well, almost. She told him how it all started. How she'd lived next to Ronald for over twenty-five years and how, in the last few year, she'd started cooking for him.

"It's shameful, isn't?" she said. "You live cheek by jowl with your neighbours for years and you never really get to know them. Sometimes you don't even know their names. I mean, what does it cost to be friendly?"

She told Graham how, out of the blue, it felt like such a long time ago now, he had suddenly asked her to show him her *bosoms*, she whispered, embarrassed to say the word out loud. It started off as a joke, but it was obvious he was in earnest. He was lonely. "Only one son and you saw what he was like." Most of the time Ronald was happy to hold her hand or just have a cuddle. "It was the human touch," she explained. "That was what he missed most of all."

"Don't we all," said Graham, sombrely.

"Just because you grow old doesn't mean you don't still *feel* things," she said. "After all, you're still human. It's just maybe things don't work so well."

Alice continued to explain to Graham how, from cooking for Ronald and giving him the occasional display of her *bosoms*, she whispered the word again, it grew from there. She didn't mention the thong episode. After all it had only happened the once. No need for Graham to know about that. She told him the truth about Arthur, that he wasn't just someone she cooked for, how Ronald had put her on to him. He was a hand-holder and a cuddler, she told him. And he liked his food. But he also just liked her being there.

"Is that why he doesn't like me?" asked Graham. "Because he sees me as some sort of threat?"

"Not so much that. He's worried that if the biscuit thing gets serious I'll stop going to see him. He's terrified that'll happen. He's finally got

214

someone to talk to, to spend some time with him and he's scared he's going to lose that." She looked him straight in the eye. "I've told him it won't. Even when I'm CEO of my own factory!"

"I'll drink to that," said Graham, taking a mouthful of lager. "Here's to Alice's." He touched her glass with his.

"And then there's the others," said Alice.

"Others?" asked Graham, alarmed. "There are others? You mean in addition to Arthur?"

"'Fraid so. Once I started showing Ronald my...er...bosoms, word spread. The cat was out the bag."

Graham leaned back as Alice continued. More than just the cat, he thought.

There was Malcolm. He liked to chat, mainly about his dead dog; Paddy liked his feet rubbed but Iris had taken him on now.

"What d'you mean, Iris has taken him on? You don't mean Iris Batterby, do you? From Bercow's?" asked Graham, astounded.

"I do. She's helping me out by taking on Paddy and three of his friends. It was just too many for me."

"How many others are doing this?"

"None that I know of," replied Alice. "It's just me and Iris. None of the others wanted to."

Graham was speechless.

Then there was Carol. She liked you to sing to her, just that; Jack liked to talk, and boy! could he talk! Dee. Now she was a mean old lady, never smiled, never said 'thank you' but was always very generous when it came to paying; George was from somewhere in the Caribbean. He'd shown her how to make a mean goat curry. Then there was Eddie. Eddie was a real cuddler. He liked to dance, which made things interesting, especially since they both had two left feet. Graham couldn't help but smile as Alice recounted the various peccadilloes of her friends. Her oldies, as Grace called them. Each one had their own little idiosyncrasies. That's what made each one of them different and special.

"But the one thing they all have in common," she said, "is their loneliness. They're all on their own. Either because they don't have anybody else or they have family who can't or won't spend time with them. And it's not just about being a companion," she went on. "I cook for most of them. You wouldn't believe what some of them were eating. When I first met Arthur all he ate was eggs because that was all he knew how to cook. Some of them don't cook because they don't know how, some because they physically can't. It's too much for them to go shopping and then carry heavy bags home. I struggle and I have a bike! And then things like peeling vegetables or opening tins. It's a bummer when you've got arthritis in your hands."

"I'm going to have another lager," Graham said, standing up. This was a lot to take in. The mild-mannered, soft-spoken Alice he'd worked with for years in Bercow's churning out biscuit after biscuit, had been leading a double life. Was she the Samaritan she seemed to be or was there more to it than that? "You want another?"

"Please."

Alice watched him as he walked to the bar. The place was filling up and he had to wait a few minutes to get served. Am I right to tell him all this? she asked herself. He probably won't believe me. He's probably going to think I'm a right trollop.

"What about Meals on Wheels?" Graham asked, returning with two fresh glasses. "Aren't they supposed to help out? Deliver the sort of meals you've been providing?"

Alice nodded. "Oh yes, and they do. It's just what with the government cutbacks and the fact that there are so many people out there who need help they can't cope with the numbers. And when they do help they don't have the time to sit and talk. That's what people want more than anything."

"So you've been doing your bit?"

"I like to think so. In a small way."

"What does your husband think of all this?"

Alice took a sip. She'd been honest with Graham so far, pretty much. May as well tell him the truth.

"Frank and I don't communicate. We don't talk. Haven't for years. He has his television and I have my oldies. He knew I cooked for Ronald but he didn't know about any of the others. I told him when Ronald first offered me money to expose myself. Frank was all in favour. All he could see was pound coins rolling in. I suppose that's when I really knew that we were finished. To be honest, until Bercow's folded I was planning on leaving him. That's why this biscuit thing and the money I get from looking after the likes of Arthur and Malcolm, that's why they're so important. They were my escape fund."

"And now?" he asked.

216

"I'm not sure. The biscuits are taking off big-style. And now that I've got all these people to look after I wouldn't want to leave them. That would defeat the whole purpose. And break their hearts."

Graham digested this. There was a lot to digest. He didn't say anything for several minutes.

"So what Ricky said. Not true?"

"Absolutely not!" Alice was outraged. Outraged at the question and outraged that he'd asked. "I have never slept with any of my oldies," she exclaimed. "And even if I had, it would be none of your business." One or two drinkers at nearby tables stopped what they were doing and looked at her. "I will have you know, Graham, that I am proud of what I've done! There is nothing, nothing, I'm ashamed of!" Except maybe the thong thing. "I don't pretend to be perfect and I know I've been paid for what I've done. Paid well, I won't dispute that. But what I've done is to make sure that a lot of lonely people have had someone to talk to. I've given a lot of them good home cooking served up with a slice of friendship and I'm afraid if you don't like what I've done, well then! You can bugger right off!" Alice stood up to go. Graham put a restraining hand on her arm. She looked down at him.

"I'm proud too," he added. "Proud of what you've done. I think it's marvellous."

Alice sat back down. "You do?" This wasn't the response she'd expected. She thought he'd hate her.

Graham nodded. "I do. There's only one thing that's worrying me."

Alice's face fell. "What's that?"

"How are we going to manage to keep this going alongside your biscuit business?"

"We?"

He smiled. "I reckon we'd make a great team. What d'you think?"

"I think I need another lager!" She looked at her watch. "My God! Is that the time? I ought to be getting back."

"Why? You don't have Ronald to cook for any more, do you?"

No, Alice thought, I don't. Not any more. Poor Ronald. It had been a sad day. But in some ways it had been a good day too.

Graham pushed the menu across the table to her. "Pudding?"

# CHAPTER 25

## LOBSTER THERMIDOR WITH CAVIAR

It was two weeks after Ronald's funeral that Alice found herself in Interview Room 2 at Smedley Police Station sitting opposite Inspector Lancaster. She'd just finished telling him pretty much what she'd told Graham in the Stumbling Parrot, without going into quite as much detail. Once again she left out the bit about the thong. That secret would die with her and Ronald, and Valerie and the rest of the girls. The young policeman had made copious notes as she told her story but had not interrupted her once. The cold grey chair was hard and unforgiving. Alice stretched.

"Any chance of another cup of tea?" she asked.

Inspector Lancaster got up and poked his head round the door, shouting to someone to bring them another brew.

"You've told me you were a companion for Ronald. And others," he said.

"That's right, I was. I offered them friendship. And I cooked for some of them."

"Did you take any money from them?" he asked.

Alice hesitated. She wasn't good at lying. "Yes, I did."

"And what was that money for?"

"Mostly for food."

"Anything else?"

"Not as such," she mumbled.

"What does that mean?" asked the Inspector.

She was going to have to tell him. "Sometimes I got money when I didn't cook for them. When I did other things for them."

"Such as?" The policeman leaned forward.

"Well, take Paddy for instance. He liked me to rub his feet."

"I'm sorry?"

"Paddy paid me to rub his feet," she repeated.

"Is that all?"

"Of course! What did you think I did? He's 95 for goodness sake! And anyway, I'm not like that."

Inspector Lancaster hid a smile behind his hand. Like what? he wanted to ask but didn't. "And what about the others?"

"Carol paid me to sing to her."

"Sing?" This was getting weirder by the minute.

There was a knock on the door and a young policeman put two cups of tea down on the table. Alice smiled her thanks. I could do with something stronger, thought the Inspector. A lot stronger.

"Mrs Coulter," he continued, "have I got this right. You were taking money from your... your customers?"

"Friends," she said quickly. "They are my friends. My companions. They are not customers."

"Were you taking any money from your 'friends' for sex?" He made the word sound dirty.

"Depends what you call sex, I suppose."

Inspector Lancaster groaned inwardly. Why were things never straightforward?

"What do *you* call sex?" he asked.

"Well, you know. It. Rumpy pumpy. That sort of thing." Why was he making it so difficult for her?

It was all he could do to not burst out laughing. Wait until he told the rest of them about this. Pity he wasn't recording it. Could have dined out on it for years! He wrote down 'rumpy pumpy' in his notes and circled it several times. He added a couple of exclamation marks for emphasis.

"Did you have..." the Inspector paused, not quite believing he was asking this, "rumpy pumpy with any of your friends?"

Alice shook her head vehemently. "Absolutely not! That's an awful thing to say. And anybody who says that is lying!"

"But you said they gave you money for..." He consulted his notes. "'Other things'. What exactly were these 'other things'?"

"Well," Alice took a deep breath, "I got paid for cuddles."

"*Cuddles?*" Had he heard right?

"Yes, Jack's the worst!" She shook her head, smiling. "Can't get enough of them. He's a little devil, he really is!"

Inspector Lancaster could not believe what he was hearing. If this was all it was why were they even here?

"And holding hands," said Alice. "I got paid for holding hands."

"Holding hands," he repeated, dazed. She nodded. "Mrs Coulter, can I ask you. Did you ever, ever, take money for anything other than cooking, cuddling or holding hands?" Let this be an end of it, he thought. Please. I've got serial fare-dodgers to arrest. Litter louts to incarcerate. Anything rather than this.

Alice looked down at her hands in her lap. "Yes," she whispered. The policeman looked at her with dread. What was she going to tell him now? "Once I showed Ronald my, er, you know what's."

"Your 'you know what's'?"

"That's right. And he paid me for it."

"Please," he said despairingly, "what are your 'you know what's'?"

Alice looked round the interview room as if to check there was no-one else there then pointed at her chest. "My bosoms." He could hardly hear her.

"Ronald Sanders paid you to show him your…breasts?" Alice flushed with embarrassment. "Is that all?"

"Is that all! Is that all? I'll have you know, young man, it meant a great deal to him. And to me. It's not the sort of thing I do every day!"

"I'm sure it isn't," said the policeman, trying to reassure her. "What I meant was that showing him your er…" he pointed vaguely in the direction of her upper body, "was the extent of your physical relationship with Ronald?"

"That and the hand-holding. And the cuddles. Yes."

Inspector Lancaster breathed a sigh of relief.

"No rumpy pumpy?" He had to say it again just for the sheer joy of hearing the words again.

"I told you. No! Absolutely not."

"No sexual activity of any kind? No sexual…services of any description?"

"Not unless you count cuddles?" she asked. "Which I don't," she added, just to re-enforce the point.

"Me neither." Inspector Lancaster put his pen down and folded his arms. The allegations that this woman in front of him, Mrs Coulter, was operating a mobile brothel were nonsensical. Feels on Wheels indeed. She wasn't engaged in sexual activity with old men – or women. She wasn't providing sexual services for money. That was a gross over-exaggeration. Yes, she might be letting them have a bit of slap and tickle, but he wasn't even convinced it went as far as that. It was a bit of harmless fun. For her and them. Inspector Lancaster wondered if he could charge Ricky Sanders with wasting police time. No, he thought. Best let sleeping dogs lie. God knows how he was going to write this up though.

"I don't think I need to ask you any more questions," he said.

"Does that mean I'm free? I can go?" she asked, her face lighting up.

"Yes, that's it. We're done. You can go. Thank you for helping us with our enquiries," he added formally.

"So that's it? I'm not going to be charged with murder?"

Inspector Lancaster laughed so loud that a policeman passing by the interview room at that moment poked his head round the door to make sure everything was alright.

"No, you're not. I'm satisfied that Ronald Sanders died from natural causes and from what you've told me, nothing you did had anything to do with his death."

Alice was so relieved she promptly burst into tears. "What about my taking money for other things?" she asked, sniffing. "Is that wrong?"

"That's between you and the tax man," said the policeman. "You should let them know. But I won't be doing anything. From what you've told me, it looks like you're doing a lot of people a favour." He arranged his papers and stood up. Alice stood too. She picked her handbag up off the floor and buttoned her coat.

"Thank you, young man. I knew nothing I did made him die. Or if it did, maybe he died a happier man. Now, if you know anyone who needs a bit of companionship..."

"I think you'd better go, Mrs Coulter, before I change my mind."

Alice shook his hand . "Thank you for the tea and biscuits," she said, ever polite.

"You're welcome."

"Any chance of a lift home?"


Alice looked at her watch. If she got a move on she could get to the market to see how Bella was doing on her first day with Grace. She arrived just as the two of them were packing up.

"How'd it go?" she asked Grace.

"It just gets better and better. We're sold out and what's more, you know that deli round the corner? The one that sells all that fancy stuff that no-one's ever heard of and wouldn't know how to eat? Well, the owner came round this morning. Wants to sell your biscuits. What d'you think of that?"

Alice was delighted. It would mean more work but she'd cope.

"I've got his business card here," said Grace. "He said to give him a call."

Alice looked at the card in her hand. Oh, she would.

"You'll have to get some of those," said a voice behind her. It was Graham. She turned, delighted to see him. "That's the next thing. Get some cards printed up. 'Alice's'. That'll show you really mean business."

"Have you been here all morning?" she asked him.

"Mostly. With it being Bella's first day I wanted to be here to help out just in case. Turned out I wasn't needed. We missed you this morning." The unasked question was there.

"Yes, sorry. I had to go somewhere. I'll tell you about it later. But, Bella, how did it go? Did you enjoy it?"

Bella took off her boater and ran her fingers through her hair. "This boat' is heavy," she said. "I don' like."

"Never mind," said Alice sympathetically. "Did you enjoy it?" she repeated.

"Yes. Good fun. You English people love biscuit'. Sweet tooths, for sure."

"That's what we're gambling on," said Graham. "That's how we're all going to make our fortune, isn't it, Alice? Sweet tooths."

Sweet tooths. Yes, she liked that. She liked that a lot.

Alice helped the girls load the empty containers into Graham's van while he took the bunting down.

"Come on," she announced to the three of them, "I'm buying."

"What?" asked Bella. "What you buyin'?"

"Drinks! Drinks is what I'm buyin'. I'm taking us all to the pub."

"Are we celebrating something?" asked Grace.

"Yes," replied Alice. "We are. We're celebrating sweet tooths."

While Bella and Grace stood at the bar waiting to be served Alice quickly told Graham about her visit to the Police Station and the interview she'd just had about the allegations that Ricky had made. About her running a mobile brothel. He was appalled.

"That's dreadful," he said. "How could he do that?"

"Feels on Wheels, the Police called it."

Graham laughed.

"That's not funny," said Alice, indignantly.

"No, of course not. So what happens next?" he asked, becoming serious.

"Nothing, I'm not going to be charged with anything but that's because I haven't done anything."

"Is that why we're having a drink?" he asked.

"Partly. I just felt like, I don't know, things are on the up."

"I'll drink to that," he said, touching her hand briefly. He sat and stared at her.

"What?"

"Did I ever tell you you're beautiful?"

Alice was spared having to respond as Bella and Grace returned with a tray full of drinks and four packets of crisps.

"Seein' as the boss is payin'," said Bella, "I thought we push the boater out."

"Nice one, Bella," said Alice. "Nice one."

She gave Grace and Bella their wages for the day from their takings and the girls finished up their drinks and went home, leaving Alice and Graham alone. She felt awkward and struggled to find something to say.

"You are, you know," he said suddenly.

"I am what?"

"Beautiful."

"Don't be so daft, Graham. How can you possibly say that?" Alice looked down. She wasn't fishing for compliments.

"You are, believe me. You are a beautiful person. You haven't got an unkind bone in your body."

"I don't think Ricky Sanders would agree with you there," she replied.

"Stuff him! The man's a fool."

"Listen," she said, changing the subject as she always did when things got too uncomfortable. "I really would feel happier if I could give you something towards your petrol and things. And for all your advice. I wouldn't be where I am if it wasn't for you and yet you won't take a penny from me." He shook his head as she opened her handbag, searching for her purse. "Oh bugger!"

"What is it?" he asked.

She pulled out a white envelope. "I've got this letter. From some solicitors." She opened it. "Snatchet, Crumbs and Stollen. Asking me to make an appointment. I forgot all about it."

"What's it about?" he asked.

"Not sure. It must be something to do with Ronald."

"Well, there's only one way to find out, isn't there." He passed her his mobile phone. "You'll have to get one of these soon, too" he said.

"No entrepreneur should be without one." Things were moving very quickly for Alice. Business cards. Mobile phones. Whatever next!

Alice took it from him. "Can I ask you a favour?"

He nodded. "Of course."

"Will you come with me?"

The offices of Snatchet, Crumbs and Stollen, Solicitors, situated in the centre of town, were grey, inside and out. But there any similarity with the décor in the Police Station ended. The walls of the Reception were covered in delicate, dove grey, hand-made, embossed wallpaper which matched the sumptuous leather sofas, which were not bolted to the floor. The thick woollen carpet was a slightly darker grey and was so luxurious Alice was tempted to slip her shoes off and wiggle her toes in it. Several pictures adorned the walls and although Alice knew nothing about art, she guessed correctly that these were not prints. A glass coffee table was covered in coffee-table books, glossy, expensive, unread. Luscious green plants, whose foliage looked as if it had been recently polished, stood in mosaic pots on the floor and on the desk of the receptionist. Alice took in the decor. I'm sure the Police would get more results if their interview rooms were more like this, she thought.

She and Graham sank into one of the sofas at the receptionist's request as she pressed a buzzer to announce their presence.

"Mr Stollen will see you now, Mrs Coalter."

"Coulter," said Alice as she tried to stand. The sofa was too soft and too low.

"I'm sorry?"

"It's Coulter. As in *cool*. You said Coalter. As in *coal*."

The receptionist looked at her. She smiled. Well, her lips did. You could hear her thinking 'whatever', but in a posh voice.

"I'll wait for you here," said Graham. "Good luck, whatever it is."

A man held a door open for her. He looked exactly like Alice would expect a solicitor to look like. Tall, suave, with half-moon glasses perched on the end of his long Roman nose. A red and white spotted bowtie with matching handkerchief in the breast pocket of his very expensive black, double-breasted suit. She would be willing to bet a million pounds he was wearing braces under that jacket. There was no doubt about what Mr Stollen did for a living. He proffered his hand.

"Mrs Coulter?" At least he'd got it right. "Come in."

He ushered her into a room that looked exactly like she thought it would. Gracious, expensive, lined from floor to ceiling with leather-bound books, a large desk in front of an old-fashioned sash window draped with dark green velvet curtains.

"Please sit down." He beckoned towards a leather chair in front of his desk. "Coffee? Tea?"

"I'm fine, thank you."

"Do you know why you're here?" he asked.

"Because you sent me a letter asking me to come," she replied simply.

"Ha, ha! Very good. I like that!" He peered at her over his glasses.

"So you have no idea at all. No idea why I sent you that letter? Asking you to make an appointment?"

Alice shook her head. You may be a very intelligent man, she thought, with a very expensive suit and a posh office, but you are getting right up my nose. Just get on with it. Good news or bad, just tell me.

"Well, in that case, what I have to say may come as a lovely surprise for you. The solicitor opened a black folder lying on his desk. "Did you know Ronald Sanders?"

"He was my neighbour for over twenty five years. And my friend."

"It seems that he was a very generous friend," said the solicitor. "He's made you a bequest in his will. An inheritance."

"I don't know anything about that. Ronald hardly had a penny to his name." Slowly it began to dawn on her. "That's why the Police wanted to talk to me," she said, nodding her head,

"The Police?" he asked, taking his glasses off then putting them back on. "What have the Police got to do with this?"

"Oh, they just wanted to ask me some questions about him. Seems his son has been saying things."

"Ah yes. Ricky."

"You know him?" asked Alice.

"Unfortunately, I have had that pleasure," replied Mr Stollen, somewhat indiscreetly.

"Well, he said some nasty things about me which weren't true. Anyway, the Police don't believe him and they told me they were satisfied that Ronald had died from a heart attack. That I didn't have anything to do with it."

Mr Stollen shifted in his expensive leather chair. It made a soft farting noise. At least, Alice assumed it was the chair. "Quite so," he said.

What did that mean? The solicitor looked thoughtful then smiled.

"I think we can forget about Ricky. Ronald's will is very clear. Very specific. In it he recognises that his son had nothing to do with him, never visited. It was as if he, Ronald, didn't exist."

Alice nodded sadly. "That's what he said to me many times. It really hurt him, you know."

"Quite so," said Mr Stollen again. "Anyway, Ronald Sanders nominated you as his sole heir." He picked up a hand written letter and Alice looked on dumbstruck as he read aloud; 'To my dear neighbour, Alice Coulter, companion, cook and dearest, dearest friend, thank you for being there. Thank you for taking away my loneliness and making me smile." So she had made a difference after all. It was all she could do to stop herself bursting into tears. Alice got a tissue out in readiness. The solicitor continued; 'You made my life whole, made it bearable. You made it worthwhile. And for that, I can never thank you enough'. Mr Stollen put the letter down, clearly moved. "He clearly thought a very great deal of you, Mrs Coulter," he said. "You must have been a truly wonderful friend." That was it for Alice. The tears came thick and fast.

Mr Stollen cleared his throat noisily. He wasn't often moved by much but the grief of this dowdy, middle-aged woman in her cheap woollen coat sitting in front of him was clearly genuine.

"Anyway, down to business. Mr Sanders left you his house at No 48 Greenfields Road. It has no mortgage so it's yours outright."

Alice looked up. "I can't take his house," she said.

"He gave it to you. He wanted you to have it," he said softly.

"It doesn't seem right."

"And there's more. Ronald Sanders left you his entire savings and investments. When it's all realised it should come to about £350,000. Give or take."

Alice blanched. "You're kidding me, right." She could not believe what the man in front of her was saying.

"No. Ronald wanted you to have everything."

"But it's so much money," she sobbed. "I don't understand."

"Well," began Mr Stollen, "as you probably know, Ronald led a simple life after his wife died. He saved assiduously and made some fairly shrewd investments."

"He always joked he had some money stashed away but I never believed him. I always thought he was joking."

"Clearly he wasn't."

"He didn't live like he had any money," she told him. "He lived ever so simply."

"That's as may be," said Mr Stollen, "but he was obviously a prudent man."

Alice sat back in her chair and thought about what Mr Stollen had told her. It was overwhelming. Suddenly a black thought occurred to her.

"What about Ricky? He's his son. Was. Isn't he entitled to Ronald's money?"

"No. The will is legal, genuine and unequivocal. I witnessed it myself over a year ago. He left you every penny. It's yours. Ricky can contest the will if he wants to but in my experience he won't get anywhere."

The solicitor stood up and unbuttoned his jacket. Alice caught a glimpse of red elastic. I knew it, she thought. Braces! "You're a very wealthy woman now, Mrs Coulter. You need to give careful thought as to what you're going to do with all this money. You don't want to do anything rash."

I've never done anything rash in my life, she thought to herself. Maybe now's the time to start.

Mr Stollen shook her hand again. "I'll let you know when all the paperwork is finalised and you can access the money. I wish you the very best of luck, Mrs Coulter, and I mean that." He straightened his bow-tie. "You clearly meant a very great deal to Ronald. Goodbye and good luck."

Alice started crying again as the solicitor held the door open. Graham jumped up immediately.

"Are you alright?" he asked, alarmed. "You look as white as a sheet."

"I'm fine," she said, taking his hand. Alice took a deep breath. "I've got something to tell you. But not here."

"Ok," said Graham. "Let's find somewhere quiet."

"You know that new fish restaurant that's just opened? Next to the bingo? Well, I'm going to treat you to the best meal of my life!"

Alice nodded at the receptionist as she buttoned up her coat.

"I'm going to have lobster thermidor and caviar. Never had them before. Probably hate them both."

"That's going to cost a small fortune," said Graham. "It must have been good news."

"Oh, it was," said Alice, with a smile that stretched from ear to ear. "It was."

# EPILOGUE

## SIX MONTHS LATER

Alice tucked her hair up into her hairnet. It was easier to do now she'd got rid of that awful ponytail. She'd had her hair cut short, layered and a few blond highlights added. Nothing too drastic. Still mostly grey but softer. Makes you look ten years younger, the pre-pubescent hairdresser had told her. Alice wasn't convinced but she did feel younger and she liked the result. She looked round her new kitchen. She liked the result here too.

Mr Stollen had been good as his word. A month after meeting up with him in his offices he rang to ask her what she wanted to do about Ronald's investments. She asked him to convert everything to cash, except his house of course. She had plans for that. Alice didn't understand about stocks and shares and things like that and anyway, she had a better use for his money. He also told her, unofficially, that he'd heard from a friend of his at another firm of solicitors who'd told him that Ricky Sanders had taken advice about contesting the will. He'd been advised that he would be wasting his time and money so had decided not to pursue the matter. Alice's sigh of relief could be heard in the next county. And two months after that Mr Stollen rang again to say that everything was sorted and that a cheque for £379,500 was in the post, a bit more than he'd originally estimated, and Ronald's house, 48 Greenfields Road, was now in her name. Once again, he'd wished her the very best of luck. That same day, with Graham's help and much to Frank's astonishment, she moved out of her home for the past twenty-five years, No 46, and into next door. The house needed a lot of work doing to it but that would all have to wait. She could manage with it as it was for the moment. There were other things to sort out first. More important things.

When Mr Stollen had told her about her windfall she'd thought long and hard what to do with it. This could be my escape fund, she thought. Make a fresh start somewhere new. Abroad, even. Somewhere warm where rain was welcomed as a pleasant, cooling diversion rather than the constant dismal drizzle almost every day of the year. I'd never have to work again. Live a life of luxury. Sit by the sea and drink cocktails all day long. It was tempting. But what would happen to all my oldies? My companions? Who would look after them? Would anyone look after them or would they go back to being on their own? Isolated once again? Alice couldn't do that to them. They relied on her and she couldn't let them down. Then there was her biscuit business. Over the past three months it had gone crazy. Bella and Grace still ran the market stall for her every Wednesday but now they both worked for her three days a week making Alice's Apple and Almond Alouettes, Ginger Crowns, Fruity Fancies and the rest. And the best seller of all? Her newly invented Crunch Time. Not only was the deli now selling her biscuits but a swanky hotel chain wanted to provide her biscuits in their rooms with their complimentary tea and coffee. She was on a roll. Alice's biscuits were taking off in a way she could never have imagined. She couldn't leave all this, not now. And then there were her friends. The girls. And Graham. Could she leave them? She didn't think so.

With the increase in orders for her biscuits it soon became clear to Alice that Arthur's kitchen wasn't up to it. After all, it hadn't been designed to handle over two thousand hand-made biscuits a day and what with her, Bella, Grace and Arthur in the kitchen at the same time, it was proving to be a bit of a squash. Reluctantly, Alice had told Arthur that she would have to make her biscuits elsewhere. He was devastated.

"This is it, isn't it?" he asked her. They were in his kitchen, tired at the end of another very long day baking. Grace and Bella had already left and Graham was waiting for her outside in his van.

"This is what?"

"You. Leaving me. For your biscuits. Always knew it."

Alice thought her heart would break. She took both his hands in hers and looked him eye to eye. "Arthur, I am not leaving you. I need a bigger kitchen, that's all. I need more space."

Arthur was not convinced. He turned to wipe down an already spotless draining board.

"So you don't want to help me, then?" said Alice.

He stopped what he was doing and put the cloth down.

"Help you?"

"I have a job for you but if you don't want it," she said, shrugging, "I quite understand."

"Job?"

"Only if you want it."

"Doing what?"

Alice didn't know. She hadn't thought that far ahead. "I'll think of something," she said. "Deal?"

"Deal!" he said, pumping her hand up and down. "Deal!"

Graham found a new kitchen for her. And what a kitchen it was. Located behind the railway station, from the outside the building looked like large shed, with a corrugated iron roof and grey pebble-dashed walls. Originally built for a small company that made Boil-in-the Bag meals for dieters, a company with high hopes and low sales, it had stood empty for over two years after the business collapsed. But inside, it was Alice's dream. Bright stainless steel as far as the eye could see. Huge ovens and walk-in fridges. Acres of worktops and cupboards. Double sinks and triple gas hobs. More shelves than she knew what to do with. And the best bit? It had an island. A bloody great island right in the middle. When Graham had first shown it to her she thought she'd died and gone to heaven.

"It's wonderful," she'd whispered. "A good clean and it'll be just like new."

"And it's going for a song," said Graham. "You can easily afford the rent. What d'you think, Alice?"

She couldn't stop looking, still unable to believe her eyes. "I think it's what they call a no-brainer, isn't it?"

He took her hand. "That's what I'd call it too."

Alice stood at her island looking round at the kitchen, taking it all in, a look of sheer bliss on her face. My kitchen, she told herself. Mine. Thank you, Ronald, she whispered under her breath. Thank you for making it happen. But she couldn't stand here all day. Time to get to work. She had biscuits to bake; freezer meals to cook for all her oldies, deliveries to organise in one of her two smart new white vans with 'Alice's' emblazoned on the side and, with Valerie's help, three more applicants to interview for jobs. It was going to be a busy day.

"Had a good day?" Graham asked her, as she locked the door of her kitchen at the end of another exhausting day.

"Every day's a good day," she replied.

Graham took her hand. "Fancy going out for dinner tonight?"

"That would be lovely. What d'you fancy eating?"

"Wouldn't mind trying that new Argentinean Steak House that's just opened. You?"

"Sounds good. Let me change first and give Frank his dinner, then I'm all yours."

"What are you feeding the old goat tonight?" he asked.

"I thought about bangers and mash."

"You spoil him, Alice. You really do."

"Yes, I do rather, don't I? Still, he is a lonely old man and someone needs to take care of him."

Graham smiled at her and kissed the back of her hand. "Alice Coulter," he said.

"What?" Her eyes twinkled.

"Nothing. Just Alice Coulter, that's all." He kissed her hand again. "Come on, let's go eat."

# CUDDLES & CUSTARD

## By

## Maggie Whitley

Maggie Whitley lives in Yorkshire with a husband (hers).
She insists this story is not autobiographical but she would like
a new kitchen.

This is her fifth book.

Printed in Great Britain
by Amazon